CAMPAIGNING CAN BE DEADLY

A DISCOUNT DETECTIVE MYSTERY

CAMPAIGNING CAN BE DEADLY

A DISCOUNT DETECTIVE MYSTERY

CHARLOTTE STUART

Walrus Publishing | St. Louis, MO 63116

Walrus Publishing | Saint Louis, MO 63116

For information, contact:
Walrus Publishing
An imprint of Amphorae Publishing Group
a woman- and veteran-owned business
4168 Hartford Street, Saint Louis, MO 63116

Publisher's Note: This is a work of fiction. Any real people or places are used in a purely fictional manner.

Manufactured in the United States of America
Set in Adobe Caslon Pro
Interior designed by Kristina Blank Makansi
Cover designed by Kristina Blank Makansi
Cover image: Shutterstock

Library of Congress Control Number: 2020943906
ISBN: 9781940442327

This book is dedicated to all of the Americans
who take advantage of their Constitutional
right to vote in political elections.

And to all of the campaign volunteers who support
political candidates with their passion and hard work.

MENU OF CHARACTERS

TABLE SETTING

A discount detective agency located in a suburban mall

· **Cameron Chandler**: an unemployed PhD and single mother of two with no prospects until Pennywise Investigations took a chance on her

· **Yuri Webster**: colleague and jokester who uses surveillance assignments as an excuse to eat junk food

· **P.W. Griffin**: agency owner with a mysterious past who hoped Cameron would be a "stabilizing influence" on Yuri

· **W. Blaine Watkins**: snappy dresser and agency's Man Friday

· **Norm**: appears average in every way, but excels at investigative work

· **Grant**: former insurance investigator and voice of calm

· **Will**: wears belted trench coat and not at all fond of Yuri's teasing

· **Adele**: researcher with weight issues and a thin sense of humor, but can sometimes deliver subtle zingers

· **Jenny**: part-time investigator and creator of Pennywise mascot

· **Pennywise mascot**: stuffed bear wearing a Sherlock Holmes deerstalker hat and a coat with a cape across the shoulders

HORS D'OEUVRES

Cameron's sometimes supportive family

· **Stella**: Cameron's mother and gourmet cook of "uncomforting" food

· **Mara**: just turned thirteen and is becoming the quintessential teenager

· **Jason**: news junkie and almost teenager

MAIN DISH

Clients with political ambitions and zealous staffers

· **Bobby Mann**: running for Congress, backed by tons of money and intimidating rich relatives

· **Ashley Price**: Mann's former Seafair Princess wife and wanna be wife of a winner

· **Candy**: limp handshake and Mann's right-hand

· **Brian Norcross**: latecomer to Mann campaign; early victim

· **Randy Mann**: attorney brother of Bobby; wears full-length, wool overcoat

· **Nathan Knight**: running for Congress as local favorite; wants to avoid negative campaigning...until...

· **Laney Knight**: wife of Nathan Knight, concerned about threats from several members of Mann's family

· **Jim Gossett**: friend of Brian's; working on Knight campaign; couldn't keep a secret

DESSERT
The Law

· **Detective Connolly**: In charge officer with dishy good looks and piercing blue eyes

SIDE DISHES
Friends, acquaintances and one sleazebag

· **Theo**: friend of Jason's

· **Gretchen,** Theo's mother and reporter working on what she hopes is a career making story

· **Dr. Benson**: Brian's university professor, duped by a student

· **Ken and Alan**: two of Brian's university friends who may know his secret, or may not

· **Lisa Brennan**: daughter of Karl and Jennifer Brennan; doesn't know pink is not a good color for her

· **Karl Brennan**: a local politician secretly dipped in oil

· **Denny**: environmental activist who doesn't answer his cell

· **Dick Devine**: sleaziest dick on the block

The hardest thing about any political campaign is how to win without proving that you are unworthy of winning.
—Adlai Stevenson

There is nothing more deceptive than an obvious fact.
—Sir Arthur Conan Doyle

ELECTION NIGHT

BILLED BY THE PRESS as "the carpetbagger versus Mr. Smith goes to Washington," the contest between the two opposing candidates for the U.S. House of Representatives demonstrated the power of money in a campaign. With huge resources behind him, the "carpetbagger" became a household name overnight by bombarding the urban Washington State district with ads and flyers attacking his opponent. "Mr. Smith," on the other hand, already a well-known local politician who had won most of the endorsements, tried to ignore the smear campaign from his opponent by consistently focusing on policy.

As the election drew near and polls suggested the race was too close to call, the candidate who had tried so hard to remain above the fray came out with an ad aimed at discrediting his opponent for moving into the district to run for office. Immediately, the press jumped on the change in tactics. They tarred both candidates with the same brush and labeled the race as one of the most negative ever run in the state. It made good headlines.

On election eve, with the race still too close to call, both candidates hosted parties for their volunteers, contributors, and supporters. The parties appeared alike on the surface. There were reporters milling about, filling the time until there was something to actually report by commenting on who was present and assessing whether the collective mood seemed upbeat or dispirited. There were snacks and drinks, lots of snacks and drinks. There were multiple television sets tuned to election returns on competing channels. And there were loud conversations buoyed by optimism about their candidate's chances of winning.

In spite of the similarities between the two election eve parties, there were also distinct differences. One was being held at the candidate's campaign headquarters in the suburbs, the now empty desks pushed against walls, the remains of campaign flyers and telephone scripts stacked in a corner. There were plastic bowls filled with potato chips, Doritos and pretzels set out on folding tables. The dips were in their original containers. People were drinking out of paper cups. In contrast, the other party was being held in a fancy downtown hotel where caterers were in charge of food and drink, and no expense had been spared.

Another difference was the size of the television screens. Two small monitors had been set up on boxes placed on wobbly tables at the party taking place at the candidate's campaign headquarters. The large hotel event space, on the other hand, had three huge screens strategically placed so everyone could see them no matter where they were in the room.

Although there were reporters at both events, there were more at the hotel than at the cramped campaign headquarters. Not only was the food better, the hotel soiree boasted appearances by important people and the local social elite, while the campaign headquarters was mainly filled with casually dressed young volunteers and staff. The handful of reporters present at the less prestigious party wandered aimlessly around the room, showing more interest in the snacks than in the guests, although they didn't look impressed with either.

After the polls closed, participants at both gatherings continued to eat and drink while chatting optimistically about their candidate's chances, pausing in a tableau of hushed anticipation whenever new data on the local race for the House seat popped up on one of the screens.

The candidates were neck-in-neck during all of the early returns. Then, as more votes came in, the numbers would appear to favor one candidate, only to reverse direction a few minutes later in favor of the other. Shouting and clapping quickly faded into booing and slumped shoulders, back and forth with the vacillating numbers.

Finally, with 66 per cent of the votes counted, one candidate started pulling ahead, slowly but inevitably increasing his lead.

TWO MONTHS EARLIER

CHAPTER 1
THE CASE OF THE VANISHING YARD SIGNS

A NEW CROP OF CAMPAIGN signs had magically appeared overnight along the highway. To me they were symptomatic of the superficial bent our political system had taken recently. Flashy slogans and graphics in lieu of policy discussions. Did anyone honestly think a potential voter was going to make a decision about a candidate based on a yard sign? The only possible good I could imagine coming from the money and effort spent on signs was to serve as a reminder of the upcoming election. Although I doubted anyone unaware of the election would be persuaded to vote as a result of being bombarded by dozens of signs bearing the names of people running for everything from Congressional representative to county clerk. I dismissed the signs as a waste of money and gave them little more than a brief glance as I drove by.

It wasn't until I got within three blocks of the mall that a tight grouping of campaign signs actually did catch my attention. They were on a vacant lot next to a small house that had somehow survived all the development in the area. It was a busy corner with open space and no visible owner, an easy target for volunteers eager to get their candidate's name in front of the public. Just yesterday, I remembered seeing a row of bright green signs with dark green print—Nathan Knight for Congress—sticking up out of the uncut grass that blanketed the property. Today, however, the row of bright red signs screamed Vote for Bobby Mann in large navy-blue block letters superimposed over a U.S. flag. The transformation was both startling and strange. As I waited my turn at the stop sign, I wondered what had happened to Knight's signs. Maybe they had been moved to another location. Or maybe someone supporting Mann had tossed them in the bushes at the back of the lot. It seemed possible. Emotions were running hot in the run for this seat in the U.S. House of Representatives.

The mall wasn't officially open yet. There were, however, a number of cars clustered near the main entrance. Once inside, most of the storefronts were still blocked by grates or sliding doors to prevent early shoppers from sneaking in ahead of time.

In spite of the hour, there was a fair amount of activity, mostly seniors doing laps before gathering around the food court's plastic tables with uneven metal legs to drink coffee and pass the time of day with other retirees. Although mall traffic generally was down, the walkers still gathered in the morning, getting their exercise in by walking back and forth the full length of the mall. Inside you didn't have to worry about the weather.

I made my way past the familiar stores, occasionally moving out around clumps of walkers who assumed they had the right-of-way. The smell of coffee mingled with the aroma of the centrally located Cinnabon Bakery. I sometimes wondered if they used a fan to disperse the smell of their cinnamon rolls, a sweet invitation to everyone within smelling distance to stop and add approximately one million calories to their breakfast routine.

There were only a few customers at Starbucks, so I opted to get a tall dark roast rather than start the work day with the office's bland breakfast blend. There was a tempting array of pastries in the display case, but I decided to wait and scarf something from Yuri. More often than not, he stopped at a bakery on the way to work.

As I passed the Sew What? storefront, I paused to admire a newly displayed quilt featuring swirls of green and gold that looked like the background for a Klimt painting. Maybe I should check out the price when the store opened. Now that I had a job, I could afford a splurge now and then, and Mara might like a new quilt. At thirteen, she was still okay with letting me pick out clothes or decorations for her room. I wondered how long that would last.

I shrugged my purse up higher on my shoulder so it wouldn't slip off as I pulled open the door to Penny-wise Investigations. The name of my employer was painted in a cobalt blue arc that spanned three quarters of the large one-way mirror storefront window. Within the arc in smaller, straight-line print was: "Discount Detection." Lower down and to the right was a tiny griffin emblazoned in gold next to "P.W. Griffin & Associates. Vigilance you can afford."

Sometimes I still caught myself wondering how in the world I'd become a detective. My dream had been to use my newly minted Ph.D. to land a tenure-track position by churning out deep, insightful papers on the intersectionality of this and that and the interconnectedness of knowledge. But just as I was about to finish my coursework in an interdisciplinary liberal arts program, my husband died and everything changed. There was no life insurance and very little in the bank. Although it was a struggle, both financially and as the mother of two young children, I somehow managed to complete the program and get my degree.

But as fascinating as a focus on interdisciplinary studies was to me, it wasn't very marketable to college hiring committees. Eventually I gave up on finding a college position and turned to the business world. Unfortunately, no one there seemed to value my interdisciplinary background either. I was either overqualified or underqualified for whatever position they were advertising for. Try as I might, I couldn't find a job, any job. Until I impulsively responded to a "help wanted" sign in the Penny-wise window.

Although I hadn't fully understood the nature of the position I was applying for, my interview with the impressive head of the agency had gone well, and I ended up being offered a job as an investigator. Well, as an investigator in training. Jason and Mara, had been stunned when I announced that I was going to go to work for a detective agency. They couldn't imagine their Mom as a detective, and, truthfully it was hard for me to imagine it, too. My own mother had been not only surprised, but disapproving. Her dream for me was that I would remarry and devote myself to raising her grandchildren. But here I was. A real-life detective. Licensed and everything. I'd even solved a case or two.

As I pulled the door open at Penny-wise, my purse started to slip. I grabbed the purse with one hand, clutched my coffee with the other, and shoved the heavy door shut with my foot. Our administrative assistant, W. Blaine

Watkins, a well-dressed "stay in the office" version of Dr. Watson, glanced up and frowned.

"Sorry." I hoped I hadn't scuffed the bottom of the door or dribbled coffee on the floor. Blaine was a stickler for keeping the plush waiting room spotless. When I'd first opened the door to ask about the "help wanted" position, I hadn't been sure what a discount detective agency would be like. But the tasteful waiting room with the gold nameplate reflecting on the highly polished wood desk definitely wasn't it.

"Good morning, Cameron," Blaine said in his usual formal and perfunctory manner. "P.W. would like to see you as soon as you're settled in." His blue dress shirt was a perfect match for his blue eyes, cool and professional.

"Thanks. I'll just drop off my purse and coffee." And take a few quick sips to charge my batteries. Maybe grab a pastry from Yuri.

"Oh, and ask Yuri to join you, please."

"Will do." Ah, a clue. Either Yuri and I were both in hot water, or there was a job afoot, one that required two people. I had been with the agency for just over a year. During that time most of my assignments had been routine investigative work like cheating spouses, employee complaints that required a third-party perspective, theft, runaways, or background checks. They were middle class and small business problems at which no one wanted to throw a lot of money. Only one case had put me in danger, but after that, neither my blood pressure nor my self-defense skills had been challenged.

Even so, I still thought of the job at Penny-wise as part work and part fantasy. No matter how small the problem,

I was a bona fide investigator at a detective agency. Not exactly Wonder Woman, but still someone trying to dispense a bit of justice in a chaotic world. It was a far cry from a professorship in the ivory tower, but I had come to terms with it. In fact, I'd decided that compared to detective work, writing papers and teaching freshmen sounded downright boring.

I let myself into the office's large workroom, affectionately referred to as the "pit" by my fellow investigators. The room looked like an oversized, well-used den for office workers. There was a row of desks separated by chest high gray partitions and rows of bookshelves, a couple of long tables along the sides of the room, an old leather couch, an assortment of chairs, and a line of battered metal filing cabinets. Yuri was at his cluttered desk, staring at his computer, his black glasses with their thick frames resting cockeyed on his nose. When he turned toward me, I realized one arm of his glasses frame was missing.

"Let's see, did someone spot you tailing them and poke you in the nose? Were you attacked by a drone? Or did you fall off your bike?" I asked.

"I was going to offer you a donut—"

I sighed and eyed the box next to his computer. "I'm afraid we don't have time. P.W. beckons." Turning slightly as if heading for P.W.'s office, I quickly snatched a donut and took a large bite.

Yuri gave me an eye roll and dramatically slammed the lid shut on the box of donuts, most likely smashing half of them. "A new assignment?" he asked. Things had been slow of late, reflecting the decline in the number of people who shopped at the mall. All of us had begun worrying about the financial stability of the business.

"Let's hope."

Yuri stood up and pushed back the mass of black hair that covered his forehead. I went to my desk, put my purse in the bottom drawer, quickly gulped down some coffee, and took another bite of the donut.

"Come on," Yuri urged. "Let's do this. I'm tired of sitting around the office."

"Me too," I agreed, although I'd been making good use of the office time to learn more about online research and the legal issues involved when handling employee and management complaints. There was a lot to know, and on-the-job training had its limits. Besides, whenever Yuri got bored, he turned to trivia to pass the time. I was tired of being asked about the lifespans of various animals or what historic events happened in a particular month. And I couldn't think of any reason why I needed to know that fish don't have eyelids or that some lipsticks contain fish scales to give them pearlescence.

Yuri knocked on P.W.'s door, a modest three-finger rap. When she said "enter," he stepped aside for me to go first. We have an on-going debate about what behaviors are "polite" versus chauvinistic. But I nodded and stepped inside, resolving to beat him to the punch on the way out.

I always enjoy seeing what P.W. is wearing. Today it was a teal skirt and matching jacket with black, angled stripes on the jacket collar that continued down the front of the jacket and rimmed the bottom edge. A large pin that looked like something from Madeleine Albright's collection dominated her left shoulder. It was a Roman era griffin studded with gemstones. A teal hat with a black ring around the brim hung on the coat rack in the corner.

As we sat in the chairs in front of her desk, P.W. looked up from the file she'd been reading, her dark eyes unfathomable. "Good morning," she said in her low, hoarse voice, accompanied by a warm but fleeting smile.

We said "good morning" back, sounding to me like obedient children. P.W. is intimidating, not only because of her height, her startling white hair and a commanding presence, but because we know so little about her. The one thing we know for sure is that she has high standards for her employees in spite of our brand as a "discount" agency and our mall location.

"I have an assignment for the two of you." She paused, waiting for us to look appropriately enthusiastic. We didn't disappoint.

She pushed the file folder she'd been perusing when we came in across the desk. "It's a straightforward surveillance. Starting tonight, if possible." She looked at me and asked, "Will that be okay?"

"Yes," I said as Yuri nodded his agreement. "My mother should be able to take care of my kids." When I'd been running low on money and morale, the children and I had left our heavily mortgaged house in another state behind and moved into the bottom floor of a carriage house that we now shared with my mother. She lived upstairs, paid her share of the rent, and frequently bought groceries for all of us. On most days I considered it a good arrangement.

"As you know, there is an election coming up. We've been hired by one of the campaigns to look into the theft of their signage."

"Which candidate?" Yuri asked.

"Does it matter?" P.W. asked.

"There's a lot at stake in this election," Yuri said.

"I'm assuming that your political affiliation isn't more important than catching a thief?" P.W. sounded more curious than judgmental. I knew nothing about her politics, but I, too, had strong feelings about the upcoming election.

I watched the question play out across Yuri's face. "Nope," he said. "I can work for the enemy – assuming it's a paying client."

"Alright then," P.W. said. "Our client is Nathan Knight." She paused to see if Yuri approved.

"He's my guy," Yuri said, giving a thumbs up. I already knew he favored Knight from frequent discussions we'd had about the upcoming election. He was my guy too, so I was also pleased. Working for his opponent was not something I would have felt good about. Although to survive as a small business you sometimes have to take on clients that you wouldn't want as friends.

"Well, then you will be spying on the 'enemy.'" P.W. said with a hint of sarcasm. I noted that she had not revealed her political preference.

"Hey, I was willing to spy on the good guys, too, but I have to admit I'm glad the good guys aren't the bad guys," Yuri said, smiling broadly.

Ignoring his attempt at humor, P.W. continued. "In my experience it's often zealous volunteers or young staffers who sometimes step over the line during a campaign. They are usually true believers, unaware of the consequences of something they consider more of a prank than an illegal act. Your assignment isn't to incriminate or castigate the candidate, but to catch those responsible and end the thefts."

"Is that what the client wants?" I asked.

"If there are charges brought, the Knight campaign will probably welcome the bad publicity it will create for their opponent. As I'm sure you're aware, campaigns are all about getting media coverage. But they are hiring us because they are tired of constantly having to replace signs."

"I can understand why volunteers think of stealing signs as a prank," Yuri said.

I bet you can, I thought. Yuri wasn't exactly someone committed to following the letter of the law. A characteristic that had from time to time gotten him into—and out of—some awkward situations. Although I didn't always approve of his tactics, I had let him teach me how to pick a lock and found his ability to make up a story to get information out of someone admirable if not inspiring.

"As you probably know, signs are not inexpensive. And it takes time from other more valuable activities to monitor signage and replace stolen signs." She paused, turning her dark eyes first on me, then aiming their solemn message at Yuri. "Our goal is to catch the thieves in the act. Just take pictures; don't make an effort to stop them. Understand?"

"Got it," I said, turning to Yuri to make sure he agreed.

"Sure," he said. "We aren't law enforcement. But do we call the cops as well as take pictures?"

"The actual theft will probably happen fairly quickly. It doesn't take long to grab a few signs. It's highly unlikely that you would be able to get police there in time to make an arrest. If, however, it seems safe, you can follow them to see where they take the signs."

"And take more pictures."

"Yes. But it's up to the campaign staff as to whether the police get involved. It's not your decision." We nodded in unison. "The best locations for a stakeout are identified on a map in the folder. Signs regularly go missing from those places. You might want to go by this afternoon and choose the best spot for surveillance."

"And if nothing happens tonight?" I asked.

"You have up to four nights to catch the thieves. Based on their experience of late, it shouldn't take that long."

Once we were back in the pit, we poured over the thin file. It came as no surprise that the Knight campaign suspected the Mann campaign volunteers of pilfering their signs. But although they had tried, they hadn't managed to catch anyone. I guessed that the change in campaign signs I had seen on my way to work might be involved. Theft and substitution.

I spent the rest of the morning doing background checks for a case Norm Nelson was working on. Norm is our resident expert on being nondescript. He's average in every way, except in his skill as an investigator. In that he excels. The work I was doing for him was tedious but not mind-numbing. You never knew what you were going to find out about somebody. They could be boringly normal, or they could have something in their past that was criminal, kinky, or just plain strange. What you uncovered might or might not disqualify them for whatever position they were vying for. It was up to the client to make that call.

After picking our location, I dropped Yuri off and headed home. There would be time to take a short nap, grab something to eat, and have a brief but inevitable tense exchange with my mother. She never really minds keeping an eye on the kids; she dotes on them. But whenever I need her to look out for them because of my work she inevitably uses the opportunity to let me know that I should be focusing my time on finding a husband, not playing at being a private investigator. After all, I wasn't getting any younger.

Jason, my pre-teen news junkie son, was, as usual, glued to the TV news when I arrived. He barely looked up when I stuck my head in the living room to announce I was home. My daughter, Mara, with her perfect oval face and thick eyebrows, was on her computer, skyping with a friend. Thirteen was apparently the year when most girls became all girlie and talked for hours about clothes, boys, and the makeup their mothers didn't want them to wear. I didn't remember going through that phase, but Mom assures me that I did. I had let Mara get her ears pierced at the end of summer, relieved that she didn't want more piercings. Actually, Mom had insisted on taking Mara to have her ears pierced or I might not have agreed to it. A love of earrings was something they had in common.

I could hear Mom moving about in the kitchen, probably creating one of her healthy gourmet dinners that the kids would only complain about behind her back. She spoiled them in so many ways they almost forgave her for her cooking, almost. As I went in to see what she was up to, I noticed another article stuck under the ceramic goose magnet on my refrigerator. How I detested that goose with its blue flowered kerchief. I had no doubt that the article would be on one of the now familiar themes: problems single mothers face, longevity and marriage, happiness and marriage, income and marriage, and ways to meet marriageable men—the articles changed, but never the themes.

"I'm going to take a nap," I announced. "And, Mom, can you keep an eye on the kids tonight?"

Mara was suddenly there, glaring at me. "We don't need a babysitter," she said in her newly discovered whiny teenage voice. Who had taken over the vocal box of my formerly sweet young daughter?

"Your grandmother isn't a babysitter," I said. I knew the script by heart. "So, what if YOU keep an eye on HER? That better?"

Jason came in and asked, "You on a new case?"

"Stakeout. Campaign signs being stolen on a regular basis."

"That's a misdemeanor," he said. "It's a $1,000 fine and up to 90 days in jail." Trust Jason to know the details as they had probably been explained on some news program.

"Whose signs?" Mara asked.

"Nathan Knight's."

Jason said, "Research suggests that campaign signs have very little impact, if any, on how people vote. But you still need signs." He paused, then added, "And I can't stand his opponent, Bobby Mann."

"Me neither," Mara said. For once they agreed on something.

"I've never cared for a man who uses a diminutive for his first name," Mom added.

"Well, that's settled," I said. "I'm going to catch a few winks and then help out our preferred candidate for Congress. Everyone okay with that?"

Jason returned to his TV news program. Mara went back to her computer. And Mom informed me she would leave something for me to eat in the fridge. I didn't ask what it would be. I planned on taking sufficient junk food on the stakeout to see me through the evening, so I didn't need to worry about what she was planning for dinner. I left her in the kitchen stirring some healthy concoction on the stove while wearing a floral apron to protect her beige silk blouse and dark slacks. She isn't as intimidating or as stylish as P.W., but she's close. I'd inherited her long legs and high cheekbones, but not her lovely chestnut colored hair. Mine is an uninteresting ash blond. My large hazel eyes are my best feature, and I have good skin. But all eyes don't turn to look at me when I enter a room. In some ways I'm okay with that.

CHAPTER 2
CAUGHT IN THE ACT

Yuri had offered to drive, but as his driving is not only haphazard but downright frightening, I was once again behind the wheel. Still, as usual, he pointed out he's never been in an accident while HE was driving, and, like usual, I reiterated my theory that his driving is so outrageous that other drivers keep their distance.

We'd decided to watch a triangular-shaped vacant lot in a commercial district along a fairly busy road not far from Mann's headquarters. There weren't too many vacant lots left in the city, and this one probably survived because of its odd shape. Signs were scattered everywhere, like wooden-stemmed cardboard weeds growing out of control, including a dozen or so for Knight. They stood out from the rest because of their color and careful placement on the lot. According to the file, Knight's signs had been stolen from the lot in the past, and hopefully they would be a tempting target for the opposition this evening. Although I liked having an assignment, I didn't necessarily look forward to spending too many nights in a car eating junk food and praying I could last the night without needing a toilet break.

"Want to start with chips or Cheez-its?" Yuri asked.

"I brought a couple of sandwiches," I said. "Egg salad or vegetarian?"

"What's in the vegetarian?"

"Eggs," I said, handing him a sandwich. "I didn't have time for dinner," I explained. "I also have a thermos of coffee and some candy bars."

"I brought Coke and candy bars."

"Think we'll have enough?"

"Only if it doesn't take all night." Yuri laughed. I like his laugh. And I like him. We work well together. Initially my kids had hoped we would end up romantically involved, but when they realized that wasn't going to happen, they seemed content to settle for his friendship in our lives. At Yuri's instigation, the three of us had gone on a camping trip to the San Juans. I'm not a fan of camping and never will be—too much roughing it and too many bugs—but the kids and Yuri had a great time.

We settled in, eating, watching, and making small talk. Yuri vented about politics and the upcoming election. I vented about my mother and the upcoming election. We speculated about the impact fewer mall customers might have on Penny-wise as big box stores left and were replaced with apartments. And we played with the idea of inviting his father to my family's Thanksgiving dinner. Both my mother and Yuri's father have been widowed for a while. Although we didn't think they had anything in common, you never knew what might work until you tried. And I liked the idea of giving my mom a dose of her own medicine.

It was less than two hours into our stakeout when a truck showed up and parked next to the row of signs we were watching. Twilight had melted into darkness. The solitary streetlight at the apex of the triangle provided just enough light for some decent pictures. Yuri took a snapshot of the truck, then zoomed in on the license plate for good measure.

"Think we have our thieves already?" I asked.

"It sure looks that way to me."

Three young people got out of the truck. One female and two males, all wearing hoodies.

Yuri snapped their pictures. "Take that," he said. "And that."

"There they go," I said as they headed for the signs. Yuri kept snapping pictures as they pulled up one sign after another and tossed them into the truck bed. Then they got back in the truck, two in front, one in the tiny space behind the front seat. "And here we go. Let's hope they don't notice they're being followed."

It seemed too easy. The truck made two more stops. One at a strip mall in front of a convenience store where they picked up four Knight signs and another at a bus stop where they plucked three signs from the hillside. By then we had more than enough pictures to prove they were the culprits. Although we still didn't have any clear shots of their faces. They pulled up their hoods each time they got out to swipe signs. Based on their silhouettes while in the truck, we knew that the person in the back seat had long hair. But that was all we could make out.

After the third stop, we followed them to Mann's headquarters. They parked in front and started hauling signs inside.

"Can you believe it?" Yuri said, snapping still more pictures. "They're storing the stolen signs at his campaign office. That's cheeky."

"And risky, I would think."

"Wonder how many they have inside?" Yuri said thoughtfully.

"Don't even think about it," I warned.

"Think about what?" Yuri asked, even though he knew that I knew what he was thinking. I was thinking it, too. But I knew we shouldn't.

The trio left after just a few minutes inside. Yuri had taken pictures of them hauling the signs inside and more when they left empty-handed, but we still didn't have any good facial shots.

"We could continue following them and hope to get a glimpse of someone's face," I suggested, then quickly changed my mind. "But that's probably a bad idea. They haven't seen us so far, and we probably shouldn't push our luck."

"Besides, catching the thieves isn't our assignment."

"You're right. We've earned our fee."

"Still, I can't help wondering..." Yuri's voice trailed off. "I agree we shouldn't follow them and that we have sufficient evidence to satisfy our client. But aren't you curious?"

"Of course, I'm curious, but that would be breaking the law."

"I bet there are a lot of them in there," Yuri said, "And there's no one around. Just one quick peek and I'll be satisfied." He didn't wait for me to argue him out of it. He simply grabbed a flashlight out of the glove box and got out of the car. I didn't move. I just sat there, my good angel arguing with my bad angel. Yuri leaned over and peered in at me. "Look at it this way, if we go inside, you can use the bathroom."

My bad angel won. I did need to go, but that wasn't what swayed me. I rationalized that there was no way to stop Yuri once he got his mind set on something, and I couldn't let him go alone. And to be truthful, I was really, really curious myself. "We can't let on that we've done this."

"Of course not. Catching the sign thieves was for the job. This is for us."

Yuri reached back into the car and pulled a couple of baseball caps out of his bag of snacks. "You never know when you're going to need a cap." He handed one to me. We put on our caps, automatically pulling the bills down low on our foreheads.

The campaign headquarters was the last office on the end of a series of connected stores in a strip mall. Out front there had been signage for a pet store, a donut shop, a nail salon, and a deli. Nothing fancy, but I still wondered about cameras. I didn't see any, but everyone seemed to have them these days.

We made our way around to the back of the building. There was no one in the alley. And there were no obvious cameras. But there was a spotlight on the corner of the end building that cast just enough light to ensure that we were clearly visible on any hidden cameras that might be aimed at the back of the campaign headquarters. We both kept our heads titled down, just in case.

"Let's try the window," Yuri whispered. I wasn't sure why he was whispering since there was no one in sight.

But whispering seems to go with sneaking around. He went over and tried to open the window. “It’s locked.”

“Surprise,” I said softly.

“No problem. The door shouldn’t be much of a challenge.” Yuri reached into his pocket for his precious lock-picking tool. “Cover for me.” He leaned down to study the lock mechanism. “Pretend like we’re making out.”

“With you bending over the doorknob?”

“Improvise. Make it look like it’s all about us.”

I leaned over him and watched as he tinkered with the lock. It was an old door in an old building that had been built cheaply and probably didn’t meet current code. I pulled out an expired credit card that I had saved for just such a purpose and pressed it into the space between the frame and the door.

“That doesn’t work on modern locks.” Yuri continued to probe the lock mechanism.

I pushed harder. “Worth a try,” I countered. Then added, “Especially if the door isn’t locked in the first place.”

Yuri grabbed the doorknob and gave it a turn. “Maybe I unlocked it,” he said, but not convincingly.

We quickly went inside and paused to listen and get our bearings. The outside spotlight reached the interior through the small, locked window, almost meeting up with the diffused light shining through the large storefront windows from the streetlight next to the parking lot. The building may have been old, but the spacious interior appeared well-organized and well equipped. There were telephones on narrow tables along one wall, desks piled high with campaign literature, flip charts scattered among the interior desks, and two glass enclosed offices. A long banner was draped above the phone bank tables, and huge pictures of the candidate decorated the back wall. I couldn't make out too many details in the dim light, but everything suggested a professional, well-run campaign. So why had a door been left open?

Yuri got out his flashlight and ran it around the room. "Impressive." Then, "Over there." He aimed the light at a door next to a small kitchen at the back.

"It could be a bathroom," I said, almost hoping it was.

"Looks like a storage room to me. You don't usually put a bathroom entry through a kitchen."

"Wait," I said when we reached the door. "We don't want to leave any fingerprints behind." I got out a pair of disposable plastic gloves and pulled them on. "Allow me—"

"Prepared, huh?"

"Between the two of us we seem to have everything needed for a break-in." As soon as I'd said it out loud, an inner voice cried out, "You're being stupid. You should leave now." Instead, I meekly followed Yuri. "Let's remember to wipe the back doorknob when we leave."

"No one is going to know we were here," Yuri rationalized. "There are a ton of people coming and going in a campaign headquarters."

"Who is always saying not to leave a trace?"

"Okay, okay, I'll wipe the doorknob when we leave."

I opened the door. Yuri was right. It was a small room, and was definitely being used for storage. Yuri pointed his flashlight at the left wall where a haphazard mess of bright green Knight campaign signs were piled. In the middle of the room, against the back wall, Mann campaign signs were neatly stacked, apparently waiting to be distributed to appropriate locations. And as Yuri trailed his light further to the right, we saw something else. Something completely out of place.

"Damn," Yuri said out loud. At the same time, I blurted out a "holy shit." My voice resonated off the walls of the windowless room. We both stood there motionless, staring at the body lying face down on the floor next to the pile of Mann signs. Fanning out from the man's head was a pool of dark red, as if the paint from Mann's signs had liquified and drooled off onto the floor, creating a bloody halo.

CHAPTER 3
A QUICK GETAWAY

"LET'S GET OUT OF HERE," Yuri said, his voice shaking. "Now!"

I started to obey, then realized we couldn't just leave. "We need to check to see if he's dead." Reluctantly, I headed into the room.

"No way he's alive," Yuri said, but he didn't try to stop me. "Don't step in the blood."

"I have to make sure. I would never forgive myself—"

"You're right, of course we have to check." Yuri stayed in the doorway, aiming his flashlight at the man's head. Or what was left of it. The man had obviously been hit with something from behind. Hard. Maybe more than once. "Make it quick."

I knelt down, trying to avoid touching the dark circle of blood on the floor, and felt for a pulse. After only a few seconds, I was sure. "Nothing. Not even a hint of life."

"Let's go then." Yuri turned away, and the room was suddenly dark.

"Hey, I need to see where I'm stepping," I yelled. Yuri quickly turned back in my direction and shined the light on the floor to guide me to where he was waiting.

Before stepping outside, we checked to make sure there was no one in the alley. After shutting the door, Yuri looked around again and asked, "Have anything to wipe the doorknob with?"

"I'm having second thoughts. Maybe we shouldn't wipe it clean. The murderer's prints could be on it."

"But if we aren't going to call the police…."

"Aren't we?"

"Dammit, Cameron. I don't want to get involved. Do you?"

"No, but—"

"Okay, let's leave the prints. We can admit we followed them here. We can even admit we tried the doorknob. But that's it. Okay? Now let's get going."

"That doesn't make sense. Why would we try the doorknob, find the door open and not go inside? I mean, why would we try the doorknob in the first place if we weren't trying to get in?"

"We can talk about this after we get away from here."

Not at all convinced we were doing the right thing by running away, I followed Yuri back to my car, pausing before getting in to state the obvious: "If there is a camera, they will know we went inside and, if there's a timestamp, they will also be able to tell how long we were in there."

Yuri got in the car and motioned for me to join him. Reluctantly I took my place behind the wheel, turning to look at him before starting the engine. "Are we absolutely sure we want to just drive away?"

"No, I'm not sure, but I want time to think about it before we do something we'll regret."

I started the car and pulled away from the strip mall, slowly, not at all certain that we weren't doing something we were going to regret, big time. "Where to?"

"My place," Yuri said. "We need to think this through."

Yuri lived only a few miles away. We didn't talk much on the way there. I didn't know what was going through his mind, but I was envisioning being questioned by the police and them offering me a deal if I would rat on Yuri. I was also thinking about what P.W. would say. Would she fire us? Even with an unlocked door, entering someone's campaign headquarters at night without permission was unquestionably still a crime. And fleeing the scene of a crime, was that a misdemeanor? A felony? What if I ended up going to jail? Worst case scenario, what if they thought one of us was responsible for the man's death? Or that we had colluded to commit murder? That was a pretty convincing argument for reporting our discovery sooner rather than later.

Yuri's condo was the end unit of five connected, three-story structures. Each was painted brown with a different color accent on the second-floor dormer and window trim. Yuri's accent color was bright green, like Knight's signs. Eerie. In spite of working with him for over a year, I had never been inside his condo before. I was surprised to see how neat everything was. Given how sloppy he was at work, I had expected clutter everywhere. It almost looked like he had hired an interior decorator to create a comfortable space with masculine accents, the overall effect softened by the artwork on the walls and coasters on the low coffee table in front of the brown leather couch with brass studded armrests.

"Have a seat," he said. "I don't know about you, but I could use a drink."

"Have any wine?"

"Red or white?"

"Red."

He went into the kitchen and came back with a glass of red wine for me and what looked like whiskey for him. "Here's what I think," he said as he handed me my wine. "I think we need to call P.W."

"What?" I almost spit out the mouthful of wine I had sipped. It was the last thing I'd expected to hear from him.

"Hopefully she'll understand why we ran, and she will be able to give us some perspective on this."

"Or she'll fire us and tell us we're on our own."

"No, I don't think so. But you have to agree to calling her. We're in this together."

I thought for a minute. P.W. was stern but fair. She probably knew we pushed the envelope occasionally, but we never talked about it. Maybe Yuri was right. It would at least be backup for our story if we were caught. "Okay, when should we call her?"

"Right now," Yuri said.

"But it's 1:00 in the morning."

"Could be worse."

"What's worse?"

"3:00 a.m." He was already on his phone. Moments later he said, "It's Yuri and Cameron. I'm going to switch to speaker."

As he did so I heard P.W. say "okay."

"We have a situation," Yuri continued.

"That doesn't sound good," P.W. said, her voice even more raspy than usual. We had undoubtedly awakened her.

"It's not." Yuri quickly explained what had happened and that we were back at his place trying to decide what to do next.

"So, you verified he was dead," P.W. said.

"Yes," I said. "He didn't have a pulse."

"And the back of his head was, ah, not looking exactly intact," Yuri added.

"Any idea how long he'd been dead?"

"No," both of us said in unison.

"Were the sign thieves inside long enough to have done it?"

"It depends," Yuri said. "One quick hit, perhaps. They didn't act like people who had just killed someone when they came out though. But they dumped the signs somewhere, and that back room had a huge pile of Knight signs."

"Was it possible for them to toss the signs in without seeing the body?"

Yuri and I exchanged looks, and I nodded. "We think so," Yuri said. "Especially if they didn't bother switching on the light."

"And your fingerprints are on the back door?"

"Yes, mine are," Yuri said. "We didn't want to wipe the knob, in case there were other prints."

"Hmmm. Someone left the door open. It's possible your prints may be the only ones." P.W. was silent for a moment. "There's nothing else to indicate you were there?"

"Not unless there were cameras," I said.

P.W. was silent again. Then she said, "We can't take a chance. I'll call it in and get back to you."

"Will we be in trouble for leaving the scene?" I asked, trying desperately to keep my voice calm.

"You might be. You're certainly on the hook for entering without permission. I'll see what I can do. Stay where you are. I'll call you as soon as I know anything." She hung up before we could say goodbye.

"Well," Yuri said, "she didn't say 'you're fired.'"

"No, but that doesn't mean she isn't going to."

The next fifteen minutes ticked by with mind boggling slowness, as if the fifteen minutes was a life sentence. We decided we shouldn't have anything more to drink in case we ended up having to talk to the police. So, we just waited. I sat on the coach staring into space while Yuri paced back and forth in front of the couch. Once he stopped and said, "I should have listened to you." Then he continued to pace.

"I could have refused to participate. But I went along with it."

He stopped in front of me again. "I didn't have the right to put you at risk."

"You didn't force me into anything," I countered. "I chose to go along. I'm an adult. I make my own decisions."

"You have kids."

"Mom can take care of them while I serve my sentence," I said, trying to lighten up the conversation and failing completely. Yuri glared at me and continued wearing a groove in his carpet.

When the phone rang we both stared at it as if it were a bomb about to go off. Then Yuri turned it on and switched to speaker. "We're here."

"I should hope so." P.W.'s voice sounded normal if somewhat cross. "Listen carefully," she began.

She definitely had our full attention.

"I've spoken with Detective Connolly of Major Crimes. He's sending a team out to Mann's headquarters as we speak. He would like you to meet him there and verify your story. Understood?"

"Yes," we said in sync.

"Be in my office first thing tomorrow morning." The line went dead.

Yuri and I looked at each other for a moment without saying anything. "Well, that wasn't so bad, was it?" Yuri said.

"Let's see, we committed criminal trespass, left the scene of a crime, and are being asked to return for a 'friendly chat' with a detective from Major Crimes. How bad can that be?"

CHAPTER 4
GUILTY UNTIL PROVEN INNOCENT

WHEN WE ARRIVED at Mann's campaign headquarters there were official cars blocking the entrance to the parking lot. Officers in uniforms were standing next to the entrance and the area in front of the office was cordoned off. I parked on the street and we got out and walked toward a uniformed officer standing next to the barrier.

"Can I help you?" he asked in that officious tone so often used with that question. It's seldom a real offer of help but more likely a challenge to whatever it is you want to do.

"We're here to see Detective Connolly," I said.

"He expecting you?"

"Yes." I felt like screaming no, we always drop by crime scenes in the early morning and ask to see the person in charge. But I kept my cool. On the way over, Yuri and I had agreed to be as truthful and compliant as we possibly could. We couldn't see anything to gain by lying or holding something back. And P.W. hadn't given us any instructions. Maybe she had demurred to keep her distance.

The officer got out his phone and turned away from us to talk to someone. Then he turned back and asked, "You

Chandler and Webster?" It almost sounded like a classy law firm instead of two pathetic investigators who had fled from the scene and were potentially prime suspects in a murder.

"Uh huh," Yuri said.

"He's waiting for you inside. The officer at the door will give you booties to wear." I guessed he was being polite because he hadn't been told why we were there. We might be related to the deceased, witnesses to what happened, people associated with the campaign or even consultants. People who deserved civility rather than reprimands. Or worse.

We thanked him, got our booties from the officer at the entrance, and went inside. This time the lights were on. As we headed across the room toward the kitchen and the storage area a man in a trim leather jacket and jeans came out of the back and walked in our direction. He was late thirties, tall and dark haired, with the Irish good looks of a cross between Colin Farrell and Cillian Murphy. If he spoke with a brogue, I feared I might swoon.

"Detective Connolly," he said, holding out his hand to me. The gesture was polite, but there was no warmth in his sharp blue eyes. And no smile. And no accent.

"Cameron Chandler," I said, looking him in the eyes to show I wasn't embarrassed to be there, even though we had perhaps misbehaved or possibly broken some minor law.

Yuri extended his hand. "Yuri Webster." Friendly yet professional. No hint of guilt or remorse for leaving the scene.

"I'll need statements from you tomorrow, but for now I want to verify that nothing has changed since you left."

His emphasis on the word "left" made me very aware that we weren't off the hook. I wanted to explain what had happened, but Yuri and I had agreed not to offer any information; we would play it as safe as possible by sticking to answering questions.

As we stood in the entrance to the storage room, I thought everything looked the same as when we were there earlier – the haphazard heap of Knight signs, the neatly stacked pile of Mann signs, and the body on the floor. But this time the room was lit up by overhead lights and there were several people hovering over the body while one person seemed to be examining it. With the lights on I could see that the man on the floor had brown hair and was wearing jeans and a dark blue sweatshirt splattered with blood.

"Well?" Detective Connolly prompted.

"Nothing's changed," Yuri said, looking to me for confirmation.

"I understand you checked for a pulse." Connolly looked at me.

"Yes."

"And after you decided he was not in need of medical assistance, you left through the back door."

"The same way we came in," Yuri offered. "The door was unlocked," he added, with a self-conscious glance in my direction.

"I assume that we'll find your fingerprints on the doorknob."

"Yes." That was one right decision we'd made. Guilty people wiped their prints, didn't they?

"Do you know the victim?"

Yuri was shaking his head "no." Too much shaking, but the answer was clear.

"I can't tell without seeing his face," I said. "But I doubt it."

"We don't work directly for either of the campaigns," Yuri said, offering information again rather than sticking to our agreed upon approach. He was obviously more rattled by what had happened than I'd realized. Probably because he was still regretting that he had gotten me involved and was concerned about consequences such as us losing our jobs or, worst case scenario, going to jail.

"Do you have a name for him?" I asked.

"Yes."

We waited, but apparently it was not something Detective Connolly was going to share with us. It felt like he was staring us down, taking our measure or waiting for us to blurt out a confession. I can usually read nonverbals, but his were a closed book to me. A very attractive book, but closed all the same.

"That's all for now," he said, abruptly dismissing us. "I'll expect you at my office by 10:30 tomorrow morning." He didn't ask if that was convenient. It was an order by someone who had the power to issue such orders. He knew we'd be there. We turned around and headed out.

Once we were outside Yuri said, "That went well, don't you think?"

I almost laughed. "You mean because he didn't put us in cuffs and haul us off to jail?"

"There's that."

After a brief pause, I asked: "Did you notice how dark the blood was? Like the body had been there a while."

"It couldn't have been there too long, depending on what time the office closed." I could see Yuri mentally making some calculations.

"Wouldn't that depend on what they were working on?" I asked. "If they were making calls, it could have been as late as 8:30 or 9:00."

"So, between, say, four to six hours, depending on what time they closed up shop."

"Does the color of blood change in that amount of time? Or is it a question of where the blood came from?"

"I'll have to ask my neighborhood coroner," Yuri quipped. When he doesn't know the answer to something he thinks he should know, he usually falls back on humor. It was one of his frustrating yet endearing traits.

"I'm just hoping the time of death at least means we won't end up being suspects." Being named as suspects would not only be bad publicity for Penny-wise, but Mom would be horrified.

"When you put it that way—"

I dropped Yuri off at his condo with a reminder to set his alarm and headed for home. Once there I quietly let myself in and just as quietly made my way to my bedroom. In no time at all, I was in bed. The last thing I remember was wondering what Detective Connolly's first name was and whether he was married.

My mother knows how to push all of my buttons and exercises her ability to do so on a regular basis. When it comes to my own kids, I believe I am entitled to use my knowledge of their habits and preferences to bend them to my way of thinking. But I don't feel that MY mother has a right to do that to me. So, when she came in to wake me up early to tell me that she and the kids had done just fine without me while I was on a stakeout, I groaned and rolled over. "Leave me alone."

"You need to get up and fix breakfast for your children. I'm leaving to have breakfast with a friend."

We both knew that the kids were perfectly capable of pouring milk into the cereal of their choice and that cold cereal was what they liked for breakfast on weekday mornings. Her comment wasn't about breakfast, it was about me not being a full-time mother. She'd probably planned her breakfast out after I asked her to cover for me during the stakeout. She knows they can sometimes last all night. Annoying and manipulative.

"Okay, okay. I'll get up." I didn't tell her that my alarm was due to go off in ten minutes anyway.

She waited until I sat up before leaving. "Have a nice breakfast," I called after her, followed by "mommy dearest" in sotto voice.

"What was that, Cameron?" When it comes to whispered comments not meant for her to hear, Mom has the hearing range of an animal of prey.

"Nothing, Mom. Just yawning our loud." I yawned loudly to make my point.

Before getting into the shower, I went downstairs to check on Jason and Mara, just in case they really did need something. They were already at the kitchen table eating their cereal while working their phones like they were important executives who couldn't afford to take time off to eat breakfast.

"Hi," I said. "Don't be late for school."

"Ah, Mom," Jason said, implying that I, too, was an annoying mother. His light brown hair was neatly combed, but his blue plaid shirt looked like it had been slept in. I hoped Mom hadn't seen him before she left. In her eyes it would be further evidence of my inadequate parenting. Jason probably had several less wrinkled shirts in his closet, but he always wore whatever was closest at hand.

"Sure, Mom," Mara said without looking up. She was impeccably dressed, well, at least in a thirteen-year-old's version of impeccable. Perhaps a better phrase would be "fashionably disheveled."

"Have a good day," I added. "See you at dinner this evening." At least I hoped I would be home for dinner and not behind bars, eating gruel off a paper plate with a plastic fork.

I got to work just as Blaine was unlocking the door. "You're early," he said.

"And good morning to you," I replied. Then added, "I have a lot to get done today." I didn't owe him an explanation, but I was feeling defensive. Everyone would know soon enough that Yuri and I had screwed up.

The coffee pot was gurgling and my computer was making its morning coming alive sounds when Yuri arrived. "You're early," I said.

"Blaine already mentioned that," he mumbled as he grabbed his mug with the fornicating penguins around the bottom and took a stand in front of the coffee pot. "We need a Keurig," he stated, not for the first time.

"The pods aren't biodegradable." I mimicked Blaine's

tone the best I could. Blaine was the reason we didn't have a faster method for making coffee. Being green was more important to him than convenience. Given how organized Blaine was, I envisioned him getting up early enough to drink freshly ground, fair trade beans from a coffee press before coming to work.

Yuri gave up and sat down at his desk, keeping one eye on the pot, even though he knew it would make a loud rumbling sound when it finished brewing, like a volcano signaling it was ready to erupt.

"I couldn't sleep," Yuri announced without looking at me. "I'm really sorry," he added.

"I'm sorry too, and, as I've already said, I wasn't an innocent bystander."

Blaine stuck his head in. "P.W. is ready for you."

"Damn," Yuri said. "She's early. No coffee."

"We shall go unfortified into the griffin's den." I headed for the door.

"Not funny." Yuri followed, glancing regretfully back at the coffee pot.

P.W. was not only her usual smartly-dressed self, but looked wide-awake as well. Her deep forest green pants suit was the perfect match for her moss green blouse covered in tiny plum colored flowers. A large plum colored flower pin picked up the motif, it's gold stem curving downward on her jacket lapel. I felt suddenly frumpy even though I'd chosen my clothes carefully for the day's meetings, subdued colors, tailored, and professional. Unlike our behavior the night before.

"I understand you will be seeing Detective Connolly this morning," P.W. said.

"Yes," I confirmed. Yuri nodded, his dark hair hanging low on his forehead, but not quite low enough to hide behind.

"This is not the first time that you, Yuri, have crossed a line while working on a case." P.W.'s dark eyes pinioned him. Then she paused, like a priest waiting for acknowledgement of transgressions. He did so with a brief nod. "I do not, however, have any complaints about your work over all," she continued, suddenly sounding like a manager during a performance review. "You are a good investigator, if overly zealous at times." She turned to me. "I was hoping that you would be a stabilizing influence on him, but it seems that you, too, are, ah, willing to ignore professional protocol to get results."

"It's my fault, not Cameron's," Yuri interrupted.

"That's not true. I wanted to see what was inside as much as he did."

"And if there hadn't been a body in there...," P.W. finished for us. "Well, let me just say that although I don't approve of what you did, as long as you don't lose your licenses over this, I don't see that there's a problem going forward."

We were "going forward," not being fired. I felt a surge of relief. Yuri straightened up and pushed his hair off his forehead. If we survived the next hurdle, our meeting with Detective Connolly, we could hopefully get back to normal.

"I want you to tell me again exactly what happened and what Detective Connolly said and asked you last night. Let's start with you, Cameron."

I went through my version of the evening's events, and then Yuri gave his version. They were similar as to the main points, but each of us had noticed some slightly different things. For instance, Yuri was able to describe the contents of the campaign office in detail, almost like he had snapped a picture of it for his memory banks. He was also able to estimate the number of signs in each of the piles in the back room. I, on the other hand, had noticed more about Connolly's reaction, or lack of it, to what we had told him. I was also able to tick off items he'd failed to share with us for one reason or another. And, of course, I could have described his facial features and his blue eyes in some detail, but I left that out.

As Yuri talked, I studied the copper ashtray on P.W.'s desk. The ashtray was a striking vintage piece, about four inches in diameter and embossed with a double-headed Imperial eagle with the inscription "War 1914." Yuri had managed to peek underneath it one time when P.W. wasn't looking, so we knew "K. Faberge" was impressed on the center base. After that, Yuri had done some research. He hadn't managed to find out anything specific about the history of this particular ashtray, but he had discovered it was worth thousands of dollars. We all assumed it had some sentimental value linked to P.W.'s secret past.

As usual, the ashtray held a single cigarette. During our narration, P.W.'s left hand with its square cut emerald ring nestled between two mine-cut diamonds reached out several times to the unlit off-white cylinder with its short cardboard tube tip. She fingered it briefly once, but never picked it up. Yuri had also researched the brand and identified it as a Russian import, a Kazbek Papirosi. Although the ashtray and cigarette were always present, none of us had ever seen her smoke. We weren't even sure she owned more than one cigarette. But we had all witnessed her hand slowly moving, as if of its own volition, toward the lone cigarette in the copper ashtray. It was a drama waiting to unfold.

"All right, then," P.W. concluded. "Let me know how your meeting with Detective Connolly goes."

We stood, mumbled a few words and left quickly, before she could change her mind about our status with Penny-wise. Once back in the pit, Yuri raised a fist in a victory salute while I held a finger up to my lips to suggest we should be quiet about our celebration. Most of the other team members were at their desks, not paying us much attention. I thought it was best to keep it that way.

Unfortunately, Norm apparently noticed Yuri's gesture and asked, "What's up?" It sounded like an obligatory inquiry rather than a request for information. I noted that he was holding a cup of coffee. Grant, our one experienced investigator prior to coming to work for Penny-wise, was there too, with a cup of coffee on his desk. Adele, our research specialist, was also drinking coffee. As was Will, our self-proclaimed expert on self-defense and obsessed with gadgets guy.

I was about to respond to Norm when Yuri swore and asked, "Why didn't someone make more coffee? The person who takes the last cup is supposed to make more." He sounded like someone had done him a real injustice. Before I could offer to make coffee, he gestured toward the door.

"Come on, Cameron. Let's go get a real cup of coffee." I grabbed what was left of a day-old donut out of a box on Yuri's desk and quickly hurried after him.

Will smiled as we left. I had no doubt he was the one who had taken the last cup. It was his way of getting back at Yuri for teasing him all the time. Of course, in my opinion, any investigator who wears a beige belted trench coat with a leather buckle is asking to be picked on. Even though I was secretly fond of the image.

One of the advantages of having an office in a mall is that there are all sorts of shops nearby, including a glut of places to get coffee. Seattle is known for its obsession with coffee. Light, medium or dark roast. Mild, bold or extra bold. French, Italian, Guatemalan. Blends. And more blends. Flavored. Caffeinated. De-caffeinated. Americano. Espresso. Irish. Cappuccino. Steamed milk. Half and half. A shot of soy. On and on go the choices. Too many choices. That's why I always order a tall drip. It simplifies life.

I finished what remained of my donut while Yuri got us each a drip coffee and a couple of pastries. I didn't even hesitate about the calories. We needed fortification to face our day.

After reviewing last evening's traumatic climax for the umpteenth time, we headed downtown for our meeting with Detective Connolly. Yuri had offered to drive, and I had wisely declined. The only thing more frightening than being a passenger with Yuri behind the wheel in residential areas is to let him drive you downtown. Especially during the lingering remnants of commuter traffic. I only made that mistake once. Although in the last few years it was getting harder and harder to tell rush hour traffic from any other time of day. The increase in population and poor transportation planning for the future makes driving in the city a nightmare. Even without Yuri at the wheel.

We weren't sure how long our meeting would take, so we parked in a nearby lot, a wedge-shaped piece of land that had been threatened for years by development that somehow never happened. It's not a secured lot, and I've heard that cars parked there are often vandalized, but it's convenient and comparatively cheap by downtown standards. As we headed up the hill, we were panhandled several times. I usually just shake my head "no," but Yuri seemed to have his pockets filled with dollar bills and gave each person who approached us a dollar. When I raised my eyebrows in question, he said, "I know it won't even buy a cup of coffee these days, but I just can't walk by someone who's down and out without giving them something."

"I know someone who hands out energy bars," I said.

"Hmmm. Not a bad idea. But I'd need bigger pockets."

We had to go through security. The guard asked Yuri to step aside to be wanded. Then he was asked to remove everything in his pockets. Except for a wad of dollar bills, a couple of paperclips and his wallet, he didn't have anything in them. Nothing to set off the machines. It was most likely a random search. But given why we were there, it almost felt personal. Finally, they gave him the go-ahead, and we made our way to the waiting area of the Major Crimes Unit. The receptionist told us to take a seat and she would let Detective Connolly know we were there.

There were several other people in the waiting room. I couldn't help but wonder what they were doing there. Were they witnesses to a crime? Suspects? Friends or relatives of victims? They were all either thumbing through magazines or on their phones. No one was looking at us. But there was no privacy, so I didn't feel comfortable talking to Yuri. He obviously felt the same because he remained silent, finally taking out his phone and playing solitaire to pass the time. I responded to a couple of personal emails and scanned news headlines so I could talk to Jason about what was happening in the world over dinner. With a news junkie son there is always something to talk about.

When Detective Connolly opened the door and motioned us in, I had the irrational urge to run away. I didn't really think we were suspects, and I knew P.W. would have warned us if we needed to have a lawyer present, so I had no basis for the panic I was experiencing. But as I went through the door into his office, I couldn't help but feel like I might be leaving my freedom behind.

Connolly's small, glass-fronted office was packed with neatly stacked files and boxes filled with what I suspected were more files. There were two uncomfortable wood chairs in front of the gray metal desk. Except for the bookshelves on the wall behind the desk, the walls were bare. No taxpayer money had been wasted on this office.

I took a seat and, for a brief moment, lost myself in the detective's cornflower blue eyes. Then I abruptly came back to earth. He was an officer of the law, someone who could judge us as wrongdoers, gorgeous cheekbones and sculpted chin aside.

"Why don't you tell me about last night," he said as he picked up a pen and retrieved a yellow pad from a desk drawer. "I understand you tailed some individuals who you saw stealing Knight campaign signs, correct?"

"Yes."

"Start from when you saw them take the signs."

Yuri nodded for me to go ahead, and I started telling our story, occasionally pausing for Yuri to add something to the narrative. I kept it brief and addressed the issue of illegal entry in a matter-of-fact manner. "When we realized the door was open, we decided to see just how many signs we were talking about. We intended to take a picture and provide the information to the Knight campaign first thing in the morning so they could act as soon as possible. We thought having more evidence would be helpful."

Connally didn't comment. Nor did his face indicate what he was thinking. Was he going to press the point or let it go? I couldn't help but worry that he was setting a trap, one that we wouldn't see until the moment we fell into it. After a long silence, he said, "Can you identify the three individuals who stole the signs?"

"No," Yuri said. "They put up their hoodies each time they got out of the truck. But I can give you the photos we took. No facial shots though. And I took pictures of the truck and its license plate. Last night I gave one of your officers the license number."

"Yes, he looked it up this morning."

I wanted to ask if they'd identified the owner, but I restrained myself. There was another lull in the conversation. Was it a trick to get us to volunteer something? Yuri doesn't do well with silence, but I told myself that I was going to wait it out.

Before Yuri broke down and blurted out something, Connolly spoke again: "You never saw the victim's face, correct?"

Change of subject. Okay. Yuri and I both nodded. Connolly pulled a picture out of a file and slid it across his desk to us. "Know this man?" The face in the picture was youngish, early twenties. In death he looked almost peaceful. It was a much better view than we'd had of him the night before.

I shook my head "no" and looked at Yuri. He was also shaking his head "no."

"I assume his identity will be made public," I said.

"Are you asking for his name?" Connolly had a hint of a smile at the corners of his mouth.

"Just curious," I said.

"You seem to display a fair amount of curiosity about a great many things." His poker face was unreadable.

"It's the nature of our business," Yuri chimed in.

"Fair enough," Connolly said. "But I assume you're aware that when your curiosity leads you to enter an unoccupied building at night and without permission, you're committing criminal trespass and that can land you in jail. Not to mention, cost you your license as a private investigator."

There was a tense silence during which I found myself holding my breath.

When Connolly didn't say he was actually going to charge us with something, I broke the silence, asking a question that was intended to remind him that we weren't the only ones who had broken the law. "Do we need to have our client hold off on doing something about the sign thefts? I mean, I can't imagine that anyone from the Mann campaign will continue stealing signs under the circumstances. And they can hardly get rid of them and claim they were never there. But at some point, our client will want to follow up on this."

"And I assume it will eventually be in the news," Yuri said. "Not exactly good press for the Mann campaign."

"We aren't particularly concerned about a minor theft at this point," Connolly said. Hopefully that meant he also wasn't concerned about our "minor" potentially criminal actions either. "And, no one from the Mann campaign has entered a complaint against the two of you," he added. His words were encouraging, but his tone was stern, letting us know we weren't home free yet.

"But what if the two are connected?" I asked. "The stolen signs and the victim." That seemed a very real possibility to me. Depending on the identity of the victim and his connection to the campaign.

Connolly actually smiled. "I know you don't hesitate if a door is unlocked, but I assume you know better than to meddle in a murder investigation." The smile vanished as quickly as it had appeared. "Do I make myself clear?"

It was tempting to point out that he had stated an assumption not a direct order, but it seemed wise to simply agree. At the same time, I could almost read Yuri's thoughts. How could we possibly continue with life as usual under the circumstances? It was almost as if we had a duty to the corpse to look into his demise. Especially if his death was linked to the sign thefts. And it seemed to me the odds were pretty good that it was. Yet, with no client, how could we justify following up?

CHAPTER 5
HIRED, NOT FIRED

BACK AT THE PIT, Yuri and I were the center of attention. Everyone wanted to know what had happened and what we had seen. Apparently P.W. had decided it was best to tell them what was going on before they heard it in the news. Will asked the question everyone else was thinking: "So, how upset was P.W. by all of this?"

"By 'all of this' do you mean us finding a dead body next to a pile of stolen signs?" Yuri's agitated tone made everyone back off, everyone but Will.

"Yeah, like what were you doing inside the Mann headquarters?"

"Looking for signs," I said, jumping in. "Knock it off, Will. This hasn't been easy."

On the one hand I found myself feeling irritated by his attitude. On the other hand, it seemed like fair payback for Yuri's past cocky behavior and teasing. Still, everyone in the room had either done or at least considered doing something not quite on the up-and-up to accomplish some end for a client. And I didn't feel like I deserved to be heckled, even though I was as guilty of unprofessional conduct as Yuri.

"You were inside their campaign office, Cameron," Will repeated. "While working for their opponent."

"This isn't exactly Watergate," I countered, somewhat defensively.

"That's true," Will conceded. "In Watergate nobody got murdered."

There was a moment of tense silence before Yuri stepped in. "I think the Mann folks are going to have their hands full dealing with a murder at their headquarters. They're not likely to be fueling the situation by complaining about who found the body. Especially given why we were there in the first place."

On one level I thought Yuri's analysis was right on. But it was still possible they would point a finger at us to deflect their own involvement. That's where I felt Will was going with his somewhat snarky remarks.

"Look," Grant said. "The question we should all be asking is whether there is anything we can do to help." Grant, always the peacemaker, had been with P.W. from the start. A former insurance investigator with a large company, he had trained all of us on several skill sets. Gray-haired and energetic, he was both mentor and colleague.

"I'm assuming we're off the case," I said. "We accomplished what our client asked for, so our official involvement is over. And I doubt anyone is going to hire us to investigate the murder."

"Plus, the police have told us to butt out," Yuri added.

"Why would they do that?" Adele asked. Adele is middle-aged, serious about her work as a researcher, and not a fan of Yuri's kidding around. She had worked for the county in records management before she came to Penny-wise.

Yuri and I looked at each other. "Well," I began, "I think they have us pegged as people with more curiosity than good sense."

"They've got that one right," Will said. Then quickly added, "I don't mean you, Cameron."

"Hey, this wasn't all Yuri's fault. I was right there with him. And to be honest, if I had it to do over, I'd do it again."

"We've all been there," Grant said. "You just got unlucky."

"So, was the detective respectful or rude?" Adele asked, looking from me to Yuri. She's very blunt herself and is sensitive to being labeled as discourteous.

"Ask this one," Yuri said with a gesture in my direction. "She's the one who drooled all over him."

"I did not!"

"You did."

"Did not."

"Okay, kids," Grant said. "Do you need a time out?"

That made me laugh. We were sounding like Mara and Jason squabbling over who was right and who was wrong. "Okay, so Detective Connolly is, well, my teenage daughter's friends might describe him as 'screamin' or 'mancandy.' Very Irish with lovely blue eyes and a remarkably chiseled chin."

"Can't blame you for drooling then." Adele gave a little sigh of appreciation.

Suddenly Blaine interrupted: "Yuri, Cameron, front and center."

"Oh, oh." Will raised his eyebrows suggestively. But he stopped short when the others frowned at him.

Blaine motioned for us to go into P.W.'s office. When we entered there was someone in the client's chair, a red leather chair that we suspected P.W. bought as a tribute to Nero Wolfe. She had a whole row of Rex Stout books on the bottom shelf in a bookcase behind her desk.

"Yuri Webster. Cameron Chandler. I'd like you to meet Bobby Mann. Bobby, these are the two who discovered the body."

Bobby Mann looked in person just like he did in his ads, crisp, well-groomed, not a perfectly trimmed hair out of place. Expensive suit, polished shoes, white teeth. He held out his hand and smiled like a politician greeting potential voters, not like a man about to pounce on two people who had broken into his campaign headquarters looking for stolen signs and ended up discovering a dead man. I obligingly shook his hand before taking a seat. Yuri did the same. Neither of us said how good it was to meet him in person. Probably for the same two reasons— we weren't fans and we were puzzled by what he was doing there. For all we knew he had come by to let us know he wasn't going to put up with anyone tailing his staffers or breaking into his office. The smile might simply be a perpetual campaign attribute. Maybe he'd had plastic surgery to keep the corners of his mouth in a permanent uplift.

"Bobby—he's asked us to call him 'Bobby'—is understandably distressed about what happened," P.W. began. "About the stolen signs and, of course, about the loss of life."

The smile disappeared, and Bobby's face dramatically conveyed his sorrow, for both the theft and the death. It struck me as strange that we were talking about them as if they deserved an equal emotional response.

"He assures me that they will make up the loss of the signs to the Knight campaign. And, since that will end our contractual obligation to the Knight campaign, he would like to hire us to monitor what's happening with the murder investigation."

I had to admit the request took me totally by surprise. Yuri, too, must have been surprised; he sat there, eyes blinking behind his slightly lopsided glasses, staring at Bobby Mann as if he had just admitted to being an alien.

"Not that I don't think the police will do a good job," Bobby added quickly. "And I'm not asking you to find the murderer. But I'm sure you have contacts that could help you keep abreast of what's going on. I want you to give me a head's up if something comes along that might impact my run for office. It's always best to be forewarned." He smiled broadly as if to let us know that in this instance forewarned was truly to be forearmed. After all, they weren't guilty of anything other than pilfering a few signs. All he was asking us to do was to be vigilant, like our motto advertised. There was nothing that might arise that they couldn't handle, or perhaps spin to their advantage.

It crossed my mind that perhaps what he was trying to do was to neutralize Yuri and me as witnesses. I wasn't sure exactly how working for him would do that, but I had no doubt there was some hidden agenda behind his request. With family money at his disposal, he could buy access to this information in a number of other ways. He didn't need us.

P.W. continued. "It may be a bit unusual to take, ah, Bobby on as a client under the circumstances. But I assume that, given our limited involvement thus far, the Knight campaign won't have any objection to us playing a modest role in monitoring progress with the police investigation and following up on any rumors that appear in the press. I will, of course, check with them to make sure. Since this assignment will not require us to take sides or assume a lead in the investigation, I'm comfortable agreeing to take it on." She might be comfortable with the assignment, but each time she said "Bobby" it sounded forced. "How do you two feel about the assignment?" She looked from Yuri to me and back to Yuri.

"I have a question," Yuri said, looking directly at Bobby Mann. "Did you know the victim?"

"Yes, well, sort of. I mostly deal with my Campaign Manager and don't have a lot of interaction with other staff. But, although I can't say if I ever talked to him, I'd certainly seen him around."

"So, was he paid staff or a volunteer?"

"I believe he was a volunteer. Candy – she's my right-hand gal on staff. She can give you all the information we have on him." He glanced at his watch. As if on cue, his phone rang. The ringtone sounded like a Souza march. He took the call and stepped out into the waiting area to talk to someone.

Yuri and I sent similar meaningful looks to P.W. Mine was intended to ask, "What the—?" And I was still fuming about the reference to his "right-hand gal." Yuri's glare was a tad stronger. But we both kept our mouths shut. I couldn't help feeling this was a good thing overall. He could hardly hire us and press charges at the same time.

"I assume that with or without a client you were going to do some follow up anyway." P.W. paused briefly to give us time to look guilty as charged. "This way we get paid for it. And it will hopefully keep Connolly from complaining, about past and future actions."

"Well," Yuri said tentatively. Before he could say more, Bobby came back.

"Look, I have to run. I'll let Candy know you'll be coming by. She'll fill you in on everything." He gave us another campaign voter smile and left without waiting for a response.

"You're sure this isn't a conflict of interest?" Yuri asked P.W.

"Not if Knight gives his stamp of approval and you stick to certain ground rules." Yuri and I listened while P.W. ticked off the list of rules she had either already thought about or was making up on the spur of the moment. "First, don't tell anyone on the Mann campaign anything you learned when working for the Knight campaign. Second, if you discover anything that might hurt either campaign, come to me immediately. Third, keep a low profile. And fourth, don't act like you are investigating a murder. Stay out of trouble."

"So, what do we say we're doing for, ah, Bobby if Connolly asks?"

"Tell him the truth – that the candidate doesn't want to waste staff time tracking the investigation and press coverage on it, but they obviously have an interest in knowing what's going on. That's your job. Not investigating. Not taking any kind of action. Just keeping an eye on things in order to keep him up-to-date. Between now and the election."

Yuri frowned. "I would never vote for the guy."

"You don't have to vote for him," P.W. said. "Just play nice and do your job." She waved her hand for us to leave. "Now go talk to Candy."

The small parking lot in front of Mann's campaign headquarters was filled with cars. Through the panoramic storefront window, we could see that inside things were hopping. The room was jammed with people moving about, doing whatever they were supposed to be doing to help their candidate succeed. A woman in a bright blue coat stood about thirty feet out from the storefront window, her dark hair gracefully cascading to her shoulders. In front of her stood a man with a large camera balanced on his left shoulder. Someone handed the woman in the blue coat a mic, and a light on the camera came on. The woman smiled and started to speak. We couldn't make out her words, but her on-the-scene reporter tone came through loud and clear. She stopped talking as we drew near. At first, I thought the pause was about us, but it was about the breeze that was messing with her hair. Gusts of wind seemed to be swirling around her, as if protesting her presence there.

As she smoothed her hair back off her face she glanced in our direction and suddenly seemed to zero in on me. I had the urge to run, but before I could, she yelled, "Hey, Jason's mom, right?"

I stopped and looked at her. She motioned for me to come closer, but my feet didn't respond. Instead I called back, "Have we met?"

She started moving in our direction. "No, but I googled you."

"Oh?" Was that good or bad? And why had she mentioned Jason?

"You found the body, right?" she said, her voice in interview mode.

Yuri poked me in the ribs. I suddenly realized the camera was now pointing at us. "I can't comment." Yuri and I moved quickly away and made a beeline for the main door. "Sorry," I said over my shoulder.

"Maybe we can talk later," she shouted after me.

The guard asked to see our identification before letting us enter. Inside everyone seemed almost frenetically busy, moving about quickly and carrying on loud conversations. Then they saw us and froze, like in the children's game Red Light, Green Light when someone yells "Red Light."

"At ease," Yuri said, smiling, causing his glasses to tilt precariously. I wondered why he was still wearing glasses with only one earpiece. Didn't he have a spare? And how on earth was he managing to keep them on?

A young woman who looked as though she was barely out of her teens headed in our direction. Her perfect peaches and cream complexion stretched across a round face that didn't need any makeup and was framed by brown hair that appeared to have been recently styled by a professional. She was wearing jeans that I thought would be challenging to sit down in and a red T-shirt with a picture of Bobby's face stretched across her ample chest above its Vote for Bobby Mann logo in navy blue block print. She gave us a dentist's dream smile full of teeth as white as fresh snow and said, "You must be Cameron and

Yuri. I'm Candy." Her handshake was limp, and her voice was high-pitched, like a Saturday Night Live comedian trying to be camp. But then her name was Candy, so what did I expect?

As we followed her to a glass enclosed room off to the side of the main space, Yuri suddenly stopped and stared at a male staffer. The staffer saw him and immediately looked down and turned away. "It's a $1,000 fine," Yuri called after him.

"Not now, Yuri," I said. "Leave it."

Candy turned back toward us. "Is there a problem?"

"No," I said. "No problem." Well, stealing signs was a problem, but no longer our problem. But I did wonder how Yuri had recognized the young man—or was it simply a shot in the dark that had scored?

She pulled up a couple of chairs for us at a table lined with telephones and scripts. "We've had to postpone our telephone campaign. Too many people want to talk about the murder," she explained. We're going to give it a few days."

"I saw a reporter out front. Has there been an official statement from the campaign yet?"

"Bobby promised them an interview tomorrow. That's one of the reasons he hired you. He wants to show our unqualified support for finding the murderer."

"And to deflect from the fact that the victim was found in a room full of stolen signs," Yuri said.

Candy looked nonplussed. "I don't understand—" she began.

I quickly jumped in. "He didn't hire us to find a murderer," I said firmly. "We're going to be tracking the investigation as it unfolds in the press. That will free up you and your team to concentrate on the real issues of the campaign." I gave Yuri the stink eye to let him know he'd better not contradict me. "We're here to learn a little more about the victim so we have a context for assessing what we learn about the situation. So why don't you tell us what you know about him."

"I'm afraid it isn't much."

"But he was a regular volunteer, right?" Yuri said.

"Yes."

"And you vet your volunteers, don't you?" Yuri continued.

"Well, yes and no. I mean, we try to, but things are so hectic. His name is, was, oh, which is it? Anyway, Brian Norcross. He was with us about three weeks. Someone, I can't remember who, knew him from the university. I never really talked with him much. And never about anything personal."

"Did he fill out some sort of application when he started volunteering?"

"Well actually, no. We were better about that when the campaign first got under way, but he came on board late, and we hadn't got around to having him fill out our volunteer form yet. It's just been so busy."

"Well, we were obviously hoping for a little more information. Is there some other volunteer or staff member you think we should talk to, someone he spent time with?" It occurred to me that the question may have crossed the line between gathering information for context and investigating what had happened to Norcross, but Candy didn't seem to notice.

"Hmmmm." Faint lines appeared on her forehead. I had a brief glimpse of how she might age. "I'm not sure," she said. "Maybe Carolyn. They may have worked on mailings together." Her forehead smoothed out and she gave us another big smile. "Other than that, I don't know what else to tell you." It was clear that she was anxious to get back to whatever she had been doing when we arrived. She was, after all, Bobby's dedicated right-hand gal.

"Okay, then," Yuri said, sounding ready to move on. "Can you ask Carolyn to come in and talk with us?"

Candy immediately stood up and started for the door. "I'll send her in," she said over her shoulder. She paused at the door and turned back as if suddenly remembering something she needed to say to us. Through a toothy smile she added, "I hope you find the killer soon. It would be so much better for the campaign."

"We're not investigating the murder—" I said to her retreating back.

"Save your breath." Yuri shook his head.

"What if it's just a PR move on their part? Does that make a difference? Hire a couple of former employees of the opposition to prove there are no hard feelings and to show that they want the murderer found as much as anybody. Hence, no one on their team is a killer. Or, if they are, they were acting on their own."

"They're using us. It's that simple. Doesn't matter what for."

"I agree. But we're using them, too. Otherwise we wouldn't have any reason to nose around."

"Well, I don't have to like it." Yuri straightened his glasses.

"You need to get those repaired."

Yuri fingered the broken end as if surprised to find nothing there.

"Oh, one other thing, how did you recognize that guy you yelled at when we were coming in as one of the sign thieves?"

"There was just something about him—his build, the way he walked, and the way he refused to look at us."

"Well, he certainly reacted to your implicit accusation."

"It's tempting to follow up on the license plate, but…"

"The police have already done that. And we're off the case. End of story."

Yuri started to say something else but was interrupted by Carolyn joining us. She was maybe mid-twenties, well dressed in conservative clothes, with a pleasant face and a firm handshake. She sat down across from us and said, "It's so awful. He was such a nice young man."

"We understand you may have talked with him more than some of the other staffers. Can you tell us what you know about him?"

"Well, I can't tell you much. We didn't talk about anything personal. Mostly about the campaign. You know, policies, strategies, that sort of thing."

"Was he a strong Mann supporter?" I asked.

"Yes … and no. I mean, he was a hard worker, but I sensed he wasn't entirely on board with some of the party's policies. And Bobby is a strong party man."

"For example?" I asked.

"Well, none of us wants to see the planet destroyed, but we are realistic about the need for more good paying jobs. We can't just put an end to oil production, logging, development, anything that doesn't fit in with the green agenda. It isn't practical. Everyone on the campaign supports our jobs strategy. But whenever issues like that came up, I sensed Brian was uncomfortable. He didn't raise any objections or argue about it. He just kinda clammed up."

I reached over and stepped on Yuri's foot under the table to stop him from saying anything political. "Can you tell us a little more about that?"

"Not really. Brian didn't say much. But it did make me wonder why he had decided to volunteer. Bobby's main support is from big business. He doesn't try to hide that. And our jobs plan is central to the campaign."

"Do you know who recommended Brian to the campaign?"

"Someone he knew from the university, I think. He mentioned it once, but I don't remember the person's name. They must have been involved early on, before I came on board. Volunteers come and go on campaigns. From conversations about his death, I don't think any of the current staffers knew him before he joined us."

"You say he kept quiet about any political views that might not be popular with other volunteers or staff, but is it possible someone took him on about his beliefs?"

"Not that I heard about."

"Did he ever express any concerns about his safety?"

"No, nothing like that. We all get along. I mean, we all want the same thing, to get Bobby Mann elected. I assumed Brian wanted that; otherwise why volunteer?"

"What about stealing Knight's signs. Was he involved in that?" Yuri asked without preamble.

Carolyn's cheeks turned pink. "Not that I know of, but he didn't speak out against it, either. At least not that I heard."

"Did anyone?" Yuri's tone was judgmental.

"You need to understand that we saw it as a kind of lark, you know?"

"A 'lark' punishable by jail time and a thousand dollar fine," Yuri said.

"We weren't thinking of it like that."

"But everyone knew about the stolen signs?" Yuri asked.

Carolyn looked uncomfortable as she reluctantly admitted that everyone knew. "They're just signs," she said defensively. I stepped on Yuri's foot again to keep him from saying more.

Changing the subject, I asked, "Is there anything else you think we should know about Brian that might be helpful to our, ah, inquiries?"

Carolyn hesitated.

I sensed she was holding something back. "Anything at all, even if it doesn't seem significant."

"Well, there is something, but it's probably not a big thing."

"You never know what might be helpful."

"Well…one night last week, I met a friend at a downtown pub and saw Brian with someone I think is a staffer for the Knight campaign. But when I asked him about it, he said it was just a friend from school. Kind of blew off my teasing about him having a drink with a member of the opposition."

Yuri leaned forward and looked her in the eyes. "Are you suggesting he might have been spying for the Knight campaign?"

"No, not really." Now she was definitely uncomfortable, color slowly creeping up her neck toward her face. "My first thought was that he was trying to get information for our side, but when he was evasive and said it was just a school friend, well, I wasn't sure what to think. I was going to try to find out more about his 'friend' when this happened."

"Could you describe the person he was with?"

"In his twenties, brown hair, slender, normal looking. I'm not sure he's with the Knight campaign, but I think I saw him with a group of volunteers at one of their rallies. We sometimes attend to see what's happening. And there have also been times when both sides are invited to the same event."

"Did you mention this to Detective Connolly?" I asked.

"No, it didn't come up."

We asked a few more questions, but didn't learn more. After Carolyn left, Yuri and I stayed in the room and discussed whether there was any reason to talk to any other staff or volunteers and decided it might be more productive to see if anyone on the Knight campaign admitted to having a connection to Brian Norcross. Was he a spy who got caught? Or was his death unrelated to the campaign? Even if he'd been a spy, the punishment didn't seem to fit the crime. It was, after all, only a race for a congressional seat, a political office that required constant fundraising and didn't even pay all that well. But then, no one likes to lose.

CHAPTER 6
MY BROTHER'S KEEPER

"SO, WHAT WAS WITH all of the hostility?" I asked Yuri as we headed for the Knight campaign headquarters. "I thought we agreed it's just a job."

"I guess the atmosphere got to me. Someone they worked with has been killed and they were acting like it's party time."

"I can kinda understand," I said. "They apparently didn't really know him that well since he hadn't been around long. His death may have momentarily dampened their enthusiasm, but they're young and committed to a cause. Just because you think they're misguided—"

"And neither woman seemed to think there was anything wrong with stealing signs."

"Oh, I think everyone knew it was wrong. But they put it in the caper category rather than thinking of it as a criminal act. Kinda like picking locks and sneaking into buildings in the middle of the night."

"That's different. We weren't trying to steal anything. Or do anyone any harm. Since their campaign has to purchase and distribute signs for their own candidate, they certainly understand the cost and inconvenience of their actions."

"No doubt." I agreed but didn't see where complaining about it would get us anywhere. And I was a little surprised by his reaction.

"And Candy," Yuri continued, mocking her name and holding out a limp hand to complete the image. "No background check, no file, no personal exchanges, no nothing. Wouldn't want her as my right-hand anything."

"Nice complexion though."

Yuri looked at me as though I was crazy. "And so oblivious as to what's legal and what isn't that she didn't even have the good manners to look embarrassed when I mentioned the stolen signs."

"So she's clueless. We agree on that. What I would like to know is whether Bobby knew about the stack of Knight signs in the back room. And whether he approved of what they were doing. That's a little different, in my opinion, than some young volunteers getting carried away and stepping over the line."

"The thefts are probably below his pay grade," Yuri reluctantly acknowledged. "But I wouldn't put it past him."

"I assume everyone knew where the signs were being stashed. Including Norcross. But that doesn't explain what he was doing in the storage room."

"I wonder if they insisted everyone take turns stealing signs to make sure no one would want to talk about what was going on."

"I doubt it was that intentional," I said.

Yuri paused, then gave me a sideways glance. "I admit it. I took a few yard signs once. When I was in high school. That is, we switched signs in a couple of yards as a joke. It seemed funny at the time."

"Did you get caught?"

"No, fortunately." He shook his head. "But I was in high school. Kids do crazy things at that age. And we weren't actually stealing anything. These volunteers are old enough to know better."

"I think it's a peer pressure thing. Easy to get caught up in the excitement of the moment." I looked at Yuri. "Okay, if it's confession time, I once hit a protester with my purse."

Yuri started laughing. "You hit someone with your purse?!"

"They were trying to prevent us from crossing a picket line to a clinic. The group I was with was trying to make a point about free access to women's health care. Then someone pushed me, and I hit back by swinging my purse at him. It was leather, with a shoulder strap. Packed a pretty good wallop. The next thing I knew everyone was fighting, and the friend I was with grabbed me and we ran. Not my finest hour."

"Did you get arrested?"

"No, my friend and I got away just in time."

"Does your mother know?"

"I'm a grown woman; I don't have to tell my mother everything."

Yuri laughed louder. "She doesn't know."

"It was a long time ago," I said. "Don't make me sorry I told you."

"Your secret is safe with me," he said. "Want to link pinkie fingers and swear not to tell?"

"That won't be necessary."

We were almost there. Yuri got suddenly serious and called Adele to ask her to see what she could dig up on the victim. When he ended the call he said, "Not much to like about the way the Mann campaign is being run, is there? In spite of the fact that the headquarters is pretty spiffy compared to others I've seen. And I definitely don't like the candidate. You do know that he's not from here, right? He's from the east coast. Rich family. Ran there for office and lost, moved to the Midwest and lost again. Now he's here trying to pretend he represents us."

"That's politics," I said. "The good news is that we can take his money and still not vote for him."

When we arrived at the Knight headquarters, most of those present were just getting ready to call it a day. Some would probably return after a dinner break, but we didn't want to hang around. We quickly scanned the room for anyone who fit Carolyn's rather generic description of the person she'd seen Brian Norcross having a drink with. There were several young men it could have been, but there was no way to be sure just by looking. We decided to make a public ask about Norcross to speed things up. We got them to pause just long enough to hear us out, but no one admitted to knowing him.

"That the guy who ended up dead at Mann's headquarters?" someone asked.

"Yes," Yuri responded. "And we have reason to believe he has a friend in this campaign." We looked around. We had their full attention now, but no takers. "It's not a crime to have a friend on an opposing team," Yuri said in a kidding tone. But still no takers. I did, however, notice two young men in their early twenties exchanging looks. Both of them were slender with brown hair. I made a note to talk to them in private. Maybe they didn't want to speak up in front of their fellow volunteers and staffers. My fear was that if I called them out in public they might shut down for good.

I took Yuri aside and tried to get him to covertly check out the two guys I wanted to follow up with. But there were too many people milling about. "Tomorrow," I said. "Let's come back tomorrow."

It was rush hour. By the time I delivered Yuri back to his car, it was time to go home. I really needed to have dinner with my kids. Even though I rebelled against my mother's constant criticism about being an absent mom, I knew she was at least partly right. The pre-teen and early teen years were tough for kids. I needed to be there for them. I wanted to be there for them.

About half the time I park on the street in front of the main house, go in through the wood gate at the side of the yard, and walk down the curving brick path to our carriage house home. The rest of the time I park in the alley. It's closer, although usually crowded with piles of this and that. The owners tended to use the alley to store their garbage cans and spillover from garages. It's also home to weeds, cats, and an abundance of spiders. Tonight, though, I decided to brave the debris and the arachnids and park in the alley.

I was somewhat surprised to see a black sedan pulled to one side of the narrow alley, close to our place, almost blocking the lane. It wasn't a car I recognized, and I couldn't tell whether there was anyone inside because of the tinted windows and fading light. Instead of backing up

I decided it was possible to squeeze my dark green Subaru Outback past the unfamiliar car. As I pulled alongside, I thought I saw movement, shadowy movement behind gray windows.

Arriving with my Subaru intact, I parked in the space behind our fence, grabbed my purse and jacket, and got out, clicking the door locks shut.

A large man suddenly blocked my exit. He wore a full-length top coat, not your typical Pacific NW attire. In the gloom of the alley I couldn't see his features clearly, but I could see enough to make me not only wary but a bit frightened.

"Cameron Chandler?" he asked.

He seemed vaguely familiar. "And you are?" I asked back, sounding more confident than I felt.

"Randy Mann."

Was he kidding?

"Bobby Mann is my brother. We need to talk."

"Would you like to come inside?" If he was really Bobby Mann's brother, he didn't pose any threat, and if he'd wanted to assault me, he probably wouldn't have found it necessary to provide his name.

"Perhaps you would join me in my car." He sounded like someone used to getting his way.

I looked at his car and said, "No, sorry, but I wouldn't be comfortable with that. Either come inside or say what you have to say right here." I braced myself to fend him off in case he tried to force me into his car, hoping I could remember the self-defense moves Will had taught me. Wishing my Swiss Army Victorinox was in my pocket instead of my purse.

He hesitated, not moving, a menacing human barrier. Then he seemed to make up his mind and backed off a few feet. "All right. This shouldn't take long."

Both the words and the tone sent chills down my back. I half expected him to whip out a weapon or pick me up by the throat with one beefy hand and toss me against the side of the building. How I wished I had parked out front where someone might be looking out their window at this very moment, a witness to whatever was about to happen. And how could he have been sure that I would park in the alley anyway?

Instead of attacking, he started talking, voice low, as if he didn't want to be overheard by anyone lurking in the alley. It was too late to turn on my phone's recorder and too late to run. It seemed like my only option was to listen.

"I know that my brother hired you to keep tabs on the investigation into the death of Brian Norcross. I just want to make sure that you understand what is needed."

"What's needed?" I echoed, my voice cracking slightly. "I'm not sure what you mean." And if this was a business call, why was he at my home, in my alley, instead of at the office taking his issue up with P.W.? Besides, I wasn't supposed to be talking about clients, not even with relatives. Although it didn't seem wise to mention that at the moment.

He took a step toward me, a black wall of intimidation towering over me as I pulled myself up to my full 5'10". It was like facing off with a bear.

"My brother is in the midst of an important campaign. He isn't necessarily thinking clearly about how this death of a volunteer could impact him. I want to make sure that you don't exceed your contractual obligations."

Contractual obligations? What the hell?

"You aren't being asked to solve the murder," he continued. "Leave that up to the police. Understood?"

"We have no intention of meddling in the investigation The police are obviously better equipped than us to find a killer." No meddling, no stepping on Irish toes.

"Good. Then there's no need for you to be asking too many questions. Use your connections with the police and the press to see what they're up to. And keep me informed." He reached into his pocket. It was all I could do to keep from flinching as I braced myself for what might come next. It was almost anti-climactic when he pulled out a leather card case holder and handed me his card. In the fading light I could barely just make out the print. He was an attorney with a law firm in Washington D.C.

"There's no need to bother my brother about any of this," he said with a firmness that wasn't to be argued with. "He has enough on his plate. If you find something that needs attention, let me know immediately."

I could have mentioned that I didn't take direction from him, we answered to our client. But in the dark alley with him looming over me, it didn't seem like the right time to get into an argument about ethics. He assumed I agreed to his terms, and I didn't say otherwise.

"Are you staying in town with your brother?" I asked. It might be good to know where he was when he wasn't spooking around alleys at dusk.

"I'll be around until the election." He put his card holder back and turned to leave, then paused, looking over his shoulder. "I'll be checking in with you." It sounded more like a warning than a simple head's up.

I watched as he got in his car and drove away down the narrow street. What he'd said about his brother and his reason for wanting to talk with me made sense in a way, but I had some serious concerns about his approach. The whole situation creeped me out. I felt like I'd been threatened by someone straight out of the Sopranos, and I didn't like it one bit.

Randy Mann might be no more than a devoted brother looking out for the candidate's best interests. All the same, it seemed to me like we needed to take a closer look at him. His intimidating appearance and manner didn't make him a criminal, but I couldn't help speculating about whether he had discovered that Norcross was a spy for the opposition and eliminated the threat.

On the other hand, we didn't know for sure that Norcross had been a spy. It was possible he had just been a volunteer who didn't agree with everything his candidate stood for. It was even possible he had met with someone he knew from the Knight team to spy on them for the Mann campaign. At this point, all we knew for sure was that Norcross might not have been just your average volunteer.

I was expecting to hear the usual sounds of activity and television when I finally made it to the carriage house and went inside, but the house was as still as death. For an instant I feared there might be a note saying that my kids were being held hostage to ensure that I obeyed Randy Mann's instructions. Then I heard someone moving around upstairs. The kids were probably with Mom. I tossed my coat and purse on the entry bench and headed up the back stairs.

"Anyone home?" I called as I reached the top.

"In here, Mom," Mara called back. Her voice came from my mother's compact kitchen. She and Mom were huddled over a recipe on the counter, their long, chestnut colored hair blending together in perfect harmony. Mara definitely had inherited her hair and eyes from my mother, her height and disposition from me.

"New recipe?" I asked, almost fearing the answer. I was hungry and wanted comfort food, not some gourmet meal designed to look good on the plate.

"We're making a truffle risotto."

That didn't sound bad. Although we'd never had one before that I could recall.

"With edamame and shitake mushrooms."

Hmmm. Not a Betty Crocker recipe then. "Is Jason okay with this?" He hates mushrooms.

"He needs to expand his palate," Mara said, obviously quoting my mother.

Oh well, it sounded like something I could get into, and there was plenty of peanut butter downstairs for Jason. I went into the living room and found him reading the news on his computer. He looked up and said, "You do know they're putting mushrooms in our food."

"I know. I'm sorry."

"I'm not going to eat it."

"You can pick them out."

"You can't get the flavor out."

"I'll ask Mom to set some aside before putting in the mushrooms, okay?"

"Would you?" He looked so pathetic that I silently vowed to order a pizza just for him if he didn't like the risotto.

Back in the kitchen I put Jason's request before Mom. She bristled as she looked directly at me. "I was already planning on doing that. I know he doesn't like mushrooms."

"I have to eat vegetables I don't like," Mara said in her best pouty voice.

"We all do," I said. At least since we moved in with my mother, that is. "But no one should have to eat something they really dislike. You agree, don't you?"

Mara read my mind, and knew that if she didn't agree with me now, she'd be looking at a plate of things she personally hated the next time I made dinner. She grudgingly went along with the plan. From everything I'd read and been told, the next few years were going to be bumpy for my kids. I remembered how difficult the transition from childhood to adolescence had been for me, and I'd had the support of two parents. To avoid or reduce the magnitude of some of those bumps for my own offspring, I wasn't above a little manipulation now and then.

After dinner we went downstairs. Mara draped herself sideways over an overstuffed chair in the living room with a book while Jason swiped a few cookies out of the kitchen, defying me to complain. I pretended not to see. In spite of himself he'd enjoyed the risotto, but I could tell he still felt put upon. Then he sat down with his computer and went back to reading news stories. We've agreed that we shouldn't have the TV on after dinner unless we all wanted to watch the same thing. Well, maybe saying we've "agreed" is an exaggeration. I've made it a rule, and they haven't managed to convince me otherwise. Jason frequently lobbies for a TV for his room, but I'm afraid we'd never see him if I gave in to his request.

Since the kids were fully occupied, I took that opportunity to call Yuri to report on my talk with Randy Mann.

"You aren't serious, are you?" he asked.

"About his name or the conversation?"

"Both."

"From one perspective it makes sense, but—"

"But it sounds like they have something to hide."

"They both say they want the same thing—to be kept up-to-date on the investigation. But if Randy is so worried about us asking a few questions, why doesn't he just talk to his brother and ask him to end our contract? That's what I don't understand."

"Maybe because whatever he doesn't want us to find is related to him and not to his brother," Yuri said. "Or maybe Norcross had enough evidence of shady, unethical or even illegal activities related to the entire Mann family that he had Norcross eliminated to save both the family name and his brother's campaign."

"I considered that. But if there was something the candidate wanted to keep under wraps, you wouldn't think he'd have hired us in the first place."

"Keep in mind he didn't hire us to solve a crime but to keep tabs on the investigation. We are a kind of early warning system for him. Or, maybe he wants to keep tabs on us. That thought has crossed my mind."

"Mine, too. So, how do we handle this? Do we tell P.W.?"

"Yeah, we should." Then he added, "But maybe not quite yet. Let's do some digging first."

"In other words, we're going to do exactly what Randy Mann specifically warned me against doing."

"He should have known he was waving a red cape in front of a couple of bulls," Yuri said with a short laugh.

"I'm not sure I appreciate the comparison."

"You should. Bulls are known for their power and have been an icon for worship in many ancient cultures."

Oh, oh. That sounded like the beginning of one of Yuri's trivia rants. "Okay," I said quickly, "I'm flattered, not offended."

"Seriously, in ancient Greece and Egypt the bull was considered sacred. In the Celtic culture it symbolized fertility and…"

I cut him off. "That's okay, Yuri. I get the point."

"I have more."

"I'm sure you do."

"Okay, what I'm trying to say is that we need to stand our ground and proceed with our version of monitoring. With discretion, of course. You okay with that?"

"Absolutely."

Even though I agreed in theory, I felt a tiny nagging doubt as to the wisdom of our decision. After all, the bull seldom beats the matador. And even if it does, the end is never pretty.

CHAPTER 7
DEEP DIVE FOR DIRT

YURI AND I WERE BOTH at the office early, but Blaine, as usual, was already there. Looking starched and alert in a light blue shirt and gray pinstriped suit, his dark grey necktie had a single blue strip angled across it from the mid-point. The tie looked like something P.W. might have given him as a gift. He raised his eyebrows when we came in together, both carrying coffee we had purchased in the mall, as if we couldn't wait to get started on our day. But all he said was his usual, "Good morning."

We returned the greeting, then grinned at each other for sounding like a stereophonic recording. It was becoming a habit. Scary.

Adele wasn't in yet, but she had emailed both of us with what she had found out so far about Brian Norcross. It wasn't a lot. He had led a fairly normal life. Grew up in Seattle, played some basketball in high school but wasn't good enough to get a college scholarship for it. Was active in campus politics. Spoke at a couple of rallies about the impact of fossil fuels on climate change. Involved in a number of protests against Shell Oil. And had been arrested but not charged during a peaceful local demonstration.

We both looked up from our computers at the same time, and Yuri made the comment I'd intended on making and asked the same question that was on my mind: "This guy shouldn't have been working on the Mann campaign. Wonder why he got arrested during that demonstration?"

"He had to be a spy for the opposition," I said. "That's the only thing that makes any sense. And I don't remember reading about any altercations at that demonstration, although both sides were there, and tempers tend to run high in situations like that."

"I'll ask Adele to keep poking around." Yuri turned back to his computer.

Adele chose that very moment to appear, right on cue. "Hi, guys," she said. She took off her beige coat and dark brown scarf and hung them on the metal coat tree. "I don't smell coffee."

Yuri jumped up and ran over to make coffee for her. "Sorry, I wasn't thinking."

"Ah," she said, "if I don't even have to ask to get someone to make coffee, you two must need something. Hmmm? On a hot scent?"

"Something like that," I said. "Although we have more questions than answers." I paused. "Thanks, by the way, for the information on Norcross."

"And, let me guess, you want more, right?"

"About the arrest, if you have the time."

"I'm way ahead of you," she said. "I checked on it from home this morning." She leaned over and whispered, "While having a cup of coffee." That made me smile. Although I like Yuri in part because of his playfulness, I knew he sometimes went too far. The idea that strait-laced Adele was teasing him back tickled me.

"Thank you." I smiled. "And?"

"He got into a shoving match with an oil company employee. It was unclear who started it, but since the guy was an employee, my guess is that not pressing charges was a company decision made as a goodwill gesture."

"Norcross was lucky no one on the Mann campaign checked him out. Protesting against oil companies would not have been too popular with his campaign cohorts. My understanding is that Mann is definitely in the pocket of big business, especially big oil."

"Democrats do sometimes support business," Adele said. "And vice versa." We had never talked politics, but it wouldn't have surprised me to find myself on the opposite end of the political spectrum from Adele. The one thing that I did know was that she considered herself a fiscal conservative, and I respected that. I might even accept the label for my own views, with a couple of policy exceptions.

"Even so," Yuri persisted from across the room, "it's beginning to sound like Norcross was on the radical side. That definitely doesn't square with supporting someone like Mann."

"Maybe he had a crush on some woman working on the Mann campaign." I threw out the idea, not really believing it myself. But it was possible.

"Hormones versus politics," Adele said. "I like it."

Yuri pushed the start button on the coffee pot and joined us. "Well, since you've already done what we were going to ask you to do, how about we ask you for something else?"

Adele looked from Yuri to me and back again. "What do you want?" Her tone said she was being put upon, but I knew she enjoyed researching people. We told her what we wanted, asking for her first priority to be whatever she could find out about Randy Mann. Then on his brother, the candidate, and finally, on Nathan Knight, the other candidate.

"Dig as deep as you can," Yuri said. "We think there's something dirty there somewhere."

"Enough to kill someone over?" Adele asked.

"Well, when you put it that way . . . You may have to dig really deep."

We were just about to leave for the Knight headquarters when my phone rang. I didn't recognize the name or the number. I answered anyway. "Hello, this is Cameron."

"Hi, Cameron, my name is Gretchen Brady. I'm Theo's mother. I talked with you the other day in front of the Mann campaign headquarters."

Suddenly it all came together. One night at dinner Jason had mentioned his new friend, Theo, whose mother was a journalist. Given his news junkie proclivities, he considered Theo's mother in the awesome parent category. For that reason alone, this was someone I needed to be friends with. But I guessed she wasn't calling to set up a mothers' tea so we could get to know each other better. She confirmed my suspicions in the next breath.

"I was hoping we could meet for coffee, partly social, partly business."

More business than social I guessed. But if we were supposed to be tracking what was in the press as well as what the police were up to, that fit my agenda too. "I would love to. How about late this afternoon? Any chance you are going to be near the mall?"

"That works for me. 3:30 at the inside Starbucks?"

"I'll be there."

Yuri raised his eyebrows in question. "Jason has a friend named Theo. His mother is a reporter, sometimes does TV spots. She was the woman outside Mann's headquarters. The one we blew off. I'm meeting her for coffee at 3:30. You aren't invited, but if there's anything you want me to ask or tell her, let me know."

"Good, get something from her that we can include in our report, something that won't make the Randy man crazy."

"Should we include her name in the report?"

"Why not? She's a journalist, not an undercover cop. If we're watchdogs, one of our tasks is to talk with the people in charge of the flow of information. Ask her lots of questions. Just be careful what you say. Don't give her the impression we're actually doing any investigating, okay? Wouldn't want that to get in the paper."

"There's something I've been wondering. Do you think Randy has someone keeping tabs on our activities?"

"Don't you?"

"Have you noticed anyone following you or us?"

"No, but we need to watch our backs, just in case."

I certainly agreed with that. We needed to be circumspect. And guarded. And observant. There was no way I wanted another encounter in the alley with Randy Mann and his full-length overcoat. The next time he might live up to his image.

The Knight headquarters was abuzz, as we might have expected with the election so near. Tables were piled high with papers and the remains of snacks. Young volunteers needed a lot of fuel to canvass neighborhoods, make calls, and put up signs. But in spite of the fact that the room looked like a cyclone had passed through, everyone seemed organized and intent on whatever task they'd been assigned. Knight was said to be running a good campaign. Not an easy thing to do on a tight budget and with a horde of young people who had never worked on a campaign before.

No one paid much attention to us as we looked around for the two young men who had exchanged meaningful glances the day before. When I finally spotted one of them, I motioned for Yuri to stay put while I headed over to see if we could manage a word in private. When the young man saw me headed in his direction, he didn't look pleased, but he didn't turn away. Maybe he didn't realize I was zeroing in on him. Until I was standing right in front of him. Then he took notice.

"Any chance we could talk outside for a minute?"

He didn't ask "about what" but seemed to be considering whether he was going to say "yes" or "no." In the end he nodded agreement, and I turned and led him through the maze of workers and out the front door. Yuri followed in our wake.

"How about a cup of coffee?" I asked. There was a coffee shop just a few doors down. He glanced back over his shoulder and apparently decided getting out of sight of his co-workers might be a good idea. Or maybe he just wanted a cup of coffee.

As we headed for the coffee shop Yuri and I introduced ourselves. He didn't volunteer his name; I had to ask. "Jim Gossett," he replied. Jim was a long-haired, scruffy looking young man with a mouth that turned down at the edges and a disposition to match. I couldn't help but imagine what it must have been like for his mother during his early teen years. He had rebellion written all over him.

We got our coffee at the counter and sat at a small table at the back of the room. There was only one other customer, so we didn't need to worry about privacy. Once we were settled in, I turned to Jim and said, "You probably know what I'm about to ask."

"No, you tell me." It sounded like a challenge, but I responded to his words, not his tone.

"You were seen with Brian Norcross in a pub. As you may know, we are the ones who found his body. We're not investigating his murder; we're leaving that to the police. But we do have some questions. For one thing, we're curious about his connection to the Knight campaign. We thought you might be able to shed some light on that."

"Am I a suspect?"

"Why would you ask that?"

"Well, you haul me away from my work and double up to interrogate me. What am I supposed to think?"

"Yuri and I were together when we caught the people from Mann's campaign who were stealing Knight's signs. And we were together when we found Brian. So, we aren't ganging up on you, we're just working together on this. Although if you don't want to talk to us and we turn your name over to the police, they might want to interrogate you." Take that, you disrespectful twit.

He looked down and didn't say anything for a minute. Finally, he reluctantly came round. "Okay, you win. What do you want to know?"

"Start with how you knew Brian Norcross."

"We had classes together. Been involved in a couple of protests with him."

"About…?"

"What's happening to our planet and what we have to do to save it."

"So, did he have something specific to talk to you about that night at the pub?"

"Yeah, he was supposed to dish some dirt on Mann. But he didn't have his shit together yet."

"But he was working for the Mann campaign, wasn't he?"

"Yes and no."

"What does that mean?"

"Just what I said—yes and no."

"Tell us the 'yes' part," I said.

"He'd inserted himself into the campaign as a volunteer," he began.

"Inserted himself?"

"Yeah, he pretended he'd been recommended by someone who'd been involved in the early stages of the campaign. He actually had a name in case he needed it, someone who had worked there for a couple of days before deciding it wasn't for him. But no one questioned him. Which seemed a bit sloppy for a campaign flush with money and volunteers. Go figure."

"Why'd he do it?"

"He wanted to see if there was some way he could keep Mann from getting elected. With all of his family money and their east coast political savvy and support, Mann has a good chance of winning. Brian thought he might learn something by being on the inside, or maybe find some opportunity to mess with Mann's credibility."

"What specific complaints did he have about Mann?"

Jim looked at us as if we'd grown horns. "Aren't you following the campaigns?" He sounded disgusted.

"We are, but we would like to hear from you about Brian's perspective and what he was up to."

Jim shrugged. As if to say, it's your dime. "Well, as you probably already know, Mann's family is in the oil business. Big time. What most people don't know is what that means in practical terms for our state. If Bobby gets elected that would broaden their reach and influence. He would undoubtedly push for offshore oil drilling, a pipeline, oil containers at the Port, increased rail transport—all of it. Everything that's good for big oil and bad for the environment. Not that Mann talks about this in any of his stump speeches or ads. But he's an extension of his family and their greed. That's why Brian got involved. What the Mann family stands for is everything we've been fighting to prevent."

"So, was he spying for Knight?"

"Not specifically. I mean, no one on the Knight campaign asked him to do it. But he was hoping to find information that would help take Mann down."

"Did he ever express any concern that someone on the Mann staff suspected his true intentions?" Yuri asked.

"He was feeling pretty confident. He even helped steal some signs to make sure they accepted him."

I wondered if Carolyn's vagueness about Brian's contribution to the sign thefts had been untruthful or ignorant. Maybe she just didn't want to speak ill of the dead.

"Any idea what kind of information he was digging up on the Mann family?" Yuri asked. "Any particular lines of inquiry he was pursuing?"

"I'm not sure. That night we met at the pub he told me he was going to send us some stuff we could use soon. Something big. But he may have just been boasting."

"And he didn't send you anything?"

"No, it's hard to send emails after someone knocks you over the head."

"Did you tell the police any of this?" Yuri asked.

"What do you think?" After a short pause, he added, "They didn't ask, and I didn't offer."

"This could be related to his murder, you know." Was he really as dense or uncaring as he seemed?

"Brian was committed to saving the planet, but how could he have learned something no one else knows about? I mean I suppose he could have asked the wrong people about the Manns, but I can't imagine why they would think of him as any kind of real threat."

"If I knew the answer to that, I might be able to point a finger at the killer," I said.

"I thought you weren't trying to find out who did it."

"We're not," Yuri said firmly. "We're tying up some lose ends and satisfying our own curiosity. That's all. But we couldn't help noticing your reaction when we asked the group if anyone knew Brian."

Jim leaned back and looked almost thoughtful. "You don't really think that he got caught snooping around and that's what got him killed, do you?"

"It's up to the police to figure that out," Yuri said, pushing his empty coffee cup aside as he stood up. "Well, I think it's time we let you get back to work."

"Thanks, for the coffee," Jim said, swallowing what was left in his cup. We parted with him at the entrance to the coffee shop and headed back to the parking lot.

"It's going to be hard doing any kind of investigation while not looking like we are investigating the murder," I said as we got back in my car.

"I agree," Yuri said. "And it seems to me that we should look into the Randy and Bobby brothers a little more before screwing with them. What do you think, you've met both of them."

"I agree with you about Bobby. He's plastic, no feeling of authenticity. But he does a good fake smile. Doesn't seem devious, but he doesn't have to be. He has his family for that. The brother, on the other hand, is downright scary. Someone used to wielding power and getting his way. It wouldn't surprise me to find out he carried a concealed weapon. He may be a lawyer, but his aura screams mobster."

"His aura?"

"He radiates menace."

"That could come in handy," Yuri observed. "Sometimes I wish I could pull that off."

"Try wearing a full-length black wool coat." I pretended to be considering him in such a coat. "Nah," I said. "I think you should go for a different look. Menacing isn't your forte."

Ignoring me, he said, "Okay, here's the plan." He began laying out what he thought we should do next. Use my meeting with Gretchen to find out what the press was looking into. Go to the university and talk to any professors and students who knew Norcross to get a better feel for his interests and what he was capable of pulling together to upset Mann's campaign. Pursue any leads Adele unearthed. Try to get one of the people who was involved in the theft of the signs the night of Norcross's death to talk to us. "One last thing," Yuri concluded. "I think you should have a conversation with Detective Connolly, tell him what we're doing, see if you can get any information out of him."

"Why me?" I tried to suppress a smile at the suggestion.

"Come on, don't give me that."

"Seriously, why don't we go together to talk with him?"

"Because he doesn't want to ask me out after this is over."

"So? You think I should act as what—date bait?"

"It's me, Yuri. I know you, Cameron. It wouldn't hurt you to put yourself out there a little. And you could do worse."

"For all I know he might be married."

"Well, you're an investigator, find out. Now, let's get going on this. Right after we grab some lunch, that is."

CHAPTER 8
STOP THE PRESS

OVER LUNCH WE DIVVIED up the tasks. I would talk with Gretchen, the reporter and mother of Jason's friend, while Yuri made a trip to the university. We would meet back at the office to compare notes and to go over whatever information Adele managed to dredge up. Then, unless she had found something that seemed urgent to follow up on, we would go together to Mann's headquarters to see if we could corner the sign thief Yuri thought he'd recognized. It would be interesting to hear firsthand what he and his fellow partners in crime had and had not noticed that evening.

Questioning one of the sign thieves definitely went beyond what our client had asked us to do. But if we didn't seek him out by checking on the truck's license plate and only happened to recognize him when we were at their headquarters for some innocent reason, we could argue to Detective Connolly that it was serendipitous and not a deliberate attempt to interfere with a police investigation. The only thing that worried me was the possibility that Randy Mann would find out. If he did, he would not be pleased. Nor would he be likely to accept our rationale. Nevertheless, I agreed to the plan.

Tomorrow we would follow up on any new leads we got from Adele, and I would contact Connolly. After that, we would re-assess. Although I pride myself on being spontaneous, I confess to feeling more comfortable if I have some idea about what's going to happen next. I suppose it's a matter of wanting to feel in control. Something I've often lacked big time in the past. Although realistically I know anything can change not only on a moment's notice, but without any notice at all.

Everything started out as planned. I met Gretchen at Starbucks inside the mall and stood there impatiently while she ordered a complicated drink with soy and skim milk and a shot of this and a swirl of that. I had to admit that when it came, the design on top was attractive, but I like my coffee unadulterated so I can actually taste it.

After we sat down, we chitchatted for a few minutes about our kids. It turned out that she too was a single mother and was worried that her son, Theo, like Jason, wasn't very social, and spent too much time connected to one device or another. She was so pleased that he and Jason were becoming good friends. She explained that she was divorced and that although she'd been devastated at the time, she was finally moving on. She said that her work kept her from having much time to dwell on the past. But from the emotion in her voice, I guessed it wasn't quite that simple. Emotions seldom are.

When our conversation turned to talk about the murder and we started comparing notes, we were both initially cautious. Just because our sons were friends didn't mean we could trust each other. But the more we talked, the more convinced I became that this was a woman with a sound moral compass, an inquisitive mind, and a ton of motivation. To be on the safe side, I intended to treat her with care, but my gut said she was a potentially valuable ally.

"I was initially assigned to cover the Norcross murder by the news station as a one-off," Gretchen explained. "I was available when our main crime reporter wasn't. That's the kind of break we in the news business are always hoping for."

"Does that mean you'll be doing more live coverage?"

"From time to time. Although my first love is print. You can be more thorough, actually do a deep dive into the facts." She took a sip. "That's why I wanted to talk with you. It's about something I'm working on. It started as a sideline for maybe one article. But at this point I'm 100 percent obsessed with the story. In fact, I'm taking some vacation days so I can devote myself full-time to it."

"Intriguing."

"I'm not ready to share any specifics, but it's something that could have an impact on the current House race. That's why I think we may be able to help to each other."

"I have a client confidentiality issue when it comes to sharing information. Not quite like a lawyer-client thing, but it still prevents me from divulging facts and details gathered for the client."

"No problem. Let's agree that we have to independently verify anything that comes out of any conversations we have. And neither of us can quote the other without permission."

Once we agreed on the ground rules, it didn't take us long to find that we were on the same page about the

Norcross murder. Although we couldn't decide whether he had been eliminated by someone close to Mann's campaign or by someone directly related to the oil industry, we were both convinced that the key to his death was related to his research on Mann's links to big oil.

"I'm not trying to solve the murder," Gretchen emphasized. "However, if in the process of working on my story I lay out the breadcrumbs that lead to his murderer, the police are welcome to follow them."

"The same goes for us." I looked her in the eye. "Okay, I admit it; I'm dying to know what you're working on. Are you going to tell me? I can keep a secret." I desperately wanted to know more, but at the same time, I told myself that I would understand if she didn't want to share any details. I would understand, but I would probably still keep trying to get her to open up. I can be a nag that way.

"You really can't tell anyone," she said, hesitating before leaning forward and keeping her voice low, even though there was no one nearby. "Timing is everything in this business. With luck, I should have the story to my editor in about a week. Just in time to rock our local political congressional race."

"That sounds promising." Now she really had my attention.

"Okay, I admit how hard it is to sit on a story like this with no one to talk to. I haven't even given my editor details; all he knows is that I'm working on something related to the campaigns. Since the election is so close though, and since you might know something helpful, I'll tell you the gist of it." She took a deep breath, glanced around, and leaned even closer. I found myself holding my breath.

"It started with an anonymous tip from someone a couple months back. About an ad campaign: Save Our Local Economy. You may have seen some of their ads. It's an attempt to rebrand big oil to make locals more receptive to things such as offshore drilling and increased transportation of oil by rail as well as through our ports and inland waterways. I never figured out for sure who the tipster was, but I later suspected it was Brian. He had talked to some of the same people I approached." The expression on her face was one of sadness tinged with enthusiasm. "Now that he's gone, I want to get my story out at least in part for him. Even if he wasn't the anonymous tipster, he was passionate about the same issues that I am—climate change denial, corporate social responsibility, and, preventing environmental degradation by the oil industry."

"It sounds like you talked to him," I observed.

"Once. He contacted me to let me know that he had some information I might find useful. He wouldn't talk on the phone and insisted that we take elaborate precautions not to be seen together. We sat at a tiny table in a shadowy corner of a bar on highway 99. He had on a hoody, and I wore a baseball cap with my hair tucked up in it. There was a TV over the bar. Everyone who wasn't looped was glued to it. It was like a scene out of a movie.

"When I asked, Brian wouldn't admit to being the tipster. Looking back, I think he just wanted to maintain deniability. And he made me promise not to bring up his name when I was asking questions about the Mann family's business connections. At the time I thought he was being overly cautious. Even when he said he was looking into potentially illegal activities, related to Mann and others, the warning bells didn't go off. He said he was almost ready to share his findings with me, but wouldn't give me a preview. And he made it clear that he would contact me, not the other way around, when he was ready."

"Doesn't it make you personally anxious knowing that someone may have killed him for asking the wrong questions?"

"That's why I'm keeping a low profile. Fortunately, there are a lot of people concerned about the impact big oil activities could have on our local environment. People have been more than willing to talk with me, although no one I've met with so far, at least no one who knows much of anything, wants to talk on the record. And no one seems to know the big picture. But they've given me bits and pieces—dates and names, for instance—that I'm starting to pull together into a coherent story. Meetings between government officials and Mann family representatives for example. Possible quid pro quo, shady stuff if not illegal. I just need to dig a little deeper."

"Are there any official inquiries going on?"

"Not that I've come across. Anyway, my short-term goal is to expose how the Mann family hopes to exploit Bobby's political clout to implement some very ambitious plans they and their big oil friends have for the Pacific Northwest. The Mann family has made a ton of money in the oil industry, but they want more. There is no place for ethics or morality in what they hope to accomplish, no concern for future generations, and the environment be damned. It really is a case of 'follow the money.'"

"So, you have evidence of collusion, maybe even wrongdoing?" I said. This was huge.

"I have enough to make a lot of people uncomfortable. Maybe even enough to set some legal challenges in motion. I would be more specific, but I've promised to keep my sources confidential, and it's hard to talk about details without revealing names. That's something I'm struggling with in writing this piece."

"I can understand why timing is critical. A week before the election an article like that would destroy Bobby's chances in a liberal state like ours."

"I didn't set out to hurt any particular person," Gretchen said. "But he and his family are the poster children for what happens when money is the driving force for everything."

"You're sure no one knows you're working on this? I mean, the Mann family is going to go off the rails when you expose their connections to the ad campaign and tell everyone their vision for expanding their oil business in our state."

"You're the only person I've talked with about it."

"You're absolutely certain that your sources won't give you away?"

"They have their own reasons for staying mum. They don't want to be identified even after my *article* comes out. That's been a challenge, filling in the blanks without being able to attribute facts to credible sources."

"Everyone pointing a finger at someone else. No one wanting to speak up for fear of retaliation. Sad."

"That's why I need hard evidence to substantiate my claims. To be honest, it's just the kind of story I've always wanted to write." She smiled. "I suppose you think I'm terrible, an expose, even for a good cause. All for a byline."

"Hey, the issue would be there whether you were going to write about it or not. Writing your story may be the only way to reveal Mann's true intentions. You could be preventing an environmental disaster in our state."

"Some would argue that jobs are more important than the environmental risks."

"There are other ways to create jobs. But I guess I don't need to tell you that."

"Actually, last year I wrote a series of articles on new energy technologies and how they can re-energize our economy."

I took a sip of cold coffee. It was better hot, but I was used to drinking whatever was left in my cup without reheating it. It was a habit that started in graduate school when I was too busy to interrupt my work to use a microwave but needed the caffeine jolt. "What I said about Mann's campaign not being happy with you if you publish this, well, what I really mean is that they will be furious. You will basically be handing the election to Knight. If Mann's family is as powerful and underhanded as you are suggesting, and as I believe they are, they could make things extremely, ah, difficult for you."

"I know, but once the story is out there, I think Mann will pack up his bags and go home, just like he did after his loss in the Midwest."

"I hope you're right." I hesitated, on the verge of telling her about Randy's threat to me, but if what had happened to Norcross didn't dissuade her, then her enthusiasm for the story wouldn't be dampened by a tall man in a dark overcoat.

"Don't worry," she assured me. "I'm taking precautions."

"But if Brian's murder is linked to big oil and the Mann family, and they get wind of you snooping around, they could think that Brian shared information with you, or even that the two of you were collaborating. That puts you in the crosshairs."

"I really don't think anyone knows what I'm working on. And I only need one more week. And a little luck." She reached across the table and put her hand on mine. "Don't worry. I have a good feeling about this."

Unfortunately, I didn't. But I couldn't think of anything that would make her give up pursuing a potentially career making story. "Look," I said, "here's my card with my work and home phone numbers. If you feel at all nervous about whether you might be compromised, give me a call. I work with people who know how to handle that sort of thing."

We agreed to keep in touch and share information that we thought would help the other, within the parameters we had already established. I was concerned for her safety, but respected her professional courage. And I looked forward to having her as a friend after this was over.

I spent the rest of the afternoon impatiently waiting for Yuri to return, annoying Adele by repeatedly looking over her shoulder. I also worked on a somewhat vague report for Bobby Mann, one that would hopefully justify our fee and not upset his brother. I wasn't sure whether withholding information gained in my conversation with Gretchen was living up to P.W.'s expectations for how we were to treat clients, but then I still had some qualms about whether we should have agreed to take on the assignment in the first place. I finally decided that as long as the client felt like they were getting their money's worth, I wasn't going to examine the ethics of the situation too closely. It was like eating a wild salmon while knowing they are going extinct; there is some guilt involved, but it probably wasn't going to guarantee me a spot in hell.

When I had almost given up on him, Yuri called to say he wasn't coming back to the office. Instead, he was going to have a drink with a professor who'd been a mentor to Norcross. No, he hadn't learned anything helpful yet, but he was still trying. At the very least, he was going to see if Dr. Benson could give him some names of people Norcross palled around with.

"Sounds like you're investigating a murder to me," I said.

"Nope. Just having a beer with a new acquaintance. Like you having coffee with a reporter, right?"

"Right. And we both need to keep our heads down."

Adele came over to inform me that all she had found on the Mann brothers was stuff we already knew, that there were hints of shady dealings but nothing had ever been proven, and that as far as she could tell Knight was squeaky clean. On that note, I called it a day.

Wanting to be a good mother I stopped on the way home to pick up the ingredients for spaghetti and garlic bread, something both of my kids like. For once, everyone was where I expected them to be when I arrived home, and the kids were pleased with the prospect of spaghetti.

Mom begged off, too many carbs, so when we finally sat down to eat, I had the kids to myself. I managed to put work out of my mind and listened with interest as Mara and Jason caught me up on what was going on in their lives. At least the stuff they were willing to share with me. I assume they held some things back, just like I had done with my mom at their age. In fact, like I continued to do.

When Mara asked what I thought about her joining the coed wrestling team, my first instinct was to question whether boys and girls should be wrestling each other. Instead I managed to squelch my inner maternal shriek and ask a few questions about the program. Then I asked if there were any other sports she was considering, and she mentioned gymnastics and debate.

"Is debate considered a sport?" If so, that was a sport I could approve of.

"It's one of the after-school options."

I wanted to explain how useful debate would be in academia and throughout her professional life, but I kept a lid on it. "They all sound interesting," I said, striving for a neutral tone.

"Come on, Mom," Jason interrupted. "You know you want her to join the debate team."

"You mean because I debated in high school and college?"

"You've talked about it a lot, how it helps you see both sides of an argument, how it's a chance to make close friends and travel to other schools. On and on."

"Well, I do believe that debate is valuable, but I want you two to do what appeals to you."

"I'm going to be a debater," Jason announced.

Mara was still considering. "I'm leaning toward wrestling."

We capped off the evening by watching a television show together. Well, we more or less watched it together. I admit to dozing off several times, but the kids didn't seem to mind. Then we called it a night. I miss tucking them in like I did when they were younger. But I still hug them before going to our separate bedrooms. Jason always acts like he doesn't want a hug, but he never disappears into his room until we've said our goodnights.

As an afterthought, I went back and made sure the front door was locked and bolted. Then I checked the windows to make sure they, too, were secure.

I fell asleep as soon as my head hit the pillow, waking up abruptly when I heard someone pounding on the front door. My clock told me it was almost 1:00 a.m. A little late—or early—for visitors. I grabbed my robe and went to the door. "Who is it?" I asked from inside.

"It's me, Gretchen. And Theo. Can we come in, please?" She sounded upset.

"Are you alone?" I asked.

"Yes," she said. "It's just us."

"Mom," I heard Theo say, "I'm cold."

I quickly opened the door and was surprised to see them standing there in their night clothes. Gretchen had on a long, green nightgown and was barefoot, her long hair tousled. Theo was wearing blue Spiderman pajamas and fleece-lined slippers. I stepped aside for them to come in and shut and locked the door behind them.

"I'm sorry to show up like this, but I didn't know where else to go," Gretchen said. She glanced at Theo who was shivering and looking very unhappy. "Could you give him something warm to put on? And maybe he could lie down somewhere?" It was clear she wanted to make him comfortable and get him settled in before explaining why they had shown up on my doorstep at 1:00 in the morning in their night clothes.

"Come on, Theo," I said. "I'm sure we can find something to fit you." I didn't want to wake Jason, so I took him to my room and gave him a sweatshirt to put on and tucked him into bed.

"Is Mom going to be okay?" he asked. I was touched by his concern for his mother when he was so obviously cold and tired himself.

"Yes, of course. Everything will be fine. We just have to sort out a few things."

"It was my idea. I mean, I told her to come here," he said. "Jason told me about your job, and I figured you'd know what to do."

"Don't worry," I reassured him. I grabbed a robe and a pair of thick socks for Gretchen before shutting the door behind me.

Gretchen had wrapped herself up in a blanket from the couch, but she was still trembling. I handed her the robe and the socks. "How about I make some tea?"

"Yes, please," she said, pulling on the lime green socks. "And thank you for taking care of Theo."

"Of course." I was trying to be patient, but I couldn't wait another second to find out what had happened and why they had shown up on my doorstep in their nightclothes.

"It was his idea to come here," she said as she put the robe on and followed me into the kitchen. "Apparently, the boys had talked enough to know our houses were only a few blocks apart."

I put on the water for tea and turned to face her. "We took off so fast," she continued, "that I left without my phone and couldn't call anyone. None of my family or friends live in the area, anyway. So no phone. No car keys—not that I wanted to risk trying to retrieve my car from the garage. And I couldn't think of any store or restaurant within walking distance that might be open at his hour. But Jason had told Theo about your job, and he seems to consider you an arm of the police. I think that was reassuring to him."

"So what happened?" I could barely keep the impatience out of my voice. At least I thought I kept it out. Maybe not.

"I heard someone in my study and panicked. I don't have a weapon of any kind, and I'd left my cell phone in the study on the charger. After our conversation this afternoon, all I could think of was that I needed to get us out of there. I hurried into Theo's room, woke him up, and said we needed to be quiet and climb out the window without letting anyone see us. He was so good. He didn't argue or ask questions, he just put on his slippers and we left."

"Did you see anyone?"

"No, and I didn't hang around to look."

"Just a minute." I got my cell and called Yuri. He didn't sound happy to be awakened, but he didn't hesitate when I asked him to come over immediately. He was just like Theo, quick on the uptake and quick to act. I assured him no one was hurt and that I would explain when he got there. Then I turned to Gretchen. "Do you want to call the police?" Under normal circumstances I would automatically have dialed 911, but something told me she didn't want to. If she had, she could have asked to use my phone the minute she came through the door.

"No," she said. I poured us each a cup of tea and sat down across from her. She immediately wrapped her hands around the cup. "That feels so good."

"I assume you don't think it was a normal burglary, do you?"

"If we go back and find the TV and my jewelry gone, then I'll be okay contacting the police. But if there's nothing missing, I mean, if they were coming after me or my research, then I don't know what I'll do. I don't want to have to explain to the police what I'm working on. Once the police know, the story will get out."

"But even if all they take is your laptop or whatever, you don't have to tell the police what you're working on."

"I know, but they will ask why that was the only thing taken, and I'll have to tell them something. Besides, some other reporter will undoubtedly get nosy. They all monitor police calls. I'd just rather know what I'm dealing with first."

"Okay. Drink up. I'll get us some clothes. I think I have a running suit that'll do for you. Never been used." Gretchen managed a small smile at my feeble joke. "And I'll need to wake up my mom and ask her to keep an eye on the kids. As soon as Yuri gets here, we'll go check it out."

"Thank you, Cameron. I can't tell you how grateful I am for this."

By the time Yuri arrived, Gretchen and I were dressed and Mom was making herself a cup of tea in my kitchen. One thing I will say for her, when she needs to step up to the plate, she does so without complaint. The complaints would come later. I could almost hear it now: normal mothers don't have people drop by in the middle of the night, yadda, yadda, yadda.

We filled Yuri in on the situation on the way to Gretchen's. I didn't ask whether he had a gun, but I assumed he did. What I wasn't at all sure about was whether the three of us would be capable of dealing with an intruder if one or more was still there. The more I thought about it, the more I wanted to call the police, but Yuri sided with Gretchen. We would check out the house first, then decide what to do.

Yuri drove around the block while we tried to figure out if there were any cars parked on the street that either didn't belong there or for some reason looked suspicious. As far as we could tell, no one was watching Gretchen's house from a car, but that didn't mean there was no one lurking nearby. If there was someone watching and waiting for Gretchen's return, we hoped the fact that there were three of us would discourage them from doing anything aggressive or violent. Still, that wasn't much comfort. Not given the murder and the sinister presence of Randy Mann.

"We aren't the A-Team," I said. "Not even the B, C, or D team. I think we should call for back-up. It's the sensible thing to do."

Gretchen looked to Yuri for support, then said, "I have a key under a pot in the back yard. We could go in the back door. Or the front door for that matter. We could even climb up to the second floor and go in through the window in Theo's room."

"Let's get the key and go in through the back," Yuri said. "I have a flashlight, but let's try not to use it, okay? Just as a precaution."

"What about a gun, you do have a gun?" I had a bad feeling about what we were about to do, but apparently there was no turning back.

"We won't need a gun, will we?" Gretchen asked, sounding as uncertain as I felt.

"You ran away from them," I pointed out. "You must have thought they were dangerous."

"I didn't really think. I just knew I wasn't equipped to confront someone, no matter what they were after."

"If we're going to do this, let's do it," Yuri interrupted. "And, yes, I have a gun. Let me go first. Cameron, you bring up the rear. And keep your eyes peeled."

The house had a large front yard shrouded in darkness by tall rhododendrons interspersed with dogwood trees that lined the driveway. The other side of the lot was cut off from the rest of the neighborhood by a laurel hedge that had not been trimmed in a long time. Although the city is never really dark, Gretchen's front yard could have been a set for a Halloween movie. Or maybe that was how it seemed to me because I was concerned about what we were going to find inside.

We made our way along the narrow driveway, trying to blend in with the rhodies and dogwood, peering through darkened windows for any signs of movement inside. Whoever Gretchen had heard could easily have searched the entire house in the time it had taken us to get there, but that didn't guarantee the house was empty. Especially if their intent was to threaten or harm her. Although if that was the case, it was doubtful they would have hung around once they realized she'd taken off. For all they knew, Gretchen could have gone to a neighbor's and called the police. They were probably long gone. But we couldn't count on it.

We were trying to sneak into the back yard when a motion sensor light at the corner of her house came on.

Instead of running, we all froze in place. Like deer who seem to think you can't see them if they stand still. Then, when nothing happened, we continued on to the back porch. The key was right there under a pot. A somewhat obvious hiding place in my opinion. She needed to do better than that. Yuri retrieved the key, put it in the lock and turned. A loud "click" reverberated in the still night. He paused a moment, then pushed the door open. It squeaked softly, further announcing our presence.

As he stepped inside, I wished that I, too, had a weapon. A gun, a baseball bat, anything. What were we going to do if someone attacked Yuri and got his gun away from him? I should at least have brought my Victorinox with me. Although I wasn't sure how a knife, reamer or cork screw would measure up against a real weapon. But it would have been better than a few seldom used martial arts moves fueled by fear rather than skill.

It felt anti-climactic when nothing happened and Yuri waved us in. But tensions built as we went room to room in the dark, listening for sounds of another's presence. I figured if someone was there, they wouldn't simply lie in wait, hoping we didn't turn on the lights. They would either make their escape or attack.

"Do you have a basement?" Yuri whispered when we'd gone through all of the rooms on the main floor and upstairs.

Gretchen whispered back, "no."

"Why are we whispering?" I whispered.

"Okay," Yuri said in his normal voice. "Let's turn on the lights. But stay away from the windows."

As soon as the lights came on Yuri went to check out the front and back doors to see if he could determine how someone had gained entrance. Gretchen headed straight for her study. I followed her and wasn't surprised when she announced that someone had taken her laptop and her phone. All of the drawers to her desk were standing open as well as the drawers on a two-drawer filing cabinet under the window. There were papers and files scattered around as if someone had gone through them in a hurry. Before I could comment she turned and ran downstairs. I followed on her heels. She stopped at the entrance to her living room and swore. "Damn, damn, damn." I felt her choice of words was quite moderate under the circumstances. The room had been tossed and the contents of her purse turned upside down in the middle of a coffee table.

She raced over and frantically went through the stuff from her purse. Then she started crying. She sat down the edge of the couch and sobbed, rocking back and forth as if pain. "Noooo," she moaned. "Noooo."

I sat down beside her and put my arm around her shoulders. "What did they take?"

"The back-up thumb," she managed to mumble. "They took the thumb."

Then it hit me. "It was in your purse?"

She nodded.

"They took your backup as well as your laptop?" I asked, sensing the worst.

Gretchen took a deep breath and sat up straight. "Everything," she said. "They took it all."

"You do have a copy at work." I said. "Or in the Cloud." It was hard to believe that she'd had all of her notes and her backup in one location. But then, she'd thought her investigation was being done in secret.

"No. I…I thought it was safer to…." She struggled to say it out loud. The fact that she'd kept her research on a thumb drive in her purse seemed absurd given what had just occurred.

"It's not that bad, is it? I mean, you can re-create everything, can't you?"

She turned her tear-streaked face toward me. "Maybe. Given time."

"I'm sorry." It was limp, but it was all I could think of to say.

Yuri joined us. "No forced entry that I can see. No broken windows. A very professional job." Then he saw Gretchen's face and froze. "What is it? What's wrong?"

"My chance at making a name for myself is over." Gretchen slumped down, her crying under control. She was like an inflated life-sized mannequin that was slowly deflating.

"They took all of her research," I said. "For an important article she was working on."

"What about back-up? You have back-up, don't you?"

"They got the back-up." I held up my hand before he could repeat what I had said about re-creating the material. "It will be difficult to meet the publication deadline."

"I'm sorry," he said, even though he had no idea what we were talking about and how devasting the loss was.

"I think it's time to call the police," I said. "Thieves often just take electronics. You don't have to explain anything about what's on your computer. You don't even need to mention the USB flash drive or that they went through your purse and didn't take your wallet."

Gretchen stood up. "You're right. Might as well call the police," she said. "Maybe they left something behind that will help nail the bastards."

"Like their images on the camera in the kitchen?" Yuri asked.

"Oh," Gretchen exclaimed. "I'd forgotten about that. It's Theo's spy thing, a nanny cam I bought him so he could see what animals traipse through our back yard at night. He said he and Jason rigged it up to see if the cat ever gets up on the counters when we're not home."

"Let's check it out."

CHAPTER 9
THE SLEEPOVER

"I'LL SEE IF THE CAMERA PICKED UP anything," Yuri said. "You call the police, Cameron. And, Gretchen, check to see if anything else is missing."

"Don't worry, Gretchen," I said. "I'll just say there was a burglary and that we are in the process of looking around to see what's been taken. When they get here, just stick to the facts, what you heard and that you were scared because you were alone with your son. They will understand why you ran away, even if that's all you tell them."

"But they went through my files and my desk. Isn't it obvious that they were looking for something specific?"

"They could have been looking for money or more electronics. I don't know. But you have to decide which is more important, getting some fingerprints or diverting attention away from what they did to your office. Your call. But make up your mind quickly."

Gretchen went off to look at the rest of the house and decide what to say about why they might have searched her office while I called the police. They asked if anyone was in danger, and when I said "no" they informed me it would be about twenty minutes before they could get someone there.

When I hung up, I wondered if I'd told the truth. Gretchen might be in danger, depending on whether whoever took her materials considered her a sufficient threat to want her out of the way. But the situation was way more complicated than that given her indecision about how much she wanted to reveal about the possible reason for the break-in.

Meanwhile Yuri was playing back the feed from the camera. "Damn," he said. "The thief obviously didn't know the camera was there, but this guy in the hoodie must have a guardian angel. There isn't one shot of his face."

"Let me see."

Yuri replayed the footage for me. "The kids had the angle wrong for catching a burglar, didn't they?"

"Well, they didn't anticipate needing to see someone's face. They just wanted to catch the cat in the act. They would have done that."

"So, all we can tell is that there was one male, normal build, probably normal height who owns a dark hoodie and wears gloves – at least when searching a house. No logos on his clothes, no tattoos on the square inch of jaw the camera caught when he checked out the refrigerator. That doesn't narrow it down much, does it?"

"I'm afraid this isn't going to help the police at all. Although they are probably going to wonder if the thief was looking for drugs in the freezer. Do you think he thought she'd hide her notes there?"

Gretchen returned. "Well, that rips it. Theo's laptop, notepad and cell are gone. The bastard. He didn't need to take Theo's stuff too."

"Don't worry," Yuri said. "Kids lose electronics all the time. He'll probably be psyched to buy all new stuff."

"I hope so. Theo loves his technology."

Ten minutes later two police officers arrived. By then Gretchen had straightened up her office and packed overnight bags for her and Theo. Since the thief had been wearing gloves, there was no need for them to check for fingerprints. Gretchen did, however, show the officers the image that had been caught on camera. Like us, they didn't think it would be of much help.

Yuri and I had gone through the house again looking for anything that might give us some clues about the identity of the intruder, but we hadn't found anything. The younger female officer told us that there had been a lot of robberies in the area of late. "Kids looking to pick up some easy cash. There's always a market for computers and phones."

"But don't most of those kinds of robberies happen during the day when they think no one's home?" I asked. The minute the words were out of my mouth I regretted them. We wanted the police to think it was a simple robbery. On the other hand, we also wanted them to make some effort to find whoever did it. "I'm just saying, it could have ended badly." Hint, hint. Be a little more thorough than you might ordinarily be.

When one of the officers noted the time discrepancy between when Gretchen said the robbery took place and how long it took to report it, Gretchen explained that her first thought was to get her son out of the house. That she had called once she knew he was safe. That seemed to satisfy the officers. In fact, one of them said, "You were smart. It's usually not a good idea to confront a criminal. Things can escalate pretty fast."

They left with a list of items stolen and a warning to make sure all of the doors and windows were locked. We left shortly after the police did, making sure all of the doors and windows were locked. Not that we thought it would make any difference. It was definitely a case of locking the barn door after the horse was gone. And there wasn't another horse to lock up.

Back at my place we decided to have more tea before trying to sleep. Yuri complained about my tea selection, said I needed something more robust, not wimpy herbals. I handed him a box of Irish breakfast tea, a bag of Tazo Awake, and some loose-leaf Russian Caravan with an infuser spoon. "Take your pick, tough guy."

"Someone needs to stay alert," he said, then added, "Did I mention I'm going to hang out on your couch? We can go to work together. Gretchen, you can work from our office tomorrow. Until we know a little more about who broke into your home." It sounded like the plan was final, like we had no say. But I wasn't about to protest. The more I thought about it the more worried I was that Gretchen might still be a target. They couldn't know if she had another back-up somewhere. Or what information she had in her head.

"Do you think it's safe for Theo to go to school?" I asked, thinking out loud.

"We could have your mother take the kids tomorrow," Yuri said. "Once they're there, it's probably okay."

I had a vision of Mom taking on a pair of attackers dressed in dark hoodies, her armed with a sharp tongue and a couple of karate moves learned in a class she had taken last year. "I'm not sure if that's a good idea."

Yuri sipped his tea. "Maybe to be safe we ought to have Theo come with us tomorrow."

"We can't hide forever," Gretchen said.

"Just for a few days. Until we see what the police find and we have a chance to think this through."

It was settled. Irish breakfast was manly tea. Gretchen and Theo would come to the office with us tomorrow. And we would all be able to function normally after about three hours of sleep. If any of us could sleep after what had happened.

Actually, I think Yuri was asleep within minutes after he laid down on my sofa with a pillow and a blanket. We could hear him snoring softly as we headed for bed. "If you stay tomorrow night, you can have Mara's bed," I told Gretchen. "She can sleep upstairs."

"Maybe I'll be able to go home tomorrow," Gretchen said, sounding doubtful and extremely tired. I gave her an old nightgown and she slipped into bed next to Theo while I went down the hall and climbed into the lower bunkbed in Jason's room where I spent the rest of the night worrying about what was going to happen next.

The next morning Mara was surprised to see Yuri, Gretchen and Theo at the breakfast table. She had slept through all of the excitement. Yuri was already on his second cup of coffee, chatting with Mom as though his being there was the most normal thing in the world. Jason was obviously delighted to have his friend staying with him, but Theo was more subdued. Even so he made quite the case for going to school rather than going to work with us.

"Hey, you'll be in the pit with a bunch of detectives, isn't that cool?" Yuri said. I wasn't at all sure P.W. was going to be thrilled about having Gretchen and Theo in the office, but Yuri made such a strong pitch to Theo that Jason ended up wanting to come along too. I had to promise that sometime in the not too distant future, he could come to work with me. Mom was definitely not thrilled by the prospect, but she held her tongue. You didn't display family discord in front of others. I wondered if she would refrain from putting articles up on my refrigerator while Gretchen was staying with us. Maybe another magnet would appear so she could put up a separate set of articles for Gretchen. Gretchen was, after all, also a single mother, although in an acceptable profession.

We all got up to go at the same time, bussing our dishes, but leaving the clean-up for Mom. As the others filtered out, she held me back and asked how many there would be for dinner. I had to admit that I didn't know. "Don't worry," I said. "I'll pick something up."

Then she asked, "Is Theo in danger?" Again, I had to admit that I didn't know. "It might be good if Yuri stayed with us until this is resolved," she said. I wasn't sure she even knew what "this" was, but I was glad she was okay with the idea and quickly agreed. "We could bring my Futon down and set it up for him in the living room if you want."

"Thank you, Mom. I'll let you know if we decide it's necessary." She was being a trooper, helpful without demanding to know all of the details. I truly appreciated her support, but I had no doubt there would be hell to pay down the road.

As we approached the office, Theo stopped in front of the small display window to the left of the entrance. The window held a single three-foot long shelf. On it was a stuffed bear wearing a Sherlock Holmes deerstalker hat and a coat with a cape across the shoulders He held a magnifying glass in his right paw. Above the toy sleuth was a flier that read: "For the man or woman who has everything—give them the gift of vigilance. Special rates for gift certificate detection services."

The display attracted a lot of attention. Originally the bear had been wearing a beige trench coat and a red plaid hat. Quite a few people had taken the time to come in and point out it was NOT the right hat for Sam Spade or the right coat for Sherlock Holmes. Jenny, a part-time investigator and the bear's creator, had admitted to me that the bear was her way of ribbing Will about his retro detective coat. Still, succumbing to popular demand, Jenny picked Sherlock over Sam Spade and had made a new outfit for the display. Unfortunately, most of the people it drew in wanted to buy a bear, not hire a detective.

"Come on," Theo's mother said, urging him to catch up.

As we went inside and headed toward the pit with Gretchen and Theo in tow, Blaine shot us a questioning glare. But he didn't yell "stop." Will, Adele, and Grant were already there. We introduced everyone and explained that Gretchen and Theo would be with us today. Everyone immediately seemed to accept the situation, as if bringing strangers into the office was an everyday occurrence. While Yuri got Theo set up at a computer on the spare desk, I took Gretchen with me to see P.W. When P.W. came around from behind her desk to shake Gretchen's hand, it looked a little like Gretchen had taken a bite off the wrong side of the mushroom. P.W. towered over her. Her brown vertically striped pants suit accentuated her height, whereas Gretchen's casual clothes made her seem not only petite but young and vulnerable.

When we explained that someone had broken into Gretchen's home and had stolen research materials she'd been gathering for a potentially explosive article about a local politician, P.W. graciously said that Gretchen and Theo were welcome to spend the day at Penny-wise. I'd encouraged Gretchen to tell P.W. more about why she might be a target, but Gretchen didn't offer any further details, and P.W. didn't press for more information.

"Once you have Gretchen and Theo settled in, I would like to talk with you and Yuri," P.W. said as we got up to leave.

Fifteen minutes later Yuri and I were seated across from P.W. "Are there some things you need to fill me in on?" P.W. asked. "About your activities, not anything Gretchen wants to keep to herself."

It was time to unload about a few things. I gave P.W. an update on the threat from Randy Mann, and Yuri told her about the victim's involvement with a group of protesters trying to stop the oil companies from doing more direct business in the State. "It's looking more and more like Norcross was spying on the Mann campaign," Yuri concluded. "If we knew what he had uncovered so far we might know why someone felt threatened enough to eliminate him."

"Do you think Bobby Mann knows what his brother Randy is up to?" P.W. asked.

"For some reason, I don't think so," I said. "It's more likely he's Randy's pawn, going along with the plan because he's ambitious and is used to being manipulated by his well-to-do family."

"Do you think Randy Mann could be behind the burglary at Gretchen's?" The question was P.W.'s indirect way of acknowledging that she guessed at least the general nature of what Gretchen was working on. By not asking for more details, we would be able to maintain the illusion that Gretchen and Theo were in the office because I was doing a favor for the mother of my son's friend.

"It seems unlikely to me. I mean, Randy Mann could have local connections that tipped him off to what she's working on, but he seems more like the strong-arm and bribery type to me."

Yuri said, "Look, I know we are trying to respect Gretchen's right to keep what she's been working on to herself, but my investigator instincts tell me it's related to the same things Norcross was looking into. So big oil and the Mann campaign are at the center of this mess. I got the names of a couple of Norcross's university friends from Dr. Benson, the prof I had a drink with last night. I say we talk to them and see if we can find out more about what Norcross was up to and if he mentioned anything to them that might point us in the right direction."

"The police may consider that crossing the line into their murder investigation," P.W. said. She frowned and looked at the cigarette in the copper ashtray on her desk, but she didn't reach for it. "Have you talked with Detective Connolly about any of this?"

"That's on our agenda for today," I said.

"Then start there." It was as close as P.W. ever came to giving a direct order about how to handle an assignment in progress.

"Since Gretchen doesn't want us to tell anyone about the story she's working on, that makes it difficult." I said.

"Tell him about what we've been hired to do by Bobby Mann and let him know about the 'visit' from Randy Mann. And explain that you're not trying to interfere with the police investigation of the murder but that we have still another client with overlapping interests. You don't have to be more specific." She raised an eyebrow. "Gretchen isn't technically a client, but I don't see how she can feel comfortable going home until we better understand the situation. And I fear that you two may also have placed yourselves in jeopardy. Although I have confidence in Major Crimes, I believe it is necessary to continue your line of inquiry. Keeping as low a profile as possible, of course."

"Thank you," Yuri said.

"And if you need help from any of the others, just ask. This is a priority."

I called Detective Connolly from the tiny conference room we refer to as "the closet" and put Yuri on speaker. I told him about being hired by the Mann Campaign and about Randy Mann waiting for me in the alley behind my home. "He made me feel uncomfortable, but he was right—we weren't hired to investigate a murder. But now we have another client, and there may be some overlap between what she wants us to look into and some activities Brian Norcross was involved with. We thought you should know." Referring to Gretchen as a client seemed like a reasonable exaggeration to justify our actions. I just hoped we didn't run into a wall of conflict of interests as we poked around in the complicated mess of potentially connected events.

"I assume you don't want to tell me the name of your new client."

"No. And I assume you don't want to tell us where you are on the investigation of the murder."

"So you can put it in your report to Randy Mann?"

"Well, I guess I would have to report on anything relevant."

"You'll have to settle for what you see on the news. You know I can't comment off the record on an on-going investigation."

"Of course."

"I do, however, expect you to call me if you come across anything connected to our murder investigation."

"Of course."

"Then we are in agreement. Just one more thing—"

"What's that?"

"You two should be careful. You may be poking a hornet's nest. And hornets can sting."

"I appreciate the analogy," I said. "We'll try to keep our distance from any hornet's nest."

"You get the idea. I just want you to be aware of what you might be getting into. And don't say 'of course' again. I get it that you are trying to appear cooperative."

I couldn't help myself, "Of course," I said one last time, but with a hint of sarcasm.

"Stay in touch," Detective Connolly said with feeling, ending the call.

"I told you," Yuri said. "The man likes you."

CHAPTER 10
POKING THE HORNET'S NEST

WHEN YURI AND I RETURNED to the pit, we ran into Gretchen and Norm on their way out. They were headed to a computer shop in the mall to purchase a new computer and phone for her and a tablet for Theo. It seemed more like a chummy shopping spree than a woman in danger being accompanied by a body guard. But then Norm always made people feel comfortable. Meanwhile, Theo was happily working away on his borrowed computer, occasionally glancing around at the occupants of the pit as if expecting them to suddenly don superhero costumes and do something outrageous. I was afraid he was destined to be terribly disappointed. Unless he considered Will's trench coat a costume.

Adele took us aside to share what little she'd been able to obtain from her research on the two candidates and the victim. She started with Bobby. As we already knew, he was from a filthy rich east coast family. His grandparents had made a fortune by extracting, refining, and selling oil. His parents had carried on the tradition of making money from oil by expanding exploration and making a number of wise investments in start-up oil companies. As far as she could tell, they weren't under investigation or hadn't recently been accused of doing anything illegal, but they definitely threw a lot of money around to persuade state officials and the federal government to ease domestic regulations. Furthermore, it was rumored that they had investments in a number of oil rich countries and were behind some moves to loosen regulations on shipping and importation of foreign oil. According to scuttlebutt, Bobby didn't have a head for business, but with his talent for schmoozing and networking, once he became a Representative, he would become the political arm of their business enterprises.

It looked as though Bobby had planned on entering politics for a while. After graduating from Yale Law School—in the bottom quarter of his class—he'd taken a job with the Public Defender's office, perhaps as a way to soften his image as a member of the one percent as well as to beef up his resume. Probably not because he believed in their mission, but you wouldn't know for sure unless you could get inside his head. And although the position may have convinced some members of the public that he valued justice over money, it hadn't helped him win in his first run for Congress. Nor in his second. This time he was relying on money and marketing to increase his chances of winning.

He had used his marriage to a well-known and attractive former Seafair Princess, Ashley Price, to gain access to the local monied families and the influence they wielded in the area. It was a politically astute move. Their whirlwind courtship had been played up by the press, and their wedding included all of the affluent and powerful families in the state. Although it may have been love at first sight, it undoubtedly crossed the mind of the aspiring politician and his family that it was strategically advantageous for him, an outsider, to marry into a local family with deep roots in the community. Not that the marriage worked only in his favor. Ashley too benefited from the union. There was considerable talk that she had been eager to marry a wealthy and ambitious man.

His brother, Randy, was a more complex character. Given his demeanor and behavior, it surprised me to learn that he had gone to Harvard Law School and had graduated at the top of his class. A partner in a large, prestigious D.C. law firm, one of his major clients was the Mann family business. There were several lawsuits of public record where he'd been on their legal team, including one in which they had been sued for a massive oil spill. That one was still in the courts on appeal.

There was also a sister, Michelle. After graduation from Yale, Michelle had joined the family business and was rumored to be a shrewd and formidable leader. She was the one who brokered some of their more significant deals, although she wasn't well known outside of business circles.

There was very little public information about his father, beyond his flair for business, but his mother was considered a strong party fund-raiser. As such she commanded a lot of power. All she was lacking was a son on the inside of the political establishment.

In contrast, Nathan Knight was from an entirely different background. A local boy who attended Stanford Law on scholarship, he was known for his political savvy as well as for his commitment to social and environmental causes. His parents were both engineers and environmentalists.

His only sibling, a sister, worked for an environmental non-profit whose mission was to preserve and protect local waters. Nathan's wife, Laney, a stay-at-home mother of three was actively involved with her children's schools as well as being a strong supporter of quality education for all children.

The victim, Brian Norcross, was the first in his family to attend college. His mother clerked at a grocery store and his father was a mechanic. His older sister was married to a farmer and raised cattle in Colorado. He had been on his way to becoming a success story in the social media for his outspoken advocacy on climate change. He had leveraged his use of Facebook, Twitter and Instagram, and he'd made several YouTube videos at protests that had gone viral. It was somewhat surprising that no one on the Mann campaign seemed to have been aware of any of this. But then, if you weren't engaged in protest activities, maybe you didn't pay attention to those who were. Norcross had obviously been banking on that when he started volunteering for Mann.

"So, that's what I know about all of the players in your on-going non-investigation," Adele concluded as she closed the file folder.

"What a strange cross-section of society," I said. "All converging on one local race."

"Given all their advantages, it's too bad the Mann campaign seems more interested in attacking their opponent than focusing on issues," Yuri said. "I hate to see them put the Knight campaign on the defensive like they have."

"Yes," Adele agreed. "The negative ads they're putting out are little more than smear jobs. The one about Knight wanting to crack down on gun ownership really irritates me. He does want to require background checks, even at gun shows. But the Mann ads make it look like he wants to do away with the 2nd amendment."

"No one ad is going to make the difference, but they may start to have a cumulative impact on the Knight campaign, true or not," Yuri added.

"I always thought reporters were supposed to seek the truth," I said, feeling naïve even as I uttered the thought. "If the ads twist the facts, why aren't reporters pointing that out?"

"The problem is that they report on what they see or hear, so even if they question the validity of the ads they end up reinforcing the message. And so what if they mention questionable facts one time, the ads just keep coming, playing over and over and over." Yuri sounded angry. "I told you I don't like our client. Neither his positions on issues nor his tactics. I just wish someone would expose him." He blinked and looked at me, then back at Adele. "Make sure Gretchen gets anything she needs. Anything."

"Isn't that working against the interests of our client?" I asked.

"No, it's being supportive of a friend of yours whose home was burgled."

I didn't entirely buy his logic, but I agreed with it in principle, so I let it ride.

"Okay," Yuri said. "Let's go poke the hornet's nest. Maybe we can make a difference."

"Low profile, remember?"

"I know, but a guy can dream."

Yuri had made arrangements to meet with two of Brian's friends after their 10:00 class. At 10:50 we found ourselves walking with throngs of students across campus. Jeans, baggy jackets in muted tones and tennis shoes, some in eye-catching colors, seemed to be the latest fashion. Even among the older students. Yuri in his disheveled outfit that he'd slept in on my couch the night before looked like he had just done an all-nighter for an exam. I suddenly felt overdressed and out-of-date.

We spotted the two young men waiting at the top of the steps to the student union at the same time they saw us. One of them waved, and we headed in their direction. "How did they know who we are?" I whispered, hoping Yuri would say something reassuring about my appearance.

"We obviously look like the professional investigators that we are," Yuri said with a mischievous grin.

"Good to see you again," one of the young men said to Yuri as we drew nearer.

Yuri turned to me: "Did I mention that I met Ken at the pub the other night? But we didn't get a chance to talk much." Two steps later he introduced me: "Ken, this is my partner, Cameron."

Ken, in turn, introduced us to the other young man, Alan. Then we went inside. Yuri and Ken went to get us all something to drink while Alan and I searched for a table for four amidst the chaos of students crowded around well-used tables scattered haphazardly throughout the room. My guess was that the tables had started out neatly lined up, slowly giving way to the creativity of various sized groups wanting to sit together.

It hadn't been that long ago that I'd been a student, but now it all felt so far away, another life. The institutional walls with posters everywhere. The noise. The smell of cafeteria food. The energy. The mix of nationalities. Good times and hard times. A rite of passage.

Once we were seated, I tried to make conversation by asking Alan what his major was and what he wanted to do after graduation. "Computer programming," he said. "Or maybe try to get my pilot's license." Such disparate choices for his future made me smile. Not that I could talk. Getting a Ph.D. to become a college professor only to end up working for a discount detective agency. Not exactly a traditional career track.

Ken and Yuri came back with coffee for me, sodas for them, and a tray full of junk food. We spent a few minutes sorting out the food before getting around to the purpose of our conversation. The picture they painted of Brian was of a young man more interested in causes than in school. They told us about editorials he had written for the college newspaper, rallies he'd attended to protest big oil's role in the destruction of the planet, and about how much time he had spent trying to come up with strategies to stop environmentally unfriendly practices.

"He wanted to become an environmental engineer," Ken said. "He was hoping to develop solutions to environmental problems. But in the meantime, he was focused on hassling companies associated with big oil. He railed against pipelines, called out companies in the campus newspaper for spills, protested rail transport and shipping of tar sands crude through local waters, and generally raised hell about potential oil drilling off our coast."

"Sounds like a committed activist," Yuri commented.

"Some of us dabble in protests," Ken admitted, "but Brian was seriously dedicated to trying to influence policy. And he believed that if he made it personal, we could leverage our local efforts."

"What does that mean?" I asked.

"Among other things, he was developing a list of names for protesters to target. Politicians, investors, management. Anyone either supporting or making money off the oil industry. It was basically an annotated list explaining each person's connection and involvement with oil. It was going to include home and office addresses, phone numbers, email, even pictures. He was also hoping to find enough evidence of unscrupulous or potentially illegal dealings to use as leverage to force them to back off on some of their projects, or to at least show some restraint. Maybe even stir things up enough to get a few lawsuits under way. He planned to put everything he learned online, to engage as many protesters as possible."

"Did he give you that list or share any of his research with you?"

"He would have eventually, but he wanted to get his ducks lined up first. It wasn't that he didn't trust us. But he wanted to do it all himself. It was a bit of an ego trip." Ken paused "Not in a bad way, you know. It was just that it was his idea, his project. He wanted to be the one at the center of the storm when it all went live."

"So, you don't think anyone else had a copy of what he was working on?" Yuri asked

Ken and Alan exchanged looks, and both shook their heads. "I doubt it," Ken said, speaking for both of them.

"I assume Bobby Mann would have figured prominently on the list," I said.

Both young men nodded. "We knew Brian was volunteering on his campaign to see if he could uncover anything shady about Bobby Mann and his family business, but if he'd found anything damaging, he hadn't mentioned it to us."

"We kidded him about it," Alan said. "Had bets on how long he'd get away with his undercover work."

Ken said, "He did once say that he was looking into influence peddling. I think he believed that if he could prove the oil industry was buying off politicians that he could stop them, or at least curb their appetite for pipelines and offshore drilling. But that kind of thing is hard to prove."

"And, sadly, now that his data has gone missing, we may never know what he found," Alan said.

"So, he didn't share his research, but did he tell people what he was working on? For instance, who else might have known he was trying to get dirt on the Mann campaign?"

"He wasn't advertising what he was working on," Alan said. "He wanted to make a splash when he decided to go public."

We sipped our respective drinks for a minute in silence. Then Yuri asked, "Is there anyone else you think we should talk to? Anyone at all?"

"Well," Alan said after a brief hesitation. "He was dating the daughter of a local politician suspected of being in the pocket of big oil. Maybe you should talk to her."

"We thought that was strange," Ken added.

"Not so strange," Yuri said. "Go behind enemy lines and find out everything you can. Gather ammunition for the final assault. He was doing it by volunteering on the Mann campaign, why not date the enemy too?"

"She's a hottie," Alan said. "So maybe not so strange for that reason too."

"Do you know her name?" I asked.

Ken leaned toward us across the table. "I can not only tell you her name, I can point her out. She's the redhead two tables over. The one wearing a pink sweater." He shook his head. "She shouldn't wear pink with that coloring."

I looked at the young woman he indicated and agreed with his assessment. Pink was not her color. But I was surprised Ken had commented on that given her appearance overall. She was definitely a hottie.

I kept my eye on her to make sure she didn't leave while Yuri asked a few final questions. Then we thanked them for their time and made our way over to Lisa Brennan, daughter of Karl Brennan, the hottie in pink. She looked up when we stopped next to her. "Can I help you?" she asked, sounding puzzled. Up close the pink wasn't any more flattering. But she was definitely attractive, her full figure accentuated by the soft clingy sweater.

"You might be able to," Yuri said. "My name is Yuri Webster and this is my colleague, Cameron Chandler. Could we speak to you in private?"

"About what?" She reached for her purse as if preparing for a quick getaway, nodding briefly at the young man across the table from her. He looked uncertain as to what he should do. Defend his friend or make tracks.

"It's about Brian Norcross."

She looked at Yuri, then at me, a vertical frown creasing the middle of her forehead. "Who are you?"

"We're private investigators..." Before Yuri could continue, she stood, pulled on her jacket, and grabbed her purse.

"See you later," she said to her startled friend.

"We just need a few minutes of your time," Yuri persisted.

"No, I have nothing to say." She abruptly brushed past us and started walking away.

I waved Yuri back and quickly caught up with her. "We know you two were dating, so you must have cared for him." She stopped suddenly and turned toward me. The look of hostility on her face made me involuntarily take a step back.

"My mother has instructed me not to talk to anyone about Brian. If you insist on pestering me, I'll report you to the police."

With that she turned on her heel and took off like a racehorse out of the gate.

Had Brian been using her and had she discovered his subterfuge? That could explain her reaction. Or maybe her mother just wanted to make sure neither she nor their prestigious local family became tainted by being associated, even distantly, with a murder investigation. For all we knew, it was possible her father had been one of Brian's targets. I let myself follow that line of thought. Maybe Brian initially asked her out to find out more about her family, but had ended up falling for her. Feeling guilty, he may have given her a head's up about what he was working on. That seemed unlikely. Still, anything was possible when youth and hormones were involved.

"Well," Yuri said. "I think we know which hornet's nest to poke."

"Maybe we've already done it."

CHAPTER 11
THE STING

WHEN WE GOT BACK to the car, I called Detective Connolly. "I think we just did what you told us not to do," I said. "I think we poked a hornet's nest. But by accident, not deliberately."

He could have immediately started blaming us for stepping in it even before he heard the details. Instead he asked, "Are you okay? Do you need assistance?" He sounded concerned. I appreciated that. Especially since he had specifically warned us not to meddle.

"We were asking a couple of Norcross's university buddies about his protest activities." I paused. Connolly didn't say anything, waiting for me to continue.

"Go ahead," Yuri whispered. "Tell him."

"They told us that Norcross was compiling a list of people and companies for protesters to target to let them know they aren't welcome in our state and to possibly expose any secret or underhanded deals they are part of. Maybe even reveal illegal or criminal activities."

"And?"

"They pointed out a young woman Norcross had been dating, and we tried to talk to her."

"Tried?"

"Yes, her father is a local politician who gets a lot of money from the oil industry."

"So do a lot of politicians."

"But this one's daughter did not respond well when approached. At first, she just said she didn't want to talk to us and walked off, but I followed her and mentioned that I knew she and Brian had been dating. Then she told me that her mother had warned her not to talk to anyone about Brian. She threatened to contact the police if I persisted. I decided to contact you before she could call anyone."

"So, she either anticipated someone would approach her about Norcross or someone else already has." He sounded like he was speculating out loud, not asking me a question. "Do you think Norcross was playing her and she found out?"

"It certainly seems like a possibility. But why mention that her mother warned her not to talk to anyone about him?"

"Maybe she told her mother about Norcross and her mother advised her to keep mum about her murdered boyfriend to protect her from an inquisitive and sometimes unkind press," Connelly said.

"Or maybe daddy was a target and he found out, either from his daughter or through another source. It's something that needs looking into."

"But not by you," Connolly said firmly. "I'll have someone check it out. Now give me their names, all of them—the two students, the young woman and her parents." It wasn't a request. I gave him the names of Alan, Ken, Lisa and her parents, Karl and Jennifer Brennan. Then he said,

"It sounds to me like your new client's interests are surprisingly close to the lines of inquiry in our murder investigation."

"I'm telling you the truth when I say that we aren't trying to find Brian's killer. But it's possible the same people who are causing our, ah, client difficulty, also had some interaction with Brian." I suddenly realized I was thinking of the dead student more and more as Brian rather than as Norcross. The more we learned about him the more I felt like I knew him. The investigation was beginning to feel personal.

"You understand that criminals don't always make discerning decisions about who is their enemy and who isn't. If you look like you're going after them, it doesn't matter whether it's to catch a killer or for some other reason."

"I'm aware of that. That's why we would appreciate it if you would hurry up and catch the person who is responsible for Brian's death. That would make our job a lot easier. And safer."

"Can I speak with Yuri?" His abrupt request took me by surprise.

"Ah, yes, of course." I handed my phone to Yuri.

I could hear Detective Connolly's voice and the cadence of his speech, but I couldn't make out the actual words. Yuri tried to interrupt a couple of times but didn't manage to get a word in until Connolly had said his piece. "Will do," was all Yuri said before clicking off.

"Will do what?" I asked.

"Will obey the law. Will stay out of police business. And will keep an eye on you."

"He thinks I can't protect myself?"

"All I can say is that you might want to cozy up to him. It would be better to have him on our side than criticizing our every move."

"No way I'm going to cozy up to a chauvinist, ah …"

"You can say 'pig,' it's okay."

"Resorting to stereotyped labels makes me no better than him."

"Don't worry about it. I'm not asking you to marry the guy, just be nice to him. Think quid pro quo, we give him information, he gives us information."

"You may notice how effective that was just now. I told him what we knew and he lectured you."

"Well, what we need to do now is take a step back, reassess, and decide what we want to do next." He yawned. "And I could use a nap." He leaned back against the headrest and closed his eyes. "Wake me when we're back at the office."

As I pulled into a parking space at the mall, Yuri's eyes popped open and he said, "We need to find the stuff Brian was working on, find out who he was planning on targeting. See if he had evidence of illegal activities or if he was just blowing smoke."

"I thought we were taking a step back," I protested. "Besides, if no one we've talked to has a copy of what he was working on or knows where he stored his research, then how do you propose we find what no one else can?"

Yuri grinned. "We're investigators. That's what we do."

"Okay, Sherlock, what do you suggest?"

"Well, if you wanted to keep some data you were collecting private, you wouldn't put it on your computer or carry it around on a piece of paper tucked into a pocket."

Or leave it on your computer with a copy in your purse, I couldn't help thinking. Although in her defense, Gretchen honestly believed no one knew what she was working on. Brian's situation was entirely different. Given his history and media visibility, he must have been aware that he could be discovered at any time.

"No," Yuri continued without waiting for comment. "You would put it somewhere safe, somewhere you could access it easily, but not somewhere others could lay their hands on it."

"I take it you have something in mind." I could tell as much by the excitement in his voice.

"Yes, I do. Want to stretch your brain a little and make a guess?"

"No thanks, my brain is currently stretched to the limit." I suddenly had an image of a brain pulled taut like a rubber brand. That's how I feel when the stress of work and family get to me.

"The university has a service where researchers can store files," Yuri said.

"Isn't that primarily for professors, researchers, and staff?" I'd known a couple of Ph.D. candidates who'd made use of the service, although I never had.

"That wouldn't stop someone with tech savvy, someone determined to use the service to hide information."

"It sounds beyond us," I said doubtfully. "But I suppose you know someone who could figure it out?"

"Let's go back to the U," Yuri said, sounding more excited by the minute. "I've got a hunch."

"We just got here," I complained, hating that I sounded like Mara having one of her snitty moments. But I had just pulled into the mall parking lot, found a space close to the entrance, and was looking forward to doing something routine until quitting time.

"You're right, maybe I should call first. Hold on."

"Who are you calling?"

"Dr. Benson." Yuri frowned as he listened to the phone ringing. "Damn, he isn't answering."

I started to say something but he held up his hand to stop me. He left a message for the professor to call him back as soon as possible. Then he turned to me and said, "Go ahead and park."

"You obviously haven't noticed, but we are parked."

"Oh, right." He opened the car door and said, "Let's go back to the office and wait until he calls."

"Is this something we should tell Connolly?" I asked as we headed across the parking lot toward the entrance closest to our office. "They probably have someone with the expertise to figure it all out. And Connolly could use the information to further his investigation of Brian's death."

"Not until I verify my theory. If we find Brian's research, we'll turn it over to him." He turned to me with a big smile, "After reading it, of course."

"And making a copy?"

"Of course."

Blaine acknowledged us with a brief nod as we passed by his desk. He didn't look happy, but we didn't stop to inquire if anything was wrong. I had my suspicions, and I think Yuri had his. They were confirmed the minute we opened the door to the pit. In fact, it was even worse than

I'd imagined. I'd envisioned Theo disrupting the work flow with questions or the restless energy of a pre-teen boy. What I hadn't imagined was that he would be playing some kind of game with a couple of colleagues. But there they were, Will, Jenny and Theo, maneuvering between the desks, shouting back and forth while tossing around a foosball.

Jenny, our part-time investigator and creator of our Sherlock bear, is a full-time hippie farmer. Whenever she needs cash she comes by and usually manages to get an assignment. P.W. has a soft spot for her and always finds her something to do. It didn't surprise me that Jenny had come by, it was probably a slow time for farming. Nor did it surprise me that she would end up playing an active game with Theo. But to see Will joining in was startling and a bit disconcerting.

Yuri immediately jumped into the fray and snatched the foosball. Then he realized he didn't know what the object of the game was and hesitated a moment too long. Jenny grabbed the ball from him and yelled, "I win."

"Enough," Adele said over the chatter.

'Okay, okay," Jenny responded. "You can have your peace and quiet back." She went over to Theo and poked him in the ribs. "Next time, kiddo."

Theo was smiling at her with adoration. "You'll have to come out to the farm sometime," Jenny added. They had obviously bonded. Theo beamed a "yes" to her suggestion and reluctantly returned to his computer. Jenny sat down at a work station across from Gretchen and immediately became absorbed in a file. Will returned to his desk, looking somewhat sheepish. Adele waved us toward the closet.

Once we were seated in the narrow chairs around the small table, she asked, "Learn anything?"

We brought her up to date and asked if she would check out Lisa's father, Karl Brennan.

"I can already tell you a little about him," she said. "He's a powerful state senator in my district. A hardline conservative with a direct link to big business, specifically big oil. He never met an oil company or an oil project he didn't like."

"Not a hidden connection then?"

"No, but he doesn't advertise it either. He needs crossover votes to win in our district. But his financial disclosures tell all."

"Any links to Bobby Mann?"

"That I'll have to look for. Seems likely, I would guess." She wrote something down on a pad of paper she'd brought with her. "Anything else?"

"No," I said. "Everything okay here? I'm not sure what we are going to do tomorrow with Gretchen and Theo. But it probably isn't safe for them to go home yet."

"Theo is a good kid, but this isn't exactly a fun place for him."

"Looked like everyone was having fun when we came in," Yuri said, wiggling his eyebrows suggestively.

"You know what I mean."

"I get the point," I said. "And I'm sure Gretchen does, too. We'll have a talk this evening and see what we can figure out."

Dr. Benson called back just as we were getting ready to leave for the day. When Yuri posed the possibility that Brian may have used the professor's research site to store some private information, the professor assured him that he hadn't. If Brian had asked him, Dr. Benson said, he would have given Brian permission, but he hadn't asked. And there was nothing unusual on the site to suggest someone had stored something there without permission.

What had looked for a moment like a promising lead had become a dead-end. The day ended with few answers and a feeling of unease about what might happen next.

We bought pizza and salad on the way home. Gretchen seemed more upbeat than she had that morning, but she still wasn't sure how soon she would be able to get her story ready for publication. "There's the issue of re-creating exact dates of meetings and remembering who was present for which conversations. But most important, even if I get all of the facts straight, knowing what someone told me and having contemporaneous notes to back it up are two different things. I don't have time to go over every detail with each of the individuals I've talked to. Especially since some of them were so reluctant to tell me anything the first time around. I obviously can't tell them someone stole my notes. That would definitely scare them off. And the paper or anyone I take the story to will be hesitant to stick their corporate neck out unless I have some fairly concrete evidence."

Mom joined us for dinner, whether out of curiosity or a yen for pizza rather than her usual healthy fare wasn't clear. We were just getting started when my cell rang. I didn't recognize the number but answered anyway. The low-pitched, intimidating voice on the other end immediately got my attention. I went into my bedroom to get away from the background noise.

"I thought we had an understanding," Randy Mann said.

"Do you have a problem with something I've done?" There were so many possibilities there was no way I could guess what he was upset about.

"You've been poking your nose in where it doesn't belong."

"I don't know what you mean."

"Consider this warning number two. I don't think you want a third." He hung up.

I sat down on the bed and tried to think. Did he know about Gretchen and Theo? Had Lisa Brennan said something to her father that got back to Randy already? Did he find out that Adele was researching his family? Had he heard that we were trying to track down Brian's research? How was I supposed to stop doing something if I didn't know what it was?

Yuri poked his head in. "You okay?" I waved him over. He came in, closing the door behind him, and took a seat on the bench at the end of my bed. "Who was it?"

"Randy Mann." I told Yuri what he had said and what had remained unsaid.

"We obviously poked something sensitive. Too bad we don't know which poke scored."

"What we do know is that the threat level has gone up."

"Okay, let's not get everyone excited, but tomorrow we need to move Gretchen and Theo to someplace safe. And we need to watch our own backs."

"What about Mara and Jason? And Mom?"

"Okay. He's calling you and not me for a reason. He knows you have family. I hate to say it, but we have no choice. We have to stop interviewing people. And we need to make sure your family isn't taking any unnecessary risks."

"You mean like living their lives like normal human beings."

Yuri reached out and took my hand. "I'm sorry, Cameron. I know this isn't what you signed on for."

"It's one thing to risk my own neck, another to put my family at risk."

"The good news is that Randy has been open about his threats. He has to know that if anything happens to you or your family, he will be the number one suspect."

"That's reassuring," I said, not meaning it. Yuri didn't miss the sarcasm.

"Let's call P.W. She could assign someone to accompany the kids to and from school for a few days. Until we have a chance to prove we are off the case. And she will have some ideas about how we keep Gretchen and Theo safe."

We returned to the dinner party. Mom gave me a penetrating look, but everyone else seemed oblivious to our brief absence. After dinner Yuri called P.W. Later, when the kids were in bed, Yuri and I filled Mom and Gretchen in on the new plan. P.W. had made arrangements for Gretchen and Theo to stay with a friend of hers on Vashon Island, just a short ferry ride away from Seattle. But hopefully far enough away to create a cushion of safety. Her friend worked from home and would meet Gretchen and Theo at the ferry in the morning. Grant would take them to the ferry and make sure they got safely aboard.

Meanwhile, Will was going to accompany Mara and Jason to school. The kids were to be told that they might be approached about a case Yuri and I were working on, and that under no circumstance were they to talk to any strangers or leave the school grounds during the day unless they got permission directly from me to do so. Will would be waiting for them at the end of the school day, and they were to come home only with him.

P.W. had offered to have Will also keep an eye on my mother, but she nixed the idea, loudly and with determination. Mom was happy to have her grandkids escorted to and from school, but she could handle herself and them after that, thank you very much.

Yuri and I also had our "orders." We were to stick together during the day, and he was to escort me home in the evening. When I asked who was going to watch over him after he left, P.W. was vague. She obviously didn't want to insult me by suggesting that I needed protection but Yuri could take care of himself. In my opinion, owning a gun didn't make him invincible.

P.W. also informed us that she would be contacting Bobby Mann to terminate our relationship with him. She added that under no circumstances were we to continue investigating anything related to the campaign or to Norcross's death. I was grateful that she was willing to give up a paying client to protect us. But it also made me feel guilty. Guilty about getting us involved in the first place. Guilty for putting my family at risk. And guilty for feeling like I was letting Brian down. After all, he had risked everything for a worthy cause. It felt like someone should pick up the torch and run with it.

The only bright spot was that the election would soon be over. The people would have spoken. Any threats connected with the campaign should end. We just needed to stay vigilant until then.

The one wild card was Gretchen's article. If she managed to get it published before the election, all hell would break loose. But making the story public would at least lessen the danger for her and Theo. If it didn't come out until after the election, the danger would linger. Those responsible for the break-in wouldn't know for sure how close she was to re-creating what she had been working on. Nor could they be certain how much she had learned from Brian. They, whoever "they" were, were still out there somewhere, potentially ready to act on their fear of exposure.

CHAPTER 12
A DEAD HEAT

THE WEEKEND AFTER WE QUIT investigating was relatively calm. For me at least. The campaigns continued their back-and-forth fight for votes, and the name-calling and finger-pointing intensified. In spite of all the hand-shaking, speech making, and money spent on ads, the polls indicated that the race between Bobby Mann and Nathan Knight was a dead heat.

Mara had friends over on Saturday, so I didn't' see much of her, except when they came out of her room to stock up on snacks. Jason was holed up watching election coverage, tracking various campaigns across the country, following polls, listening to speculation and analysis, totally immersed in the political process. Saturday afternoon Mom went out with friends to a movie. They planned to have dinner together afterwards; she told me not to wait up. My big evening consisted of ordering pizza for everyone, then seeing Mara's friends off as parents came by to pick up their daughters. Afterwards, my exhausted daughter disappeared back into her room while I hung around and moped.

On Sunday I checked in with Gretchen. She and Theo had decided to stay with P.W.'s friend on the island until after the election. Theo was doing daily homework so he wouldn't get behind at school, and Gretchen was continuing to work on her article. She was fairly certain she wasn't going to be able to regroup and complete the article in time to have any impact on the election. However, she still hoped to have a more extensive exposé published at some point in the future.

Although Gretchen was disappointed that she wasn't going to meet her self-imposed deadline, both she and Theo were thrilled with where they were staying. She sent me some pictures of the house. It was on a bluff overlooking the sound and had an incredible view. It had been built in the forties but had been updated in the late 90's. It was a lovely old house surrounded by trees with a pond off to the side of the wraparound, covered deck. As a bonus, P.W.'s friend apparently enjoyed cooking and fussing over her guests. Neither Gretchen nor Theo was eager to return home. There was even some talk about them renting the friend's guest house the following summer.

Monday dragged by without a peep from Randy Mann. There were no threats from anyone. And no more deaths.

Yuri and I survived Tuesday by hanging around the office making phone calls and doing paperwork on another case, trying not to think about the upcoming election that was now one long week away. Will was still escorting my kids to and from school, and Mom was monitoring their activities when I wasn't there. In short, we were all shuffling along toward the finish line.

Just before quitting time on Tuesday, Adele asked Yuri and me to meet with her in the closet. "What's up?" Yuri said as we pulled up our chairs.

"I know we're no longer looking into anything associated with the campaign, but..." She paused, looking guilty.

"But?" I prompted.

"Well, you asked me to check out Karl Brennan, and I admit I continued to nose around a bit, just out of curiosity. You understand."

Both Yuri and I nodded.

"Discreetly, of course. I don't think anyone would attribute my research to your previous investigation. I mean, I didn't want to put anyone in danger."

"But?" I prompted again, anxious for her to get to the point.

"And this isn't anything important. I mean, I don't think it's important."

Yuri couldn't take it anymore. "Spit it out," he said. Adele looked offended and clamped her mouth shut.

"It's okay, Adele," I said, trying to smooth things over. "We understand that you may have learned something that doesn't seem important on the surface, but you still think it's something we should know."

Adele gave Yuri a look that let him know she was only going to speak up because I was asking her to. "It's about Lisa's mother, Jennifer, the one you said told her to keep her mouth shut."

Yuri and I waited. It was the longest drumroll in human history.

"Jennifer went to the same high school as Ashley Mann. They were in the same graduating class. See? Just a coincidence. It probably doesn't mean anything."

Yuri and I both leaned back and looked at each other. "Probably," I agreed. "But quite a coincidence." So, Brian was dating Lisa whose mother had gone to school with the wife of the candidate he was spying on. And after Brian's murder, Lisa was told by her mother not to talk to anyone about Brian. Furthermore, Lisa's father was most likely in the pocket of big oil. And the Mann family had the big pockets. What an intertwined mess of facts and coincidences. But what did it mean? If anything.

After Adele went back to her desk, Yuri and I stayed for a while and tried to come up with a theory that would tie everything together, but nothing we thought of withstood the barrage of counterarguments that came to mind. Maybe Brian had indeed been using Lisa to get information on Mann. Maybe he was even out to bring down her father. Maybe her mother found out. Maybe she confronted Ashley. Maybe, maybe, maybe. It seemed just as likely that it was simply a case of young love and coincidence.

Wednesday morning Yuri was drinking his coffee and checking out the headlines on his computer when he came across a new negative ad targeting Nathan Knight.

"Can you believe it?" Yuri said loud enough for people out in the mall to hear.

"I saw it," Will said without looking up. "I was wondering when you were going to explode."

I went over to Yuri's desk and looked over his shoulder. "Play it for me," I said. When he did I, too, almost exploded. "None of it's true," I said. The ad claimed the Knight campaign had received a large contribution from an out-of-state company that was lobbying for offshore drilling. "It's the pot calling the kettle black," I added.

"I won't ask you to explain what that actually means," Yuri said. "But I think you're right."

"Doesn't matter," Will said. "It will stick."

"Not fair," I said.

"Politics isn't fair," Will assured me. "Never has been, never will be."

"Paid for by the Citizens for Government Excellence. What a joke."

Everyone fell silent, as if mourning for the loss of a simpler time when people at least claimed to value truth in politics. A time when being a reporter was considered an enviable job and when there seemed to be fewer lies to track and report on.

My cell phone broke the silence. When I saw who it was I excused myself and went into one of the conference rooms. I noticed that Yuri was also answering a call and going into the closet to take it. My antenna was up and wiggling.

Minutes later Yuri and I were both back in the office. Yuri looked around and announced that he was going out for a coffee. Since when did that require telling everyone? And what about the cup of coffee on his desk?

I quickly said I'd join him. He gave me a strange look, but I didn't give him a chance to say "no." Once out in the mall I said, "Okay, come clean."

"You first," he said with a grin. Then we both laughed.

"Think anyone is suspicious?"

"I hope not. I don't like doing anything behind P.W.'s back. And I know we promised to stay away from anything and anyone related to the campaign. But this is too good to pass up."

"And 'this' is?"

"Dr. Benson came across an unfamiliar link on his research site when he was searching for something. He said he hadn't noticed it before because it looked legit. But when he investigated, he discovered it didn't belong to anyone who was supposed to be using the site. He tried to open it, but it's password protected. It was at that point that he remembered me asking about whether Brian could have used his site to hide some information."

"Think you can get in?"

"I'm not sure, but if I can't, I know someone who can."

"If you get the data Brian was putting together, will you give it to Gretchen or to Connolly or both?"

"Connolly wouldn't be happy if I gave it to Gretchen," Yuri said, sounding like he was way ahead of me but still debating what he would do.

"If there's anything that smacks of illegal activities in the data that can be laid at Bobby's feet, Gretchen might be able to at least do a mini article before election day. I can't see why Connolly would have any exclusive claim to it."

"I do think we owe it to the people of our district to expose the SOB." We were almost to the parking lot when Yuri turned to me and asked: "And you, where are you off to in such a rush?"

"I'm headed to that Starbucks just down the road," I said, pointing. There were several Starbucks near the mall. They seemed to sprout like weeds in a flower garden. "To meet Laney Knight, Nathan's wife," I added. "She said she has something to run past me; she wants my advice. I doubt it's about what to wear on election night."

"Why did she call you?" Yuri asked.

"Don't know. I'll find out when we meet."

"Well, make sure she understands we are no longer working for either campaign," Yuri said without a hint of irony. "And be careful."

Laney Knight was already in the coffee shop when I arrived. I had seen her in ads and on campaign flyers, but we had never actually met. She was a petite woman with straight blond hair that could have been featured in a shampoo ad, shiny and smooth. She was wearing a running outfit in dark blue and white tennis shoes with blue trim. The entire look was classic Pacific Northwest. Even dressed casually she was a striking woman.

She waved at me when I came in, then stood up to shake my hand. "Hope you like lattes," she said, gesturing at a paper cup on my side of the table. I hate lattes, but thanked her anyway as I sat down across from her.

"You were probably surprised to get a call from me," she said.

"To be honest, yes, I was."

"I was the one who researched agencies when we were looking to hire someone to find out what was happening to our campaign signs. Penny-wise has a good reputation. And you came through for us." She paused. "Although I'm sorry it turned out the way it did."

I nodded agreement and waited for her to continue.

"Well, I need advice on something campaign related. I didn't want to make it 'official,' but I wanted to talk to someone who knows about the kind of thing I'm dealing with."

"You do know that we recently did some work for the Mann campaign," I said. I felt like I needed to tell her that.

"Not that I support his candidacy," I added quickly. "I fully intend to vote for your husband."

She smiled. I couldn't help thinking that Knight was lucky to be married to a good-looking and personable woman. Even without connections to high rollers in the area, like Mann's wife, she was undoubtedly an asset.

"Well, what I want to talk to you about is a bit, ah, odd. I hate to bother Nathan with it; he's got so much on his plate right now. And his campaign manager is barely keeping his head above water; there is just so much to do. Most of our campaign staffers are young and so passionate about the campaign that I don't think they would have much perspective." She took a sip of coffee. "I'll be happy to pay you for your time, but I'd like to keep it off the books if possible."

"I can't do any 'off the books' paid work as an investigator, but I'm happy to be of help if I can. Your husband is a good candidate."

"Thank you." She took another sip of coffee followed by a deep breath, as if steeling herself for our conversation. "It's about something that happened at a campaign forum two nights ago. A group of candidates running for various officers were given a chance to speak at an event sponsored by United American Voters. In the past the event has drawn a large audience, so quite a few politicians agreed to make brief presentations. They were given three minutes each to say a few words about their reasons for running for office.

"Bobby Mann's family was there, and although we've seen them at a number of events, I'd never actually talked to any of them. Everyone is always so fixated on reaching out to potential voters. But it's drawing near the end of the campaign, so, as what I hoped would be considered a goodwill gesture, I introduced myself to Bobby's wife, Ashley. And, ah, it didn't go well." She took another sip of coffee, holding her cup with two hands. To keep them from shaking was my guess.

"What happened?" I prompted.

"Instead of being friendly or even coldly polite, she was extremely hostile. She told me in no uncertain terms that we are going to lose. Then she informed me that they are going to be running a series of ads that will make us wish my husband had never entered this race."

"That sounds almost like a threat."

"It certainly felt like one. I always thought she was so attractive, but if you could have seen her face when she was talking to me. Hard and mean. Filled with hate. As if I personally had done something terrible to her. Then she left me standing there wondering what had happened, and moments later I saw her talking to a group of reporters, all smiles, posing like she was some sort of pageant winner. It was scary."

"Campaigns don't always bring out the best in people. But I admit that seems a bit extreme. And not something I would have expected from her. Not that I know her; I'm just talking about her image." I had always assumed Ashley Mann was a bit of a lightweight, eye candy, not someone sufficiently invested in the details of her husband's campaign that she would consider Laney to be "the enemy."

"That wasn't all that happened at the event." Laney took another deep breath.

"You and Ashley had another conversation?"

"No. Bobby Mann's mother literally backed me into a corner and told me we would be wise to get used to losing. She said that they plan on spending whatever it takes from now until election day to make sure that we do. And then she told me that, given our lack of personal resources, she knew that we couldn't afford to compete, so we shouldn't waste what little money we have and that we should set it aside to pay off creditors after the election."

"Bizarre."

"She's a big woman. I felt physically threatened. Especially when her daughter, June, joined in on the, ah, verbal attack. June laughed when I said that my husband was trying to run a clean campaign and that there was good reason he'd captured most of the endorsements."

"You fought back. Good for you."

"It was hardly a fight. They ganged up on me. I was intimidated by their domineering physical presence and stunned when they told me that after this next weekend, my husband's reputation would be 'transformed.' That was the word they used—transformed. I wasn't sure what they meant at the time. Then that ad came out this morning linking my husband to offshore oil drilling, a complete and total lie, by the way. And now the ad's everywhere. On every channel. And the media has picked up on it, repeating the lie over and over again. That's when I decided to call you. I'm hoping you can help me think through what I should do, what I can do."

"Sounds like they were trying to psych you out," I said. "Although I can't imagine what they actually thought that would accomplish. Your husband isn't going to drop out at this point. No matter how many negative ads they run."

"No, he can't. But they are right about the money. We don't have enough to fight back with a lot of ads of our own. And I'm not sure telling him about what happened to me would make any difference. It would just make him angry. He wouldn't dream of threatening members of their family. That isn't the kind of person he is." She paused and looked me in the eyes. "What do you think? What should I do?"

"Any idea whether they said something similar to your husband directly? Or to members of the staff?"

"I wondered about that. But no one from the campaign mentioned it. Maybe we are all keeping quiet for the same reason, so we don't upset everyone at this late date."

"Let's look at this from the Manns' point of view. Do you think they were trying to provoke you so that you would go to the press with the story? Then they could act innocent and claim you have become unhinged. Or maybe they wanted you to tell your husband so he would get mad and say something they could turn against him. Make him seem desperate and defensive, something like that."

"Well, I certainly feel defensive. And we are all concerned about the impact of them spending a lot of money on attack ads during the final days before the election. The campaign is getting a ton of calls about this morning's ad. And the volunteers calling to encourage people to get out to vote are having to spend most of their time explaining that the allegations are false."

"I can imagine. I remember the Swift Boat attack ads against John Kerry claiming he wasn't the hero he represented himself to be. And the birthers claiming Obama wasn't born in the U.S. Both lies, but the campaigns had to spend time and money addressing those allegations rather than talking about the issues."

"I've been researching negative ads and their impact. Whether they're truthful, shade the truth or tell outright lies, they apparently can be very effective."

"Is your husband going to run any negative ads?"

"He doesn't want to, but his campaign manager is pressuring him. He claims it's the only way to counter the ads Mann is running. The other problem is money. Developing effective ads and paying to air them isn't cheap."

"This is sad. Really sad. The thought that this kind of thing can make a difference in a campaign rather than what the candidates stand for."

"That's why I called you. I just don't know what to do. And as a neutral party, and someone who deals with these kinds of issues for a living, I'm hoping you can give me some practical advice."

I took a sip of coffee to give myself time to think of something to say, remembering too late that it was a latte. Somehow, I managed to swallow. I really dislike milk in coffee. And I still didn't have any ideas. "I need to run this past a colleague," I said, stalling for time. "He's politically savvy and knows a lot about this campaign. He might have some thoughts on the best way to handle this."

She leaned forward, gave me a searching look and asked, "As a woman, tell me truthfully, do you think I should tell my husband?"

If someone had asked me whether I believed in total transparency in a marriage, I would have said "yes." But this situation was complicated. Being the wife of a politician was a bit like being married not only to your spouse but to his constituency. You needed to make decisions with both in mind.

"Don't you have a friend you could talk to about this?"

"Friends tell you what they think you want to hear. And my friends are also my husband's friends. That puts them in the middle."

"Of course. I understand. But this is a lot to digest. I'd like to talk to my colleague and look into a few things before suggesting anything, okay?" I wasn't sure what those "few things" actually were, but I desperately wanted to run it past Yuri. Between the two of us we might be able to come up with something. I sure wasn't doing so hot on my own.

She looked down at her latte and nodded.

"I know you feel the clock ticking on this campaign, and the longer you wait to tell your husband, the harder it will be. But I'm sure he'll understand why you didn't share this with him right away. I'll get back to you some time tomorrow. I promise."

"Thank you," she said. "I really appreciate this."

She sounded as if it had been settled, as if I was going to work a miracle and solve her problem. All she had to do was wait for my call.

After we said our goodbyes, my mind started racing. Maybe I should give Gretchen a call to get her take. If anyone was knowledgeable about the Mann family, it was her. But she would have to agree not to use any of this, not just for now but never. That was asking a lot. It might be best to just run it past Yuri. Maybe even P.W. She couldn't blame me for talking to Laney Knight; after all, Laney had called me, not the other way around. And she might have some ideas about how best to handle the situation.

As I drove back to the office my sixth sense was working overtime. Unfortunately, what I felt was a sense of dread. It seemed a sure bet that the Mann family was going to pull out all of the stops to win, and it wasn't going to be pretty. I wasn't sure what that might mean—not only for the Knight campaign, but for me and the people I cared about.

CHAPTER 13
DEAD RIGHT

I GOT BACK TO THE OFFICE ahead of Yuri and went in to see P.W. before he returned and could talk me out of it. I'm not sure what I expected, but it wasn't vehement indignation.

"How dare they," P.W. said, her fingers snaking out to grip the slim cigarette in the Faberge ashtray. "Our democracy is based on principles of honor and fair play. Our elections require transparency and integrity." She paused. Her fingers let go of the cigarette. Then she stood up and walked over to the clothes rack and back before sitting back down and continuing. "We need to be very careful if we pursue this."

If we pursued this? I agreed but didn't say anything. I was torn between wanting to charge full speed ahead with something, anything to stop the Mann juggernaut, and wanting to play it safe.

"We can't know how serious they are about the threats they're making. It may be all show and bluster. On the other hand, I don't see how we can sit back and let things play themselves out. We have too much skin in the game at this point." She stood up again and began pacing. "This is a tough one. We don't have many cards to play. It seems to me like our best bet is to find Norcross's research and give it to Gretchen. If there's enough there on the Manns, she could go public with it. That would stop all of this nonsense, maybe even put a damper on some of the negative ads." She paused for a moment, then asked, "You're quite certain Norcross didn't share his information with anyone?"

"Well, I think Yuri might know something about that." I didn't want to betray Yuri by saying more. But P.W.'s dark eyes were boring into me, probing my psyche for the truth. "He's away from his desk but he should be back soon," I said. "I'll have him come talk to you as soon as he returns."

She frowned but didn't ask for details. "Do that. As soon as he comes in. And, is there anyone you think it would be helpful to circle back to?" That sounded suspiciously like she was suggesting we re-open our investigation in full sight of everyone involved.

"Well, his two buddies from the Knight campaign seemed the most likely people he would have confided in, but they both denied having been told any details about his research, including where he might have been keeping a copy."

"Tell me about them."

I filled P.W. in on what I knew about the two men and my impressions of them. Then I told her about Jim Gossett, the fellow from the Knight campaign that we met with initially. When I finished, P.W. said, "You sound as though you weren't totally convinced that Gossett was telling you the truth."

"You're right; I felt like he was holding something back. But I have nothing to support my suspicions."

"It wouldn't hurt for you and Yuri to have another talk with him. Make him aware of what's involved." She paused and eyed the cigarette. "You do think he would want the information made public, don't you?"

"As opposed to trying to protect someone or some company Brian was targeting?"

"Or, consider the possibility that his interest in the information may be financial. Perhaps he wanted to sell it to the highest bidder and Norcross didn't. Or maybe that's his plan now that Norcross is dead."

"You're suggesting that Jim had access to Brian's research and may have killed him over a disagreement about what to do with it?" That hadn't crossed my mind.

"Don't close your mind to any possibilities," P.W. warned. "I know the Manns seem like the obvious suspects, but we don't know for sure why Norcross was killed. Sir Arthur Conan Doyle said 'There is nothing more deceptive than an obvious fact.' And let's not forget how money can warp someone's sense of right and wrong, especially if they don't have a strong moral compass."

I was about to leave when she added, "Keep in mind that the door you entered at the Mann campaign headquarters that night was unlocked. It could have been by accident. But I'm assuming it wouldn't have been that hard for Norcross to obtain a key. In that case, either the person who killed him also had a key, or Norcross let his assailant in. The question is what he—or they—were doing there in the first place."

I went back to my desk and reflected on why the door was unlocked, why the murder had happened in the storage room, and whether I thought Jim might be the murderer. One likely scenario was that Brian had been caught searching for something that he didn't dare look for during the day. Maybe his death had been an unplanned, spur of the moment act. On the other hand, he could have agreed to meet someone there, out of sight from passersby, and the blow that killed him had been premeditated.

Even if Jim wasn't the murderer, he was definitely hiding something. But murdering his friend to make money by blackmailing people and companies to stay mum about what Brian had learned? I resisted the idea, but it wasn't impossible. The old cliché "follow the money" so often turned out to be the best advice for an investigator, no matter what the crime. In my brief time on the job, I had learned that, in general, criminals don't display a lot of originality.

When Yuri returned, he was fuming. He motioned for me to join him in the conference room and didn't even give me time to sit down before he pulled up a chair and began beating a rhythm with his fingers on the desk. Like a maniacal drummer angry with his instrument. "You won't believe it," he announced as I sat down across from him.

"What won't I believe?"

"Someone hacked into Dr. Benson's research site and deleted Norcross's files."

"What?" For the second time that day I was totally surprised by unfolding events.

"My hacker friend managed to get into the folder fairly easily. Norcross apparently figured the location itself was the main safeguard. But he was obviously wrong. The entire site was wiped clean the day after he was murdered. They probably left the folder label so it would appear as though nothing had changed. The question is whether he was somehow forced to reveal where he'd stored the data or whether he'd already shared the location with someone."

"It's possible he told someone about the site in case something happened to him. But who would he have confided in? We've already talked to the people everyone says were closest to him. At least I think we have. Although, maybe someone who knew what he was researching guessed where it might be on their own after he was dead. After all, we figured it out."

"But too late." Yuri shook his head. "Okay, so we know he talked to Jim, Alan and Ken. And maybe Lisa knows more about this than we give her credit for."

"You know," I interrupted. "When we talked with Jim, I felt like he wasn't telling us everything. Maybe he knew about the site but didn't trust us. It could be that simple. Or, maybe, as P.W. suggested, Jim wants to sell the information to make some money and knocked off his friend who wanted to use it for the public good."

"You talked with P.W. about this?"

"Yeah, I'll explain in a minute. The thing is, she suggested that as a possibility. And it is possible. But I don't want to believe he did it."

"I know, you want it to be the butler with a candlestick in the library."

I had once admitted to Yuri that my favorite game as a young girl was Clue. Unfortunately, the game sanitized the act of murder. As I had since learned, the actual act was much messier and more complicated than simply following a few clues to closure.

As soon as I filled Yuri in on my conversations with Laney and with P.W. he went off to talk to P.W. Their meeting did not last long. She didn't even bother giving him a hard time about following up with the professor. And, most important, she gave us her blessing to talk to Jim. So much for staying uninvolved.

"Okay," Yuri said, pulling out his cell phone. "Let's make this happen." When Jim answered, Yuri told him he had some information that Jim would find interesting and asked if we could meet with him. He was about to leave for a class and suggested we come by the house in the University District where he lived with two other guys around 5:00. We agreed and went to grab a bite to eat and to strategize.

During our meal we went round and round about what we should tell Laney. If we somehow managed to come up with Brian's research, that would probably mean the Knights didn't have to worry about any threats made by the Mann family. Laney could then tell her husband what had happened, and together they could wait for the bomb to drop on the Mann campaign. If we couldn't find the research, then the solution wasn't as clear.

Yuri agreed with me that Laney shouldn't go public about what had happened. Voters wouldn't know who to believe, and the Manns had enough money to flood the airwaves with their point of view. One complicating factor was that we couldn't decide whether her husband would want to go public if she told him. He could easily get hung up on the unfair and unethical nature of what the Mann family had done, especially because they had confronted his wife rather than him.

Telling the campaign manager and letting him handle it was another option that we didn't like. Theoretically, he should have enough emotional distance to be able to think strategically about the incident, but if he decided it was best not to tell Nathan, that put Laney in an awkward position with her husband.

Still another alternative was for Laney to keep her mouth shut until after the voters had spoken. If her husband won, that would soften the impact of her confession. If he lost, well, in that case she might want to give it some time before telling him. Knowing what had happened to her would only make losing more bitter.

Even after talking it to death, there didn't seem to be any obvious response to Laney's request for advice. We decided to pursue the preferred solution by trying to get our hands on Brian's research. We would start by finding out what, if anything, Jim Gossett had been holding back. Depending on what we learned, our next moves might become clear. If not, we wouldn't be any worse off than we were now.

The house Jim and his two roommates rented in the University District was one of a small number of homes built in the early 1930's that had escaped demolition, not necessarily because it was a lovely example of American Foursquare architecture, but more likely because of the need for cheap communal housing near the University. It was a two-story, box-shaped structure with a hipped roof, a wide front porch and large windows. The front yard had once been landscaped. Currently it was in desperate need of tending.

There was a young man sitting on the front steps drinking a beer. Up and down the street you could hear the beginning of Friday night revelry getting underway.

"Hi," I said. "We're looking for Jim, Jim Gossett."

"He in trouble?"

"Why would you ask that?" Yuri said. "Do we look like cops?"

The young man looked us over carefully. "Narcs, maybe."

I felt insulted. He could have thought we were FBI. Or maybe the investigators we were. But narcs? Ignoring the comment, I said, "He told us to meet him here."

"Sorry, haven't seen him." He tilted his head back and took a long swig on his beer.

"Does that mean he isn't here?" Yuri asked, sounding impatient.

"No, just means I haven't seen him." The young man smiled at his own clever response.

"Well, what should we do, shout out his name?" Yuri was getting testy. That made the young man smile even more before replying.

"Or, you could go on up and have a look. His room is on the 2nd floor."

We stepped past him and went inside. The house was a mess of littered clothes, empty bottles scattered everywhere, and stacks of papers and books. There were even books piled on the stairs. They looked new, like they had been purchased for classes but never opened. Maybe they were props for parents footing the bill.

When we reached the second floor, Yuri called Jim's name, but there was no answer. "What do you think?" he asked me.

"Maybe he has on head phones."

"That's our story, huh?"

"We can try knocking." There were four doors, one partially open. Music thrummed from the room. I knocked and a half-dressed young man opened the door the rest of the way.

"Hey," he said, giving me a onceover. "You looking for me?"

"Jim Gossett," I said. "Which door?"

"Too bad," he said. "It's Friday night." When I didn't respond, he pointed a thumb at the door directly across the hall. "Haven't seen him come in. Although I just got here." He watched while we went over and knocked. There was no answer.

"He's expecting us," I said. "Any chance he has on headphones and can't hear us knocking?"

"You could bust in on him, hope he isn't up to something." He smiled at the not-too-subtle pun.

Yuri, still fueled by irritation with the entire situation, reached out, turned the knob and pushed the door open.

To say that I had a premonition as to what we would find wouldn't be entirely honest. In fact, it happened so fast I barely had time to take in the scene before Yuri started swearing and Jim's roommate started screaming. Jim wasn't on the bed with some co-ed. Nor was he dancing naked around his room to some pop song transmitted through a pair of JBL headphones. No, he was on the floor next to his desk, one leg thrust out at an awkward angle like he had fallen while trying to turn away.

He wasn't moving. His eyes were open, staring at the ceiling. The hardwood floor was splattered with blood.

There was little doubt that we were looking at the "late" Jim Gossett.

CHAPTER 14
NO ENEMIES

WHILE YURI CURSED, the lyrics "Too late, my brothers, too late," ran through my head. Although I doubted Jim would echo the "never mind" sentiment, we were definitely "too late."

"Damn," Yuri said. "Damn it all to hell."

It looked as if Jim had been hit multiple times with some kind of weapon. I'm no expert at assessing cause of death, but the red welt across his bloody face would have been my guess. Someone had taken him by surprise, someone he didn't expect to attack him. Not a pleasant way to die. If there was a pleasant way to be murdered.

While Yuri and I were standing there, processing what we were seeing, the roommate from across the hall was totally freaking out. He was half crying, half shouting and shaking uncontrollably. Yuri stopped swearing and turned to him, "Snap out of it," he ordered, as if he expected that to work. When it didn't, he took the young man by the shoulders and turned him around. "Go back to your room. We'll call the police."

When the young man didn't move, I took him by the arm and said, "Come on, you need to sit down." He had stopped making noises, but he didn't seem to grasp that we wanted him out of the room. "Jim," he gasped. "Jim."

It occurred to me that they might have been more than roommates, but it might also have been his first messy death. Either way, I needed to get him out of there, and it seemed to me that under the circumstances, he probably shouldn't be left alone. Instead of leading him back to his room, I steered him toward the stairs. He didn't resist, meekly allowing me to lead him down the steps, softly sobbing and murmuring Jim's name. At the bottom I called to the other roommate who was still outside. When he came in, he looked from his friend to me and asked, "What did you do to him?"

"Look, I don't have time for this now. Jim is dead. I'm going to call the police and you are going to take care of your friend. Got that?" It was an abrupt way to announce a friend's death, but I wanted the two of them out of the way.

"Dead? What do you mean?"

"I mean dead. Murdered. I'll explain as soon as I call the police. Wait down here." I left the two young men together and ran back up the stairs. I found Yuri going through Jim's desk drawers. He was wearing a pair of disposable plastic gloves.

"Have you called the police?" I asked.

"No, why don't you do that while I look around some more. Dammit, Cameron, whoever killed Jim searched the place. If the list and research was here, it's probably long gone."

I dialed 911 and reported the situation and location, assuring them I would be there when they arrived and that I wouldn't touch anything. They didn't ask me whether there was anyone else searching the room where the body was.

"No computer, no notebooks, very few papers," Yuri mumbled. "Shit."

"The police will be here soon," I pointed out.

"Look around," Yuri ordered. "Do you see any good hiding places?"

I got a pair of gloves out of my purse and pulled them on as I scanned the room. It was a small space with a desk, bed, bureau and single bookcase. All of the books had been tossed on the floor and the bureau had already been searched. "Do you think they found what they were looking for?" I asked as I knelt down and looked under the bed. Nothing there. "Do you think he surprised whoever was searching his room and that's why he was killed?" I lifted up the mattress and checked it out side-to-side and top-to-bottom. Nothing. "Or do you think he was killed to keep him quiet?" No vents in the walls that I could see.

Yuri was still concentrating on the desk, checking for hidden pieces of paper when I opened the window and found a bag hanging from the ledge. For a moment I thought I'd made a discovery. I had, but not the kind I was hoping for. The marijuana itself was legal, but the amount was questionable. I left it where it was and turned my attention back to the room.

"Didn't find his cell, did you?" I asked.

"No. Dammit. There's nothing here."

"It looks a lot like the same M.O. as with Brian. A blow to the head with some kind of weapon that they took with them."

"It would be interesting to know more about that. But first—"

"I'm going downstairs," I said. "You'd better finish up quickly. I pulled my gloves off, rolled them into a ball and put them back in my purse. "And be sure to take off your gloves before the police get here."

Both young men had drinks in their hands when I came down. "Don't overdo it," I said. "The police are on their way."

"Who could have done this?" the young man from upstairs asked, still sounding like he wasn't entirely functional.

"What's your name?" I asked.

"His name is Evan," the young man from the porch said. "Mine's Neal."

I introduced myself and asked how long they had been home. Both said they'd arrived shortly before Yuri and I showed up. Then I asked if Jim had left his laptop, a cell or a backpack downstairs. Neal said he would check. While he was looking around, I told Evan that everything was going to be okay. Exactly the wrong thing to say.

"Okay?" he said, a little too loud. "How can it be okay that Jim is…." He buried his face in his hands and started sobbing again. At that moment Neal came back carrying a pack. He dropped the pack and went over to Evan.

"What did you do to him?" he asked for a second time. I seemed to be getting that question a lot lately.

"He's just upset about his friend," I said. "Is that Jim's backpack?"

Before he could answer, the police showed up. They came storming in as if they anticipated meeting up with a murderer, not two upset roommates and a couple of investigators who just happened to discover their second dead man in less than a week. "Yuri," I called up the stairs. "The police are here."

One of the officers asked me what someone was doing up there as the other raced up the steps. "He stayed with the body," I said. As if that made any sense. But the officer seemed to accept my explanation. Admonishing us to stay put, he headed upstairs after his partner.

"I'm going to make some coffee," I announced to anyone who was listening. "I assume the kitchen is back there." Evan and Neal were in a world of their own at that point, so I casually picked up the backpack and headed for the kitchen, checking out the first-floor layout on the way. There was a hallway that ran from the dining room to a back door. There was also a back stairway. My recollection was that there was an alley behind the row of houses. It would have been easy for someone to slip in without being seen.

The kitchen was even messier than the rest of the house. There were pizza cartons and take-out food containers piled everywhere. There was no way I was going to be able to make coffee, but maybe I'd have enough time to check the pack's contents before going back and admitting defeat.

I didn't find Brian's research, but Jim's cell was in the front of the pack. I took out my gloves and pulled them on again. Hopefully I would hear anyone before they caught me wearing gloves while browsing a dead man's cell phone.

It wasn't locked. That surprised me. I thought everyone locked their cells these days. But I was also thankful for his carelessness. It allowed me to quickly access his recent emails and texts. When I found a text from Jim to Randy Mann, I wasn't surprised. Unfortunately, all it said was, "We need 2 talk." It had been sent late last night. I couldn't find a reply. Maybe murder didn't require an RSVP.

I took off my gloves and went back into the living room, casually dropping the pack on the floor. Neal turned around and asked where I'd been.

"In the kitchen. I was going to make coffee for you, but, well, to be honest, the place is a disaster. I gave up."

"Well, ah, thanks."

Two more officials arrived, although these were not wearing uniforms. Yuri and one of the officers came downstairs and the two plain clothes detectives went up. Yuri said he was going to step outside and make a phone call, but the officer informed him he needed to remain inside. "I'll leave her as a hostage," Yuri said, nodding his head in my direction.

"Thanks." I stared meaningfully at Yuri. "Well, you do whatever, I'm going to go to the bathroom. Neal, which way is it?"

"It's to the left of the kitchen," he said.

Based on the state of the kitchen, I was quite certain their bathroom wouldn't earn a 5-star rating, but then, all I needed was a chance to call P.W. and let her know what had happened. I was fairly certain that had been what Yuri had in mind.

The bathroom wasn't as bad as I'd imagined, but it smelled faintly of urine and mouthwash. Blaine answered and immediately put me through. When I finished telling P.W. about finding Jim dead and no sign of his research anywhere, she did not sound like her usual stoic self. "We can't have people dying like this," she said. Then I told her about the message Jim had sent Randy Mann. "I'm going to call Detective Connolly," she said. "He will understand the significance of the cell message given everything he knows about Norcross's murder. It would take too long to bring the other detectives up to speed. Just make sure the backpack is secured."

"Will do." After I hung up I thought it might be a good idea to flush the toilet for show, but although I'm not a germaphobe, I really didn't want to touch the handle. I finally did it with two fingers and quickly turned to the grimy sink to wash my hands. The water was lukewarm, and there was no soap and no towel. I returned to the living room with questionably clean and wet hands.

"You need to have the maid come by," I said to Neal. "You need fresh towels. And a bar of soap would be nice."

"No need to be a smart ass," Neal said.

"Sorry," I said, meaning it. "I get flip when I'm upset."

We were interrupted by one of the detectives. He wanted to know, once again, if anyone had touched anything upstairs. I shook my head "no." As did Neal and Evan. Yuri explained that he had gone in to make sure the deceased was indeed deceased and that he may have leaned on the desk. While he was explaining why he had opened the door, using my headphones excuse, I noticed a jacket that I recognized draped across one of the chairs in the living room. At least I was fairly certain it was the jacket Jim had been wearing when we met him the first time. I tend to notice what people wear.

When you're trying to act natural, everything you do feels unnatural. But somehow, I managed to saunter over to the jacket, pick it up, and turn my back to the rest of the group while quickly searching its pockets. I removed the two scraps of paper I found and stuffed them into my own jacket pocket before turning toward Neal and asking, "Isn't this Jim's jacket?" When he said he wasn't sure but thought it was, I went over and handed it to the officer.

"You recognize the dead man's jacket when his roommate isn't sure it belongs to him?" the officer asked.

"It's my job to notice things."

"Well, we've got this one covered, so you can relax." He sounded irritated, but he took possession of the jacket. I also pointed out the backpack belonging to Jim and he put that with the jacket.

Since Yuri had only admitted to possibly "leaning" on the desk, I doubted he had mentioned the bag of marijuana hanging from the windowsill. I wondered if they had that "covered" too. I didn't care; I was relaxing as ordered.

Evan wiped his eyes, let out a loud sigh, and said he was going to make tea. With a dazed look on his face, he looked around the room and asked if anyone else wanted some. Given that the kitchen looked more like a lab for cultivation of infectious disease cultures than a place to eat, I didn't say "yes," even though a cuppa really sounded good.

While Yuri continued to talk with the detective, I went over and sat next to Neal. "I am sorry about your friend," I said. "I only met him one time, but he seemed like a nice guy."

"What every young man aspires to be—a 'nice' guy."

"I didn't mean it like that."

"Now I'm sorry."

"Truce?"

"Truce."

I gave it a few seconds then asked, "He didn't say anything about, ah, following up on a lead about Brian Norcross's death, did he?"

"No. Aren't you going to ask me if he had any enemies?"

"Did he?"

"Not that I know of. Listen, he was just a regular guy. He was liked by some, not so much by others."

"Did he deal in anything besides marijuana?" I asked, throwing out a surprise volley.

Neal hesitated.

"Don't worry. I'm really not a narc. I don't care about the marijuana. But I'm interested in who might have had a reason to want him dead."

"Do you think the police will find the weed?"

"They might, but I didn't say anything."

"How did you…?"

"I stood next to the window when I was calling the police and just happened to see it." Not true, but close enough.

"The weed was just a sideline," Neal explained. "Jim wanted to make a little extra cash. You know. He wasn't into it big time."

"Was he short on cash?"

"Not that short. Just typical poor student short."

"So, he wouldn't have been averse to making a few extra bucks."

"Who would?"

"But no real enemies that you know of."

"No. What were you here to talk to him about?"

"Some information he and Brian had discussed that might be relevant to one of our clients. It involved some environmental research Brian was working on."

"We never talked about stuff like that. Sorry."

"Can you suggest anyone that he might have talked with about environmental issues? A classmate? A friend? A girlfriend?"

Neal thought for a moment. "Maybe Denny. I think they went to a few protests together."

"What about Evan?"

"Evan isn't political. He just looked up to Jim, admired his moxie."

Two hours later we were finally allowed to leave. By then I'd called home and asked Mom to make sure the kids ate something. She'd mumbled something about my irregular schedule but agreed to take care of dinner. P.W. had texted that she wanted us to stop by the office before heading home; she would wait for us. So, after a long day that was at times both unsettling and boring, we went back to the office. On the way we went through a drive-thru and bought a couple of burgers and fries. As I wolfed down the greasy goodies, I only managed a tiny bit of sympathy for what Mom might have fixed my kids for dinner. Whatever it had been, it was far healthier than what I was eating.

P.W. wrinkled her nose when we sat down across from her. My guess was we reeked of French fries. But she didn't complain. Yuri is known for his bad food habits and for always being hungry. And although I try to maintain a somewhat better nutritional image, to be honest, I enjoy sinking to his level.

When P.W. asked what we had learned since we last talked to her, we had to admit there wasn't much. Yuri poked me in the ribs and said, "Show her what you found." I tried to ignore him, but the expectant look on P.W.'s face forced my hand. I took the two pieces of paper I had taken from Jim's pocket and handed them across the desk.

"These were in Jim's jacket pocket," I explained. One is Randy Mann's cell number. The other is just a receipt for a bag of chips, a corn dog and a coke."

"You can't win them all," Yuri said with a grin.

"I don't see that either would do the police any good, but you need to know that I took them."

"You said they have Gossett's cell, so they will see that he texted Randy Mann," P.W. acknowledged. "Having his cell number written on a piece of paper in his pocket doesn't really add much." She seemed to be going along with my reasoning, but I could tell she was concerned.

"Sorry. I probably should have put them back, but it took me quite a while to get alone long enough to read them. By then the police had his jacket and I didn't have an opportunity to slip them back into the pocket."

"I wonder where Jim got this number," Yuri mused. "How did he know about Randy in the first place? And what were they communicating about?"

"You think there might be players involved that we aren't aware of?" P.W. asked.

"That's not only possible, but probable," I said. "The only new lead we have is another activist friend, Denny. We definitely need to talk with him."

"Tomorrow," P.W. said. "You two need to go home now. And once the story about Gossett's death breaks, you will probably be named as the people who found his body. That means whoever did it will know you are still nosing around. Whoever they are, these people are dangerous. Be careful, that's an order."

CHAPTER 15
A SHOT IN THE DARK

BY THE TIME WE LEFT the office, the mall was closed and the parking lot practically empty, a few cars scattered randomly across the vast expanse of blacktop. As Yuri and I headed for our respective cars it suddenly occurred to me that Jim's friend, Denny, might be in danger. Why hadn't I thought of that before?

I turned around and ran after Yuri. "Hey, wait up," I yelled. Yuri turned toward me just as a shot rang out. I raced to a nearby car and dropped down behind it as a second shot split the air. Disoriented yet hyper-alert, my fight or flight response couldn't quite make up its mind what to do.

"Cameron, are you okay?" Yuri yelled.

"Yes!"

"Stay down!" Did he think I was going to stand up and make myself an easy target?

As I crouched behind a silver Ford, all I could hear was my own ragged breathing. There were no more gunshots, no one talking or yelling, no cars moving, no animals skittering, nothing. Just silence.

Had someone taken a shot at me? At Yuri? Whether

they'd taken aim at one or both of us, it had to be personal. Mall shooters went inside and looked for crowds. I wasn't sure where the shots had come from, but unless there was a sniper out there who could pick us off at a distance from some carefully chosen location, they had probably come from somewhere near the back of the mall. There were lights around the perimeter of the parking lot, but the mall itself was dark and lifeless this time of night.

I looked around at the handful of cars in the parking area. I always wondered why anyone would leave a car there late at night. But there were always a few, for which tonight I was very grateful. Especially grateful for the one I was hiding behind. I prayed I was not hiding in plain view of someone on the other side of the lot. And I hoped that Yuri, too, was out of sight of the shooter.

I waited for what seemed forever. No other shots were fired.

Finally, Yuri yelled, "Stay where you are."

"You mean me?" I called back.

"Yes, you."

I didn't hear anything for another few minutes. Then I heard someone running and saw Yuri dart behind another car about thirty feet away. After a short pause, he headed in my direction, bent over, with a gun in his hand. Unless he knew where the shot had come from, the gun was more of a prop than a weapon.

When he dropped alongside me he said, "I think they were just trying to scare us."

"Well, it worked."

"He or she must know our cars."

"That's reassuring."

"I think we should stay together."

"Then, why don't we take my car and you go home with me?"

"It's a plan." He smiled. "I just wish you were inviting me up to see your etchings."

"Even if I had some, I don't think Mom and the kids would approve."

"Did you know the French version is 'do you want to come up and see my collection of Japanese stamps?'"

"You're making that up."

"In Italian it's 'come up and see my butterfly collection.'"

"I know you're trying to calm me down, but it isn't helping. For the record, in England, it's 'fancy a shag'?"

"Now you're making things up."

"Are we going to stay crouched here exchanging trivia, or should we see if we can make it to my car?"

"I haven't called 911, have you?" Yuri asked.

"No."

"So, no use waiting to be saved by the cavalry. Unless you think some Good Samaritan heard the gunshots and called them."

"I think it's unlikely, don't you?"

"Someone in a car wouldn't necessarily know that what they heard were gunshots. Besides, people have a tendency to avoid getting involved."

"We could call the police and wait for them to get here, but personally, I'd like to get the hell out of here."

"Do you want to stand up first, or should I?"

"After you, Alphonse."

"Before my time. Compromise … let's stay low and at the same time zigzag toward your car."

I couldn't think of a better option, so we did a version of the gorilla shuffle, zigging one way and then another, until we reached a large truck. My car was still about 100 feet away, across an empty space. "Do we just make a run for it? It feels kinda exposed out here."

"Unless you want to spend the night behind this truck." He took a deep breath and stood up. "You go to the drivers' side; I'll go around to the other side."

"We split up so whoever is out there has to choose which one of us to shoot first?"

"Something like that." He took off running, and I quickly followed suit.

When we arrived without either of us taking a bullet, we simultaneously leapt inside. I switched off the internal light, started the car without turning on my headlights, and raced toward the nearest exit.

There were no more shots, and after we turned onto the main road leading away from the mall, we were fairly certain no one was following us. Although if they knew our cars, they probably also knew where we lived. So not being followed wasn't much consolation.

"P.W. should be glad she parks on the other side of the mall," I said.

"You don't think they would have shot at her, too, do you?"

"We need to call her."

"First, let's decide whether we're going to call the police."

We started to list pros and cons and realized that we were coming up with mostly cons. First, we couldn't be 100 percent certain we'd heard gunshots. We'd already left the parking lot and didn't want to go back and wait. We didn't know for sure that any gunshots fired were aimed at us, and we didn't want to tell the police why we thought someone might be shooting at us.

The last "con" was a biggie from my point of view. If we started talking about specific people who might want to either scare us or worse, things could get complicated fast. Especially if we named Randy Mann as a potential shooter or as someone who may have hired a shooter. To anyone who didn't know the entire story, that might seem a bit farfetched. Worst of all, an accusation like that could piss Randy off big time.

In the end we decided not to call the police. We did, however, call P.W. She answered almost immediately. After being assured that nothing untoward had happened to her when leaving the mall, we quickly explained what had happened to us. Then we gave her our reasons for not calling the police. She hesitated at first, then finally agreed that there was little to gain by calling them unless we were willing to spell out all of our suspicions. She even threw out the possibility that it had been a random shooting.

"They were trying to scare us," Yuri argued. "It wasn't random."

"If they'd been serious about, ah, taking us out, they would have stayed around and tried again," I added. "It could be one person's desperate act to try to warn us off, or it could be part of a larger effort to keep Brian's research from seeing the light of day."

"In either case, I think we need to be vigilant but not overreact," Yuri said.

P.W. thought about that a minute. In the end she said that she was okay with us not reporting it to the local police but that I should call Connolly. He needed to know that things were escalating, even if it was just a scare tactic. And she warned that he might insist that we file a report. On the off chance that it actually was a random shooter who could decide to strike again.

I promised I would call him, although I was quite certain that he would be calling me once he found out that Yuri and I had discovered another body.

Next we called Denny to warn him to be careful. When he didn't answer we left a message saying we thought he might be in danger and asked him to call us as soon as possible, night or day. We didn't know if either of Jim's roommates would have called him about Jim's death, and we didn't want to leave a phone message telling him that his friend had been murdered. Instead, we simply said there had been an accident and that we would give him the details when he called us back. We speculated about whether the police would answer Jim's cell if it rang. If Denny called Jim and they did, then Denny might learn about his friend's death through them. If so, he might not think he needed to return our call. We would have to keep trying to get in touch.

Even though we hadn't seen anyone following us, we knew there was the possibility that someone could be waiting at my place with the intent to frighten us more, or maybe even to shoot us for real. They—whoever he, she or they were—had shown a willingness to kill other people. Although unless they were really poor shots, we were both still assuming the attack in the parking lot had been a scare tactic.

We parked out front and stayed in the car a few minutes to check things out. The main house on the large lot was a turn-of-the-century Tudor, brick and stucco with ornate half timbers inside and out. The front yard was nicely landscaped with mature trees and meandering beds of flowers and greenery interspersed with the occasional statue and pieces of eclectic yard art. There was a large antique light illuminating the entrance alcove on the front porch. Only faint wisps of diffused light reached the gate that lead to the carriage house out back.

Everything seemed normal. A bit spooky under the circumstances, but normal. We got out of the car and reconnoitered some more.

The brick walkway to the carriage house out back was lined with bushes and trees. I usually liked the feeling of privacy the foliage provided, but this evening I would have preferred more line-of-sight. It wasn't going to be hard to stay in the shadows as we made our way down the path. On the other hand, someone else could be doing the same thing. We had agreed that it was unlikely anyone was going to assault us, but I couldn't help but feel uneasy. Especially when I saw that Yuri had his gun out.

"Hey, it's just a precaution, nothing more," he said when he saw me eyeing his weapon "I don't anticipate having to use it."

No one jumped us as we made our way down the path toward the brightly lit entrance to the carriage house. The damn spotlight next to the porch was always burning out, but now, when visibility wasn't something we wanted, it was like a lighthouse beacon that had been upgraded with super bright halogen lights.

Once past the bright lights and safely inside, we both took audible breaths, and I could feel the tension leak out of my shoulders.

The TV was on in the living room. I locked the door behind us as Yuri moved quickly toward the living room. Apparently, he was still on full alert. He motioned for me to stay back, but I hurried after him. The last thing I wanted was for him to surprise Mom and the kids by bursting in on them with a gun in hand.

The door to the living room was half open. Yuri and I peered around the corner. There was no intruder. Just Mom and Mara watching TV and Jason on his computer. It all looked so normal, so far removed from what we had just experienced. Yuri quickly put his gun away, went inside, and challenged Jason to a video game. That told me he had no intention of leaving right away. Him staying with us was becoming a habit. Maybe I should have Mom bring her Futon down.

Mom raised her eyebrows, stood up and motioned me toward the kitchen. I would have tried to bluff, but she can sense when I'm stressed or upset about something. In no time at all I was blabbing the entire story about the shots fired in the parking lot. Instead of sympathy, she gave me a head shake of disappointment that I knew all too well of late. Then she went into the other room to see if Yuri wanted anything to eat or drink.

I poured myself a glass of wine and sat down at the kitchen table to check my phone for messages. There were none. I dialed the number we had for Denny again and waited while it rang eight times before giving me his voice mail. I left another message urging him to be careful and to call as soon as he could. It was entirely possible he'd heard about Jim's death by now. The college grapevine is active 24-7 through a number of media channels. Still, that didn't explain why he wasn't answering.

Next I called Connolly and got his voice mail. I left a message saying I had something to report.

After delivering a plate of food and a glass of wine to Yuri, Mom came back into the kitchen and sat down across from me. "It does seem like things are getting a bit out of control," she said.

"I recognize that is your way of saying, holy shit, what have you gotten yourself into."

"Rather a vulgar way of putting it, but yes, that's what I'm saying."

"I'm not sure," I admitted. "As you know, it started with a few stolen campaign signs and has mushroomed from there. I'm concerned, but we're trying to stay on top of things."

"I do appreciate Yuri looking out for you."

I felt myself bristle at the idea that I couldn't take care of myself, but then, I too was thankful to have him around.

"It's hard to believe two people have been murdered just to help someone win a congressional seat," Mom commented.

"Well, it may be more complicated than that." I explained about Brian's research and what we assumed he had hoped to accomplish. The facts he'd uncovered might not only link the Mann campaign to money from the oil industry but could possibly identify illegal campaign donations and reveal whatever illegal things big money does to influence elections and control politicians. Maybe even including direct bribery. And his research hadn't been limited to the Manns. We had no way of knowing who was on his list or how many.

She sighed and asked if I would like a cup of tea. I nodded. My wine glass was empty, although I didn't remember drinking anything. I reached into my pocket for a Kleenex and came up with the two pieces of paper from Jim's jacket pocket. I put them on the table and smoothed out the receipt.

"What's that?" Mom asked.

"A receipt that was in the dead man's pocket."

She didn't ask how it came to be in my possession but leaned over to read it. "Looks like he was killing time near the Four Seasons Hotel."

"What makes you think that?"

"Well, that's where this market is, and that's a lot of junk food. Anyone you know staying at the Four Seasons?"

"Ah, Randy Mann could have been staying at the Four Seasons. That sounds like his kind of hotel. But how did you know where this market was?"

Mom rolled her eyes. "I have eyes. You don't have to shop somewhere to know where it's located." She tapped the receipt. "Besides, the address is right there on the receipt. And if I knew someone I wanted to talk to was staying at the Four Seasons, I might wait out on the street or in my car until he showed up. I mean, you could hang around the lobby but that would be a bit conspicuous. Especially if you were eating junk food. And waiting for someone to show when you don't know what time they will arrive is boring, right? Isn't that what you say about stakeouts?"

My mother the detective was out-detecting her daughter. If Jim had hung around the hotel until he managed to catch up with Mann that would explain both the receipt and the phone number in Jim's pocket. And maybe when he finally caught up with Mann, he overplayed his hand. Then again, their meeting might have had nothing to do with Jim's murder. But if P.W. was right and Jim had been trying to make some money off Brian's research, it was certainly a convenience to the Mann family when he was removed from play.

"Thank you, Mom. That's brilliant. I mean it." I turned toward the living room and yelled, "Yuri. Come in here when you get a chance."

"I'll take that as a compliment," Mom replied with a touch of sarcasm. She handed me my tea and continued puttering around the kitchen, probably to give herself an excuse to listen in on the conversation I was about to have with Yuri. Since she was the one who had come up with the theory, I felt she deserved listening rights.

Yuri came in and took a chair at the table. "Look at what Mom pointed out." I handed him the receipt. "Jim purchased this at a market just down the street from the Four Seasons—"

"Where Randy Mann might be staying," Yuri finished for me. "That's easy enough to check out."

"I need to call Connolly again."

"Did you tell him about someone shooting at us?"

"I didn't get through; I left a message."

I clicked on his number and was surprised when he answered on the second ring. "Sorry for calling so late. Something has come up since I left you a message earlier.

Yuri's here. I'm putting you on speaker." We quickly filled him in on our visit to Jim's, finding his body, and being shot at. Then Yuri waited for me to explain about the receipt, and I hesitated, struggling to think of a way to mask the fact that I had taken something from a dead man's pocket at the scene of a crime.

Connolly took our silence as a sign that we had finished telling him what we had called for. "I'll get in touch with the officers covering the homicide," he said. "Not sure there is much we can do about a possible shooter. It's doubtful they would find any evidence without a massive search of the area. And since you aren't certain where the shots originated from..." He left the thought hanging.

Yuri motioned for me to continue. "Right. But there's one more thing. We, ah, have reason to believe that Jim may have talked with Randy Mann last night outside the hotel where Mann may be staying. You can check that out. If we're right, there could be someone who saw them, or maybe there are cameras in the area. You might want to follow up on that."

"You have reason to believe...?"

"Well," I said, struggling to find words to get out the facts without confessing to more than necessary in the process. "I might have looked at Jim's cell phone texts. And...we might have found Randy Mann's phone number on a piece of paper, as well as a receipt that suggests Jim was near the Four Seasons not too long before he was killed."

"I'm not going to ask you to say more now. But you'd better be prepared to answer some questions tomorrow." Connolly did not sound pleased. "And you might want to consult a lawyer."

"But you will follow up," I said to make sure. I didn't want to feel like I had committed a crime for nothing.

"Yes. Of course." After a brief pause, he added, "Anything else I should know?"

"That's it," I quickly assured him.

"I'll be in touch tomorrow." He hung up without saying goodbye.

Mom sat down at the table. "It sounds to me like you've crossed a line and Detective Connolly is not happy with you."

"You are so perceptive, Mom."

"Don't use that tone with me, Cameron. I'm simply stating the obvious."

"Sorry, you're right, Mom. I intended to put the papers back but didn't get a chance."

"You didn't need to look in a dead man's pockets in the first place," Mom said pointedly.

Yuri jumped in to defend me. "It was actually very sharp of her to recognize his jacket. And if I'd seen it and knew it belonged to Jim, I would have done the same thing. Although," he grinned, "I wouldn't have been caught."

I made a face at him, and Mom shook her head. Then, having listened in to our conversation with Connolly and made her disapproval known, Mom said she was going to retire for the evening. When Yuri suggested she should make certain that all of her windows were locked, she rolled her eyes at us and mumbled something about how her life was turning into an episode from Law & Order.

Yuri and I joined the kids in watching part of a movie before Yuri fell asleep and I tactfully suggested to Jason and Mara that we all call it a night. Mom had left a pile of sheets and blankets next to the couch for Yuri to use. I managed to wake him up to let him know it was time to go to bed and offered to help make up the sofa. He waved me off, grabbed a blanket and fell back onto the couch. "I've got this."

"Don't fall asleep on your gun and accidently shoot yourself," I said instead of wishing him pleasant dreams.

CHAPTER 16
"WHO'S THERE?"

THERE WERE NO ATTACKS in the middle of the night. No ninjas sneaking in through the windows. No zombies slouching in through the front door. No creatures from outer space. Not even a rabid dog. It was a quiet night. Except for occasional sounds of snoring from the couch.

Yuri and I were both up before anyone else. He was making coffee when I dragged myself into the kitchen, checking my phone messages on the way.

"Anything from Denny yet?" Yuri asked.

"No, nothing."

"Okay, let's drink a cup of coffee and get going."

"Shouldn't we let Connolly check out Denny?"

"You want to call him and see if they've done it yet, and, if so, what they've found out?"

I made a face and reached for coffee.

"My guess is that, unless he's a suspect, the whereabouts of a friend of a dead man won't be a priority."

Even as doubts washed over me as unsettling as a rogue wave, I prepared a cup of coffee to go. It was asking too much of us to sit around and wait without knowing what was going on. "You have his address?" I asked.

"Yeah, I got Adele to look it up for me." He gestured toward my travel mug. "Don't have a spare one of those do you?"

I pointed at a cupboard to his left. Just then Jason stumbled into the kitchen. "What's up?" he asked, rubbing his eyes.

"You can go back to bed, Jason. It's early."

"Mom. I know that."

"Yuri and I are going to be leaving for a while, but we won't be long. Will you stay inside until we return?"

"Why?"

"Because I'm asking you nicely. And because..." I was trying to think of some reward when he finished my sentence for me.

"...you'll let me choose whatever I want for dinner and stay up late and..." His young mind was struggling to come up with as many requests as he could think of that I would say "yes" to without argument. "And you'll let me have a puppy," he concluded.

"Don't push your luck," I said. "Just stay inside with Mara until we return, and you can be the king of the house for 24 hours."

That seemed to satisfy him. He headed back to his room, undoubtedly thinking about what a king could reasonably expect as concessions and rewards from his dowager mother. I gulped down the rest of my coffee and went to put on some shoes. Five minutes later we were on our way. I called Mom and woke her up to tell her about being gone for about an hour and about my deal with Jason. She muttered something about needing her rest before agreeing to make sure the kids ate breakfast if they got up before we returned. Not that they needed a reminder; I just wanted to make sure someone kept an eye on them so they wouldn't go out on their own.

"I think I told you that I promised Laney Knight I would call her today, after talking with you about her situation."

"That can wait, can't it?"

"I suppose." Since we hadn't come up with anything, I still didn't know what I was going to say. Putting off making the call wasn't a hard decision. "But remind me later to call her, okay?"

With little traffic at that hour, it didn't take us long to drive to Denny's rundown apartment building on a side street at the foot of a hill on the north end of the University. It was two stories with tiny windows looking out onto the street. There was an arrow indicating that the main entrances were around back on the alley that divided the block in half, with apartments on one side and a row of small businesses on the other. We managed to find a parking space on the street just beyond the building and were headed back toward the apartments when we saw someone in dark clothes and a hoody hurrying around the side of the building. We automatically picked up the pace.

As we rounded the corner, we saw the dark figure on the second-floor landing. It looked like he was stopping near where I estimated Denny's apartment would be. I was already running when Yuri said, "Let's hustle."

The man glanced at us as he pushed open the door of the apartment and disappeared inside. The door clicked shut just as we arrived. It was Denny's apartment. Yuri knocked, but there was no answer. "Call him," he said. I was already dialing the number. Moments later I could hear a ringtone from inside.

"Hello?" The voice was low, tentative. Caller ID can be a disadvantage when you're an anonymous caller.

"Hi, I'm Cameron Chandler. My colleague, Yuri Webster, and I are standing outside of your apartment. We are the investigators Jim talked with. Could you come to the door, please?"

"What do you want?"

"We want to verify that you are okay and that you are taking precautions."

The door inched open. "Precautions?" Denny peeked out through the crack. "Do you have some ID?"

Yuri got out his ID and held it up. "Didn't Jim mention talking with us?"

"Yeah, he did. But what are you doing here so early?"

"I left you several messages," I explained. "When you didn't answer, we got worried."

"Worried? About me? Why would you worry about me?"

Yuri and I looked at each other. It didn't sound like he knew about Jim. "Ah, have you by any chance been out of town for a few days?"

"Yes," he said slowly. "Why do you ask?"

"For one thing, you haven't been answering your phone."

"Well, I didn't pick up any messages because I left my cell here. I thought it was in my pocket when I left. But it wasn't."

"Then we need to talk. Do you want to let us in or come out here?"

He seemed reluctant to let us in, but he finally opened the door. The interior of his apartment was sparsely furnished and uncluttered. It had the look of someone who didn't spend much time at home. I took a seat on a very large overstuffed couch in tired burgundy velvet. The velvet had been worn down in places, creating shiny lily pad shaped spots. The couch didn't match anything else in the room. It looked like something left behind by previous tenants because it was too much trouble to move. Yuri sat down beside me and Denny took a chair across from us.

"So, what's this about?" Denny asked.

Yuri nodded for me to tell him. Thanks a lot. "We assume you haven't heard about Jim," I began, waiting for him to acknowledge my assumption.

"What about Jim?"

"There isn't any easy way to tell you," I began again. He was starting to look worried. Before he could ask whether Jim had been in an accident, I blurted out the fact that we had found Jim's body early yesterday evening and that he had been murdered. "We think it had something to do with the information Brian Norcross was compiling, but we don't know for sure."

"Murdered? Jim was murdered?"

Perhaps I'd once again been too abrupt. But no matter how you sugarcoat the message, the end result is the same. "We're sorry to be the ones to tell you," I said. "We know you were friends."

"Jim's my best friend," Denny said. He sounded confused. "What do you mean by 'murdered'?"

Before I could explain, he suddenly slouched down in his chair, his face rapidly losing color. "Stay here," I said, standing up. "I'll get you some water." I nodded at Yuri to take over.

"Look, Denny, I know this is tough. It's never easy to lose someone close to you. Especially under circumstances like this."

"What happened?" His voice was barely audible.

"All we know is that Jim is dead, and the police are investigating."

"But you two found him?"

"Yes, we had an appointment with him. To talk about Brian's research."

I handed Denny a glass of water and sat down again. He looked at the glass a few moments as if not recognizing what it was for before finally taking a sip. "Thank you."

"We know this is not a good time," Yuri continued, "but we need to ask you some questions."

"Why?" he asked. "You aren't police, are you?"

"No, we're private investigators. We aren't looking into the murder. We're here to see if you can tell us anything about Brian's research. And because we think you may be in danger."

He sat there not saying anything, as if trying to make sense of what we just told him. We waited, feeling uncomfortable with the silence and our reasons for being there.

"Why would I be in danger?" he asked finally.

"Do you have a copy of Brian's research?" Yuri asked.

"No."

"Do you know if Jim did?"

"He didn't say anything to me about having anything like that."

"Do you know what's in the research?"

"No, not really. Brian was going to share it with Jim and me, but, he hadn't yet."

"Has anyone tried to contact you in the last few days, someone whose name you didn't recognize?"

He took out his cell. "I haven't checked for messages," he said.

"Would you?"

He checked for texts and messages. "Just you," he said. "No one else."

"That's probably good news," Yuri said. "They may not know that Jim was a close friend of yours."

Denny looked suddenly concerned. "Ah, did I mention that my door was unlocked?" he asked. "Just now, I mean. I don't remember leaving it unlocked, but it was."

Yuri glanced around at the sparsely furnished room. "Can you tell if someone searched your place while you were away?" Denny and I surveyed the room from our seats while Yuri got up and started looking more closely at everything.

Finally Denny stood up. "Let me check the other room." He came back moments later. "My laptop is gone." He seemed surprised, as if he hadn't quite accepted the fact that someone could consider him a target.

"I wonder why they didn't take your cell?" Yuri said. "That seems strange."

"Maybe they didn't see it. It was under some gloves on the shelf above the coat rack. That's why I forgot it."

"Do you mind if I ask where you were?" Yuri said.

"My girlfriend's. I went over there Sunday night. Her roommate went out of town. It's a nice place. They aren't students; they both have jobs. But I had to come back. I have a chem test this afternoon."

We asked a few more questions but didn't learn anything. Whatever Jim had been up to, it didn't appear to be something he'd shared with Denny. Unless Denny was an incredibly good liar, which didn't seem likely to me. I gave him Connolly's number and urged him to get in touch. Then we suggested that he get out of his apartment as soon as possible and stay with a friend for a while. Yuri and I both gave him a card and told him to feel free to call us any time.

We were about to leave when there was a knock on the door. "Police," a voice called. "Open up." Yuri and I instinctively moved off to the left of the door, just out of sight.

"Ask to see some ID," Yuri whispered as Denny approached the door. Denny opened it a crack and asked to see the man's ID.

We could see Denny leaning down to check out the ID, but it didn't seem like he had enough time to actually take it in before the man outside pulled his ID back and asked to come in. Well, more like he demanded that Denny let him in.

"Hey," Yuri said suddenly, "I know that voice." He motioned Denny aside and opened the door. "What the hell are you doing here?" he asked.

"Why, Yuri Webster, I could ask you the same thing."

"Come in." Yuri stepped aside. "It's not the police," Yuri said to Denny and me. "It's Dick Devine, sleaziest dick on the block."

Dick came in and looked around. He was a short man with a husky build that wasn't quite the right shape for his off-the-rack jacket from some discount store. "You sneaked past me," he said to Denny. "I didn't see you come home."

"You were probably busy peeing into a bottle," Yuri sniped.

Dick gave him a finger and asked, "So, who's your client?"

"I could ask you the same," Yuri countered.

"Why don't you two cut it out and sit down," I said. "This is serious."

Neither man looked particularly embarrassed by their behavior, but they obediently went into the living room and sat down. Yuri joined me on the couch and Dick took a seat on a wobbly wood chair with a thin Victorian print cover.

"What's going on? Denny asked the group before looking directly at Dick. "Why are you spying on me?"

"I'm not spying. I was just looking for the right opportunity to talk with you. You are a hard man to find."

"You're here about the research, aren't you?" Yuri asked.

"What research?" Dick said, unconvincingly.

"You do know someone was murdered for that information, don't you? I asked. "Maybe even two people."

Dick scoffed. "Murdered? Someone was murdered?"

"Yes, Brian Norcross a few days ago, and Jim Gossett yesterday," I said.

Dick looked surprised. "Jim Gossett was murdered?"

"Yes, you know him?"

"Damned inconvenient," he said.

"That's one way to put it."

"I was supposed to talk to him next."

"About the research?"

Dick seemed to consider the question, then asked, "What's your story?" He looked from me to Yuri.

"We're looking for the research," Yuri admitted. Before he could say any more, there was a knock on the door. "Police," a voice called. This time I, too, recognized the voice.

CHAPTER 17
THE DIRT SLINGING BEGINS

DETECTIVE CONNOLLY WAS NOT pleased to see us in Denny's apartment, but he seemed even less pleased to see Dick Devine there. Based on first impressions, my guess was that Devine made everyone's list of least favorite private detectives.

I respectfully explained that we weren't "detecting" but had come by to check on Denny because we were worried about him when he hadn't returned my calls. Connolly frowned but did not reprimand us for our visit. Devine, on the other hand, was all bluster and deflection. But Connolly was having none of that.

"I asked what you are doing here, and I want a straight answer. You know the drill. It's either tell me now or tell me at the station. It's up to you." I was somewhat surprised Connolly didn't ask us to leave. Perhaps he thought he could get more out of all of us by keeping us together. Or by not letting us have time to synchronize our responses.

Devine gave Connolly a flash of white teeth in what was probably intended to be a charming smile. It made me think of Batman's Joker, but more buffoon than evil. "My client wants that list of wrongdoers that seems to be so popular with everyone." He winked at Yuri. An actual wink. I didn't think people did that, except in movies.

"And just who is that client?" Connolly asked. "And don't tell me it's confidential. There have been two murders."

Devine glanced at us. "Not in front of them," he said.

Connolly hesitated, then suggested we take off. "I'll get back to you," he said. "Don't—" he began.

"Leave town," Yuri interrupted and finished for him.

"That wasn't what I was going to say." Connolly sounded irritated. "Don't get in the way of the investigation. Got that?" he said, looking directly at me.

"Got it." We nodded at Denny, ignoring Devine's smirk.

Once outside, Yuri said, "That went well." The phrase seemed to be his mantra of late. But definitely more fanciful than factual.

"If you mean that Denny is alive and we weren't arrested, then, yes, it went well."

"Always the realist," Yuri countered. As if that was a bad thing.

We arrived back at my place in time for waffles, an unusual mid-week treat. Mom was wearing one of her designer aprons and looked like a TV ad for some gourmet cooking show. She removed a large waffle and put it on a flowered platter in the middle of the table. "Divide it up," she said to Jason and Mara. "And give one to Yuri. I ignored the fact that she hadn't mentioned me. There were four squares, and I intended to get one of them.

Yuri quickly sat down, grabbed a waffle and raced Jason for the syrup. He let Jason win, I think, although maybe Jason was just quicker. Mara said, "Hey, I want some, too." Yuri graciously let her go second. Then he leaned forward and grabbed the syrup before I could make a play for it.

Mara and Jason left for school, and Yuri and I were fighting over the last waffle when Detective Connolly arrived. Mom treated him like an honored guest, asking if he wanted some breakfast and offering coffee when he declined food. He accepted the coffee and joined us at the kitchen table. Mom discreetly made her exit, but not before giving me a suggestive look to signal that she wouldn't be averse to seeing more of Detective Connolly.

"Are you going to tell us who Sleazy Dick's client is?" Yuri asked.

"And a 'good morning' to you, too," Detective Connolly said in a very appealing brogue.

"Sorry, but he gets to me," Yuri said.

Connolly took a sip of coffee. "Good," he said to me.

"My mother makes good coffee."

He smiled. "She seems very nice."

Dammit. The last thing I needed at the moment was for Mom and Connolly to form some kind of bond.

"Yes," Yuri agreed, "Very nice."

I flashed Yuri a look to keep him from saying more. "Okay, my mother's nice, and Dick Devine is a sleaze. Now, are you going to tell us who his client is or not?" I knew I sounded unreasonably testy, but that was how I felt.

"If you don't have a professional interest in this case, then you don't need to know," Connolly said, not unkindly.

"Wouldn't it help us protect ourselves better if we knew?" I could tell by the look on Connolly's face that I'd scored a hit with that question.

He took another sip of coffee before replying. "You've got a point. Under other circumstances I might feel that discussing this with you posed an ethical dilemma. But if he was telling the truth, I can't see why I shouldn't. Although I doubt it will be helpful. It seems he was hired to destroy Norcross's research. Claims he never even met his client. He got a call from a burner phone with someone making an effort to disguise their voice. He's doubtful he could identify them from their brief conversation. The money for the assignment was dropped off in cash at his office by a young kid who Dick questioned. But the kid told Dick he didn't know and couldn't describe the person who paid him to do it. We'll follow up, of course, but it doesn't sound hopeful.

"There was the promise of more money if he found the research and destroyed it. They required proof of the report's destruction, pictures sent to the burner phone, showing the step-by-step process. He was threatened with severe consequences if he lied about any part of the assignment."

"And that didn't set off any red flags for him?" Yuri asked.

"He says he didn't know about the link between the research and the first murder, and he didn't know that Gossett had been murdered."

"And you believe him?" I asked.

"Sounded plausible," Connolly said. "For him, that is. It was easy money from his point of view. We'll check out his story, of course."

"I can't believe anyone would trust that dirtbag to live up to his end of any bargain," Yuri said.

"I sensed he thought his client was serious about the 'severe consequences' threat. Still, he may have had some thoughts about trying to squeeze more money out of his client by holding something back, but if so, he's out of luck now."

"Another dead end," Yuri complained.

"Probably."

"Unless you can use Devine to lure out his client," I said.

"We're working on that angle," Connolly said. He gulped down the last of his coffee and stood up. "Your assignment is to stay put today. Here or your office. I'll check in later and let you know how things are going."

After Connolly left, Yuri went into the other room to check in with the office, and Mom came back into the kitchen. "He's nice," she said without mentioning any names.

"He thinks you're nice, too," I said. "And he likes your coffee."

"Is he single?"

"You interested?" I teased.

"It seems to me that you should be." She leaned in for the kill. "So, is he single?"

"How would I know?" In spite of the fact that I found Detective Connolly appealing, I wasn't about to encourage my mother. She and Yuri needed to stay out of my love life. Not that I had one. I'd had a brief encounter with someone last year but hadn't seen him since. Occasionally I thought about getting in touch, but for one reason or another I kept putting it off.

I started to get up, but she waved me back down.

"More coffee?" she asked. "I thought we might have a little chat."

It was then that I noticed she had closed the door between the kitchen and the living room. That did not bode well for our "chat."

"About what?" I asked.

"You know I try to be supportive," she began. "But I can't help but have some concerns about your, ah, career as an investigator." She paused as if waiting for me to say something. I couldn't decide if I was angry or defensive or both. When I didn't respond, she continued. "I know it's been hard for you since Dan passed away. And I know how difficult it was for you to find a job. I just hope you don't feel like there aren't other options."

"You mean like getting married?" Now I was definitely more angry than defensive.

"No, I mean like trying to find a teaching job. A job where you don't have to be looking over your shoulder all the time, a job that doesn't put your family in danger."

She'd scored with the "family in danger" comment, but I wasn't ready to concede the argument. "You know, Mom, a lot of jobs that used to be safe aren't anymore. Take teaching for example. How many classroom shootings have there been recently?" I paused to let it sink in. "I do realize that I've run into a few risky situations in the last year, but just being alive is dangerous. I could get in a car accident or be attacked by a … a rabid dog … or hit in the head by a golf ball."

"No need to get defensive, dear."

"I'm not being defensive." Oops. That sounded defensive even to me. "This was supposed to be a simple surveillance job. See who was taking Knight's signs and tell the Knight campaign. That's what most of my assignments with Penny-wise have been like. Routine stuff."

Mom gave me a knowing look. "I just never saw you as someone who would get involved in things of a, ah, questionable nature. I always pictured you more like, oh, you know, one of the wives in the campaign. Doing good works, supporting their husbands, raising a family. That sort of thing."

"Laney Knight had a successful career, but she had to put it on hold so her husband could run for Congress," I pointed out. "How desirable do you find that?" Mom claims to be a feminist, although many of her ideas about what that means don't jibe with my view of feminism. Not that my married life would have passed the Gloria Steinem test.

"If he wins, she'll have some doors opened for her," Mom argued. "And she can go back to work after the campaign. If that's what she wants to do."

"Then there's Ashley Price Mann," I said, trying to distract Mom from her point about me and my life. "I think she married Bobby to become a politician's wife. For the prestige of being in the limelight. Before that she was some rich man's daughter who couldn't make it on her own. What kind of a role model is that for young women?"

Mom leaned forward in a way that told me I had succeeded in changing the conversation just enough. "You know she failed as a television personality, right? And she tried local theater and got panned. Looks, but no talent." She sat up straight. "But she did try. You have to give her that."

I considered telling Mom about Ashley's verbal assault on Laney, but quickly dismissed the thought as a betrayal of the confidence I had promised. "I'll grant her that," I conceded. "But I'm not convinced she ever considered herself a professional in any career category. She's all about appearances and social status."

"You could look at that from a different angle. Maybe all she wants is to feel important. And the only way to do that once you've failed on your own is to attach your ego to someone else's persona. Sad, really, when you think about it. That's probably why she had some cosmetic surgery. At least that's the rumor. She's definitely older than she looks."

I leaned forward, still intent on distracting Mom from a discussion about my life. "Can you keep a secret?"

Mom looked offended and intrigued. "Of course."

"Well, as you know, we've been trying to find a link between the two murders and the Mann campaign. And one interesting tidbit has come up."

I definitely had Mom's attention. She loves gossipy tidbits.

"It seems that Ashley went to school with the mother of the girlfriend of the first victim. And the girl's father is both a politician and a recipient of money from big oil. Small world, isn't it?"

"Yes, it sounds a bit like the 'curious incident of the dog in the night.'"

"What do you mean?"

"The connections may actually mean something." Mom looked contemplative. "Poor Ashley," she said finally.

"Why 'poor Ashley'?"

"Because she isn't stupid. She must feel somewhat used at this point. Although if Bobby wins, then she will probably conclude it was worth it."

"And if he doesn't?"

"If I had to guess, there will be a divorce in her future."

"You don't think Bobby loves Ashley?" The pairing sounded like a bad movie title.

"Men like him use people, even wives. When they're no longer of any use, they move on. Ashley may be a player in our little pond, but she doesn't have clout at the national level. If he loses, I say he'll leave her behind in a heartbeat and go on to bigger and better things."

"If he loses."

"He is pulling out all of the stops to keep that from happening," Mom said. "I heard a radio spot that mentioned something about how Knight's tour as a soldier is shrouded in secrecy for a reason. It was a teaser ad with hints of more to come."

"What's secret about his service record? He served in Afghanistan. Won a Medal of Honor for bravery."

"The ad made me wonder whether he was involved in some atrocity or lied about the Medal of Honor."

"Great. Money and a willingness to say anything, whether it's true or not. How does a campaign with a limited budget fight something like that? Especially with only a few days left before the vote."

We sat there in silence a few moments.

"Maybe you're right, Cameron. Life can be ugly no matter what choices you make." She stood up. "I just want you to be happy. You and the kids."

I experienced a wave of warmth and appreciation for my mother. "Me too, Mom. That's what I want for all of us."

CHAPTER 18
DEFINE "FAMILY"

FRIDAY CAME WITHOUT FANFARE. I hadn't heard from or seen Randy Mann in recent days. Yuri had moved back home. My delayed conversation with Laney had produced nothing but more indecision. Mom acted as if our congenial chat about wanting me to be happy had never happened. Jason kept trying to exact rewards for his one act of obedience. Mara placed second with a science project. And things had returned to relative normal. Except for the need to be constantly vigilant, just in case.

Then, with just a few days to go before the election, the Knight campaign finally came out with a negative ad about Bobby Mann. It was their first negative ad and it was based on a single true fact: Mann was not from the area. Given that he was from the east coast and had only recently moved to the Pacific Northwest, the ad claimed he didn't know or relate to local issues as well as Knight did.

The press went wild, focusing on the fact that both sides had gone negative, labeling the entire race the most negative ever seen in the state. No one seemed to care about the number of negative ads put out by each side or what was true and what wasn't true. The headlines were that both candidates had gone negative. Both were equally "bad."

In spite of all the money being spent, and in spite of the heightened sense of urgency and negativity, the polls suggested that the race remained a dead heat. Both sides were no doubt frustrated by that. I know I was. No matter what the candidates said or did, the voters remained evenly divided.

Shortly after the evening news, it happened. An event that would change our lives.

A barking dog shattered the silence of early evening. It barked and barked, right outside our front door. Under normal circumstances I would have simply gone out to see what was happening. But for all we knew, it was a trap. What kind, I wasn't sure. Jason and Mara both wanted to take a look. Then Mom came down to complain, and I finally got up the courage to see what the commotion was all about.

When I opened the door a crack, a black, moist nose tried to pry the door open more. The barking changed to whining.

"It's a dog, Mom," Jason said. "He wants in."

That much was obvious, but why?

"Oh, just open the damn door," Mom said. She grabbed the doorknob and a medium-sized black and white dog came bounding in and ran right into Jason's outstretched arms. I was staring at Jason, trying to figure out what was happening, while he rubbed the dog's head and buried his face in the dog's neck fur. That's why I didn't notice the dark figure looming in our doorway until Mom said, "You might as well come in. The damage is done."

When I saw Yuri standing there, all I could think of to say was, "You didn't."

Yuri at least had the decency to look guilty. "Well, I knew Jason wanted a puppy, and when my neighbor moved out and abandoned his dog…." He raised his eyebrows looking for approval that I denied him with a glare. "I thought since this guy is already house-trained." He looked down at Jason and the dog. "He's had his shots. He's been neutered. And … he's cute."

"He is cute." Mara said as she patted him on the back. "What's his name?"

The dog looked up, one ear flopped forward, the other stood straight up as if he was anxiously awaiting Yuri's answer.

"I'm not sure. I never paid any attention."

"We'll have to figure that out," Jason said. "Max, he looks like a Max."

The dog stared blankly at Jason.

"How about Gizmo?" Jason waited but the dog didn't respond.

"Beau?" Mara ventured. Still no response.

"Thor?" Jason tried.

"Spike." Mara said.

"Tucker."

"Duke."

"He doesn't look like a Duke," Jason said firmly.

"Well, he doesn't look like a Tucker either," Mara countered.

The dog sat down and watched while Jason and Mara sparred. I knew that I needed to nip this in the bud right away, before the naming ceremony ended and the dog officially became part of the family. "Jason," I began, but Mom cut me off.

"There's no reason why we couldn't have a dog. It might be reassuring." The dog turned toward her, and she took a step back. "As long as you keep him downstairs."

I looked at the kids. "Who's going to feed him and clean up after him?"

Just as I anticipated, Jason said, "I'll do that, Mom. He's my dog."

Everyone was staring at me, waiting for me to give in. And even though I knew Jason would soon tire of the feeding and cleaning up, I felt like there was only one answer.

"We'll give him a try."

Mara and Jason whooped and the dog leapt up and started barking.

"For a week," I added, trying to look firm. Unless he bit one of them, I knew in my heart that a week would only make it more difficult to get rid of him. I wondered if a tiny bite would leave a scar.

Friday evening, I was home alone. Except for the still-unnamed dog. I thought of him as "Nuisance," but I didn't dare suggest naming him that. Jason and Mara were trying to think of a name that was either cute or clever. I just wanted it to be something easy to shout when I was trying to get him to come in. For that reason, I'd already vetoed T-Rex, McDuff, Columbo, Hamlet and Beethoven. I was leaning toward Fang, although Pest or Devil-dog seemed like possibilities. Cerberus was too much of a mouthful.

The animal did seem to have a good disposition, but he wasn't all that happy being stuck at home with me. He kept trying to lay on my feet, and whenever I nudged him aside, he would stare up at me as if I'd treated him badly. I just didn't like having a dog on my feet. But there I was, me and no-name, my feet covered in dog, while everyone else was off having a good time.

Mom was out on a date with a man she'd met online. They had agreed she could bring a friend along so she would feel safer. They were all meeting at a nearby restaurant for dinner. Before leaving she had pointed out how easy it was to meet someone if you were willing to "extend yourself a little." HINT.

Jason was staying overnight with Theo. He and his mother had finally returned to their home, reluctantly leaving their temporary Vashon Island hideaway. With only the weekend to go and nothing published or even in the queue for publication, we decided whoever it was that had burgled Gretchen's house probably knew she was no longer an immediate threat. But if she was going to continue pursuing stories about corporations with a lot to lose, she would have to figure out how to do so and remain safe. For the time being, she had asked a friend to stay with her, the theory being there was safety in numbers.

At first, I'd hesitated when Jason asked to stay overnight with Theo, then decided I was being hypocritical. If I truly believed that Gretchen and Theo were safe in their home, why wouldn't I let Jason stay with them? Anyway, what made me think he was any safer at home with me? Reluctantly, I'd given him permission. I'd wanted to send his dog along with him, but Gretchen had vetoed it. I couldn't blame her. She had enough to worry about.

Mara was at a sleepover with half a dozen friends. I was just thankful it was happening at someone else's house. Letting a group of young girls spend the night together could be exhausting for them and for the host parents. I anticipated the girls would stay up most of the night and that Mara would return mid-morning happy but bushed.

Yuri called a couple of times to talk about how the various campaigns were doing. And probably to check up on me. He knew I was still miffed about the dog. And he was worried about me being at home by myself. I assured him that having a watch dog was just as good as having a friend with a gun hanging out on our sofa.

On the one hand, it was nice to have some time alone, even alone with a dog. On the other hand, things seemed unnaturally quiet. I had the television on low, watching for campaign ads and updates while trying to read the same book I'd been reading for the last month. I couldn't remember the plot but resisted starting over. It was only a page turner in the sense that ever so often I would turn over another page.

I glanced up at an ad, and something caught my eye. I paused the TV and hit rewind to watch it again. There she was, the former Ashley Price. Previously a professional loser, now perhaps about to become the wife of a member of Congress. The ad featured the entire family, all looking friendly and happy. Except for Ashley. The campaign had not been kind to her. She looked tired. I wondered if Mom was right about the cosmetic surgery. I didn't remember seeing references to her age anywhere. Although it would have been easy to check. Not that her age made any difference. Except how she might feel about getting older. Thinking about her life and what lay ahead.

Looking at her standing there, hoping to become the wife of a winner, a thought crossed my mind. I wondered how far she was willing to go to save her husband's campaign. And to secure her own future. She hadn't hesitated to harass Laney Knight, but that was a far cry from committing or facilitating a murder to prevent Brian's research from being made public. But what if the murder had been an impulsive act brought on by anger and fear of failure? Of course, that didn't explain what she had been doing at the campaign headquarters after hours. Unless she had specifically gone there to meet with Brian.

Could Brian have contacted her and requested a meeting? Maybe everyone had misjudged him, and he wanted to make some money off of his discoveries. Or maybe he thought he could trick her into revealing some damaging information about her husband or his family. On the other hand, it was even possible he had some connection that made him sympathetic to her situation. Maybe he'd gone there to warn her about what was going to happen.

Then again, it was possible it had been the other way around. She might have learned about what he was doing and asked to meet him there. Perhaps she hoped to pay him off, and, when that failed, she'd eliminated the threat.

For the sake of argument, I gave her the benefit of the doubt. The murder may not have been premeditated but an impulsive act of desperation. I imagined Ashley standing over Brian's body, frightened, appalled at what she had done. What would she have done next? Would she have simply run away and hoped there was nothing to link her to the crime? Or would she have calculated her options, thought about who she could call for help. And if so, who would she have turned to? Certainly not her husband. That might not only have placed their marriage in jeopardy, it would have put him in an untenable position in his run for office. But what if she had called on his street-wise brother and protector? How would Randy have responded? Would the Manns have rallied around and helped her hide the heinous crime from the law? And if so, for how long? I could picture them wanting to keep the lid on things, at least until after the election. If Bobby won, a wife, even a trophy wife with connections, might be considered expendable; the Congressional seat was everything. And if he lost, she would definitely be a disposable liability.

But, in my imagined scenario, killing Brian hadn't made the problem go away. Cornered by Gossett, had Ashley struck again? Or had the Manns stepped in to save their family reputation by eliminating him?

Realistically I knew that threatening the opposition and looking tired in an ad didn't make Ashley a murderer. And there was probably no way to prove she had somehow found out that Brian Norcross had been compiling a list of companies and illegal activities that could potentially have sabotaged her husband's campaign. And if she had managed to locate his research, she would hardly have left any evidence behind.

But what if Jim Gossett had a copy—or made Ashley believe he did—would he have used the information to try to extort money from her? She may have seemed an easy target, wealthy in her own right and desperate for her husband to win. Easier to manipulate than the Mann family members. If only I could find a direct link between Ashley and Brian. Or between her and Jim Gossett.

I called Yuri and ran my theory past him. He liked it but didn't think it was something we could or should pursue. He encouraged me to call Detective Connolly. "Maybe he doesn't have a date tonight either."

After hanging up, I gave calling Connolly some serious thought. But it wasn't much of a theory, and there were more questions than answers at this point. Like, how did the murders relate to the threats against Gretchen? And the shots fired at Yuri and me in the parking lot? It didn't seem reasonable to lay all of that at Ashley's feet. Maybe Randy Mann was responsible for the burglary and threats but not the murders. Or maybe Jim Gossett wanted to make sure he was the only one with Brian's information so he could blackmail Ashley. And maybe some bored kid with daddy's gun had taken potshots at us for fun. There were too many loose ends.

For an insane moment, I fanaticized about calling Randy Mann and asking him if he had included Ashley in his family disclaimer. Assuming he'd told me the truth when he'd said no family members were responsible for Brian's death. The key question was whether, if Ashley was guilty and the family knew, would they close ranks and protect her? At least until after the election?

In the long run, it seemed to make more sense to noodle on the idea a while longer. There were a couple of things I could look into in the morning. Until then, I would have a glass of wine, put my feet up and try to enjoy the silence.

Unfortunately, no-name had other ideas. He wanted to go out. At least that's how I read his head-butting-my-knee message. With a groan, I got up and attached the leash to his collar, both recent gifts from Yuri as an attempt to make amends for giving us the dog in the first place. Even though the last thing I wanted to do was take a dog out to relieve himself, I couldn't let him out on his own. If I did and he ran away, Jason would never forgive me. Even without a name, the dog was already part of the family.

When Mom got back from her "date" I was asleep on the sofa, dreaming about being lost in the woods, looking for a dog. She woke me up and told me to go to bed. At first, I was confused about where I was and what was happening. There was a dog lying on the floor next to the sofa. I must have found him in the woods. Then I remembered why there was a dog in our living room. As I came fully awake and sat up, no-name woke up and jumped in my lap. "No, dog," I said, pushing him off. Then, feeling guilty, I rubbed his head behind his ears. He seemed to like that. Then I turned to Mom and asked, "How was it?"

She sat down at the end of the sofa, avoiding contact with no-name, and sighed before replying. "He was older than his online picture."

"How much older?"

"Let's put it this way, he looked his age."

"So, no second date?"

"No, but the threesome idea worked out okay. As a safe way to meet someone. And the two of them hit it off, my date and my friend. She is apparently attracted to older men."

"Oh, I'm sorry it didn't pan out." I hesitated before adding, "At least you tried." When she didn't follow up with a snide comment or a reference about my lack of trying, I knew just how disappointed she actually was.

She stood up. "Go to bed," she said. "Tomorrow you need to clean this place up." No-name was eyeing her as if trying to decide whether she was friend or foe. I wondered if I should warn him not to take food from her. "Vacuum the house," she added. "It's a good thing he's a short-hair." With that she turned and went upstairs.

Without anyone to wake me up, I slept in much later than usual, surprised to find the dog stretched out next to me on the bed when I woke up. Of course, I didn't realize he had joined me until he licked my face with his rough tongue, apparently urging me to get up so he could get on with his day.

"Yuk," I said, pushing him aside. "No licking, got that? I don't like to be licked." He grinned at me, jumped off the bed and headed for the front door, glancing over his shoulder to make sure I was following.

There was no way this was going to become the norm. Letting him lick my face to wake me, waiting to get dressed until after I took him outside. We needed to get him an official bed and make him sleep in it at night. And I would have to make sure my door was securely shut after I went to bed.

We had agreed to train no-name to always go to the bathroom in the same place off to the side of the house, but it seemed too far from the front door when I was still in my pajamas. I was also supposed to say "go potty" when I took him to his bathroom spot so he would learn to go on command. But I felt stupid saying that, so I just shortened his leash and motioned at the ground next to the porch. Fortunately, no-name got the message, and I dutifully scooped up his efforts. I wondered if no-name would defend me against an assault. Maybe we could have him trained as a guard dog and personal protector, aggressive on command.

I quickly put down some food for our new family member and grabbed a cup of coffee for myself before heading for my computer. No-name wolfed down his food and was resting on my feet before my computer booted up. At least I wasn't going to have to worry about cold feet in the future.

Sometime during the night I'd thought of one possible way to check out whether Ashley and Jim had ever come in contact. There were a number of times when the two campaigns were at the same events, including the recent Oktoberfest parade. Both candidates and their wives had walked in part of the parade, followed by a tour of the food booths, stopping to sample brats, pretzels and other German specialties while shaking hands with potential voters. Both candidates had been judges in the costume contest. It was all very upbeat and congenial—on the surface.

What I needed was a picture putting Jim and Ashley in close proximity. The two of them talking together would be even better, but I thought that was probably too much to hope for.

Two and a half hours later, I'd gone through four cups of coffee and an endless stream of online campaign pictures posted by the campaigns and various news organizations.

I googled rallies, parades, sporting events, forums, speeches. On and on it went. Not all of the pictures were in chronological order. And many weren't labeled. If I found something, I might still not be able to identify the time and date with precision.

No-name had disappeared into the other room. I wasn't sure whether his silence was a good sign or not, but I was too obsessed with my online search to go check.

When Mara returned from her sleepover at noon, I was still in my pajamas at my computer. She stuck her head in and informed me she was home and was going to take a nap. I asked how the sleepover had been and she mumbled a "good" before disappearing.

"Check on the dog, will you?" I called after her. I think I heard a mumbled "sure," followed by "not my dog."

Gretchen popped in to say hello when she brought Jason home. She was surprised to see me disheveled and still not dressed for the day. "I can't stay; my friend is in the car with Theo." She sounded like she thought she had an obligation to help me get my act together.

"Just a minute," I said, "I have something to show you." But first I had to make sure Jason was tending to no-name. I needn't have worried. The two of them were rolling around on the floor, happy as can be. I went back to my computer and told Gretchen my idea and what I was looking for.

"No way," she said. "Not the lovely Ashley."

"Being good looking doesn't mean you're an angel."

"But murder?"

"Why not? It's an equal opportunity act."

"Well…." She couldn't think of any reason to counter

my suggestion, except for, well, lack of facts. "Maybe I can help," she said. "I can log into newspaper archives for pictures. You never know."

"That would be great."

"One thing though—you have to promise that if you find something, you will give me an exclusive."

"Deal. Although I wouldn't count on it if I were you."

I finally got dressed Saturday afternoon. I did a few chores, mostly to please Mom. I couldn't believe I was a grown woman with two children and still trying to please my mother. But that's my reality. Every so often I would return to my computer and search for pictures or some other evidence that would place Jim and Ashley at the same event.

Gretchen called later to tell me that the only thing she'd found so far was a blurry picture from the Oktoberfest parade. It was definitely Ashley, and it could be Brian. But it wasn't clear enough to tell for sure, and she had no way of making the image any better. She was sorry and would keep looking. But she wasn't hopeful.

Saturday ended on a downer. No leads. And the race was still neck and neck.

CHAPTER 19
EAU DE INNOCENCE

IF SATURDAY WAS A DOWNER, Sunday wasn't much of an improvement. Mom took off with a friend, and Mara spent the day on an essay for her English class, making it clear that she didn't want any help. "I have to be able to say that I wrote it by myself," she told me before locking herself in her room. Yuri came by to check on the dog, and Jason and he took it for a walk, trying out different names as they exited the house. When they returned, they played some video game that made a lot of crash sounds punctuated by Yuri and Jason screaming about their successes and failures and the dog barking in joy or pain, it wasn't clear.

I did some laundry and messed around with a new recipe for Pad Thai that I didn't have the right ingredients for. It wasn't going to taste like Pad Thai, so I was going to have to tell everyone it was something kinda like Pad Thai. Either that or make up a different name for my concoction.

When my cell started making popcorn sounds and I saw the blocked caller message, I almost didn't answer. But I was bored and still had an hour to go before serving dinner.

It was Randy Mann. He wanted to meet me out back in the alley. I said that I didn't think that was such a good idea. Impulsively I asked if he wanted to come in. He hesitated a moment, then asked, "Do you have security cameras?"

"If I did, do you think I would tell you?"

"That's fair," he said.

"Just come in if you want to talk. Otherwise, forget it."

He hesitated before acquiescing. "Okay. I'll come in."

I ran into the other room to let Yuri know what was happening. He decided to stay out of sight and eavesdrop, but promised he would be ready to come in instantly if needed. Yuri asked Jason to go to his room. When he didn't give Yuri the pre-teen grief that I usually got when I requested that Jason do something, I was both thankful and annoyed. Jason simply picked up his computer, motioned for the dog to follow and disappeared. Moments later there was a light "tap, tap, tap" on the door.

Randy Mann looked just as menacing standing in my doorway in the full light of day as he had in the dimly lit alley. There's just something about a full length, dark wool coat that screams mobster. For a moment I wondered if I had made a tactical blunder by inviting him into my home. Should I insist on frisking him for weapons? Or make him state his intentions before letting him cross the threshold? I did neither. Instead, I turned and led him into the kitchen, wishing I had eyes in the back of my head, half anticipating he would attack me from behind. When we reached the kitchen without incident, I asked if he wanted anything to drink. "Where are your kids?" he asked instead of responding to my question.

"In their rooms. You can talk freely."

"Got any Scotch?" he asked as he took off his coat and folded it up carefully before laying it across one of the kitchen table chairs.

"Scotch?" I had expected him to decline hospitality and get right to the point. But a guest was a guest, so I went into the other room and retrieved a bottle of Monkey Shoulder Blended Malt Scotch Whisky that I bought one time when Mara was with me because she liked the name. Then I grabbed a glass and set both before him on the table. "Help yourself."

He glanced at the label before pouring himself a healthy shot and knocking it back. I doubted he was used to low-end whiskeys, but he apparently wanted a drink bad enough not to complain. He refilled his glass and began twirling it between his thick fingers. "I'm not sure where to start," he said.

"How about with why you are sitting at my kitchen table drinking my Scotch."

"I just heard about Jim Gossett's murder," he said bluntly.

"And...?"

"Given the circumstances, well, it occurred to me that you might think my family is involved."

"No kidding."

"Seriously. We talk big. Maybe sometimes we get a little, um, pushy."

"Like putting out ads filled with lies. Or threatening investigators and candidate's wives."

"Okay, so we push the limits sometimes. But, for god's sake, we don't murder people."

"That's why you're here? To tell me your family doesn't murder people?"

"That, and … I was wondering if you ever found the research report you were looking for."

"Oh, you mean the one that resulted in the murder of two people? The one that lists people and companies who have committed illegal acts? With evidence to back up the claims? Is that the report you're referring to?" He was making me mad, really mad. "Do you think that if I had the damned information, I would be sitting on it? No way. I would have turned it over to the police and the press. So, you can rest easy if you think I have it. Because I don't." I hoped that by telling him what I would have done with the information if I had found Brian's research that I was perhaps buying some safety for myself and my family. If the Mann family was behind the murders.

"Okay, okay, I get the message. You don't have copies of the stuff Norcross was working on. What about your friend the journalist? Do you know if she got hold of any of the Norcross research?"

So, he knew about what Gretchen was working on. Did that mean he was responsible for the burglary? "For what it's worth, she never had Brian's research, and what she did have was stolen from her home. But then, maybe you know about that?"

"Now you're accusing me of burglary?" He sounded sincerely offended. But then, lawyers have to know how to put on a show when it's called for.

"No, I'm not accusing you of anything. Just speculating, that's all."

"Look, I don't steal things. I'm a lawyer. I don't want to be disbarred."

"But you know people who do steal things, right? You have the money to pay for whatever you want done, right?"

"I'm not here to argue with you. I'm just concerned about how all of this could impact my brother's campaign. I need to know what we're up against."

The nerve of the guy. His family threatens everyone in sight, slanders the opposition, and then he worries that his family might get some bad press. "I think you should be talking to the police, not me."

Ignoring my suggestion, he asked, "What do the police think? You're staying on top of their investigation, right?"

"Look, from where I'm sitting you may be responsible for two deaths and a burglary. I'm not going to help you by providing confidential information, even if I had any, which I don't."

"You really don't understand. We're not mob. We're east coast, old money. Maybe we're used to getting what we want. But we don't resort to anything physical."

"You consider lying and intimidation somehow better than getting physical?"

"It is what it is." He drank down his remaining Scotch. "I don't suppose you'll call me if you get a lead on the missing report." He stood up. "I could make it worth your while."

Yuri took that moment to make a dramatic entrance. "We don't want your money. We earn ours through honest labor."

Mann glared at him. "You've been listening?" He sounded truly indignant, like eavesdropping was more of a crime than threatening people.

"I have one question: if you're telling the truth, then someone else must have an interest in keeping what Norcross found under wraps. Can you give us any names?"

Mann shook his head. "You understand that for us it's more a question of timing than the actual details. We'd fight any accusations in court, drag things out, maybe even win, or pay a fine and move on. But this is a tight race...." His voice trailed off. Then he added, "I honestly can't think of anyone who might be on that list who would murder someone to keep the information from surfacing. I mean, big companies get accused of things all the time. They go to court or settle. Whatever."

"You do realize that you're making a case for the murderer being someone who wants to see your brother elected," I said.

"No," Mann countered. "I'm telling you our family is innocent. And I don't know what is in that report Norcross put together. It could be anything. But one thing for sure, it's something that someone desperately wants to keep secret."

He was changing his tune a bit to defend his family. I wasn't sure I was buying his "our family is innocent" argument, but it was possible Brian's research included the lowdown on several local personalities and companies. It was about big oil, not just Bobby Mann. There were a lot of people who stood to lose bigtime if the information Brian had gathered was as significant as we suspected.

But even if Randy Mann was telling the truth, and no family members were responsible for the murders, the Manns were definitely neither pure nor blameless. And the other big question that was still lingering in my mind was whether or not the Manns considered Ashley "family."

CHAPTER 20
A LITTLE LIE

THE LAST TWO DAYS before the election the campaign got ugly, really ugly. The Knight organization struggled to maintain a dignified approach while being slammed with one negative ad after another. Sometimes there was a smidgeon of truth in an ad, but most often they contained made up stories to get the voters agitated enough to turn out and to cast their ballot for Bobby Mann.

By the time Monday morning rolled around, I was going stir crazy. Hopefully my chat with Randy Mann had assured him that I was harmless, because I was headed for the office. Even if someone else was responsible for the two murders, I doubted I was in danger anymore. Just in case, I had my Victorinox, pepper spray and a siren alarm with me. Overkill perhaps, but it gave me some confidence that I could defend myself if necessary.

When I reached my Subaru, I almost set off the siren alarm instead of the remote to the car door. I would have to learn how to juggle the two more efficiently if I was going to carry both on the same keychain.

Nothing unusual happened on the way to the mall. If someone was following me, they were very good at it. Once there, I was lucky enough to find a parking spot close to the entrance. As I made my way through the sparse crowd, I didn't notice anyone paying unusual attention to me, and I arrived at the office without incident.

I barely had time to pour myself a cup of coffee when I was told that we had a new client. I vowed to put the campaign murders, as I had come to think of them, out of my mind. But it wasn't easy. Assisting Adele with an asset search in a child custody case wasn't engaging enough to hold my attention. And Yuri wasn't helping. He was on another trivia kick. This time it was on names of animal groups. He and Jason had been trying to come up with names that suggested the animals themselves. The names were supposed to be authentic, and they weren't supposed to look online for answers. Although I was pretty sure Yuri was cheating when he suddenly shouted: "An obstinacy of buffalos."

"A shrewdness of apes," I called back. I had done my homework in preparation for just such an opportunity to one-up Yuri.

"A piddle of puppies," he said with a smirk.

"A jerk of jokers. And a clatter of clowns."

"Not nice," he tut-tutted.

"Next time check with me first."

"He's a sweet dog."

"He's an additional dependent. And he doesn't bathe or feed himself."

"Jason is thrilled with him."

He had me there. I had even caught Mom giving him a doggie treat and mumbling something in dog language.

The rest of the day dragged by. I left early and sat in the parking lot trying to decide whether to call the number I had looked up earlier. It was just a hunch, partly the result of a conversation with my mother. But the possibility had been at the back of my mind for a while. And now that the election was almost upon us and Brian's research seemed to be long gone, I was feeling more secure. Finally, my fingers took over for my better judgment and I dialed the number.

I heard the voice of Ashley Mann tentatively say, "Hello?" She obviously hadn't recognized my number on her private cell. But she had taken a chance and answered. Too bad for her.

"My name is Cameron Chandler," I said. "I knew Brian Norcross and Jim Gossett." I paused, waiting for her response.

"Sorry," she said after a tick too long. "I'm afraid those names mean nothing to me."

"I'm certain you will remember Jim when I show you the picture of the two of you together at the Oktoberfest parade."

Another pause. "There were a lot of people at that parade," she said. But she didn't hang up.

"Perhaps we should talk face to face," I suggested on impulse.

"It's the night before the election. I have a lot to do."

"The returns won't be coming in until tomorrow. And you may not need to get ready for a celebration. It depends."

"On what?" She was beginning to sound nervous. I had a feeling my little lie was actually based on fact, an elusive fact that I didn't actually possess.

"On what I'm offered for the picture."

"I have no idea what you're talking about."

"Then I guess this conversation is over." I pretended to be about to hang up.

"No, wait," she said hurriedly. "I'm sure there's been a misunderstanding, but perhaps we should talk."

"Where can we meet?" I was going to leave it up to her. It would be interesting to see what she proposed.

After a moment's pause, she said, "How about that park near our headquarters? I could be there at the kiddy swimming pool at 8:00."

Aha, after dark in the middle of the park. That was fast thinking on her part, and from my point of view, the location did not bode well for a date with a murder suspect. "I'll be there," I said and hung up before she could change her mind. And before I could change my mind.

If I was really going to do this, I would need back-up. I saw Yuri leaving the building and hurried to catch up with him. When I told him what I'd done, he seemed angry. "If you really believe she's a murderer, then why on earth would you agree to a meeting in the park?"

"She won't confess in a public place," I said. "It's not as if I have any proof."

"So, what are you going to do? Ask politely if she killed two men?"

"I was hoping you could help me figure that out."

"Dammit, Cameron, if you're right, this could be a dangerous move."

"I don't have to go," I said.

"But you gave her your real name. And you called her from your cell phone. You can't say, 'Oh, sorry, just kidding.'"

"But what if she's responsible for the murders of two people? She might not have done it herself, but she could have hired it done. Given how she responded to my call, we have to at least consider the possibility."

"We aren't in the criminal prosecution business. Our mission is not to 'right wrongs' or 'seek revenge.' We're investigators; we work for other people, not for ourselves." Yuri got out his cell. "Let's see if P.W. is still around. Although I think she left early to go somewhere."

Yuri confirmed through Blaine that P.W. was occupied for the evening and shouldn't be interrupted except for an extreme emergency. Fortunately, Grant was still in the office. Blaine put Yuri through to Grant and he agreed to meet us at the nearby Starbucks without questioning why. After all, we were a team.

A half hour later we were sitting across from Grant, explaining the situation. When we finished, Grant looked at me and said, "I do understand why you called her, but I'm not sure it was a good idea."

Yuri jumped in to defend me, sort of. "Well, it's done. The question is how we make the best of it. You in?"

"I will understand if you don't want to be," I said quickly.

"I didn't say that. I've done stupid things before." He smiled. "Maybe we'll nail a murderer. That would be good."

"It's too bad you didn't get her to admit to something on the phone," Yuri said.

"She was hardly going to confess on the phone," I argued. "But I should have been recording our conversation. I don't know why I didn't think to do that."

"That would have been a good idea," Grant agreed. "But I doubt she would have said anything specific in an initial call. Still, the only way this is going to work is to record her saying something incriminating that we can take to the police. We need to figure out what bait you can dangle. She will want to know what evidence you have and who else might know about it before she shows her hand. But that doesn't mean she isn't dangerous right out of the starting gate."

"We can't take anything for granted," Yuri said.

"You armed?" Grant asked. He sounded so matter-of-fact, like asking whether I wore clothes when I went to work.

"No."

"I have a gun she can use. I don't live far away," Yuri said. This was sounding far more serious than I'd originally planned for.

"And I have a couple of in-ear two-way communication devices we can use," Grant said. Of course, he did. He was, after all, experienced and cautious, not like me, putting myself out there without thinking it through.

We spent the next half hour discussing what I could say that might provoke Ashley into making an admission and that could be used to prove her guilt, or to at least provide sufficient cause to consider her a suspect. It was a balancing act. If I didn't push hard enough, she wouldn't confess to anything. But if I pushed too hard, she might retaliate in the moment. Even with back-up nearby I needed to be prepared.

We agreed to meet about two blocks from the park at 7:30 to set everything up. Meanwhile, I went home to organize the kids' dinner and make sure Mom knew I would be gone for a few hours. I didn't tell her the truth about what I was up to, just that Yuri and I had an errand we needed to run. She gave me a look that let me know she guessed there was more to it, but she didn't object. I'm lucky she likes spending time with her grandchildren.

I arrived about 7:20 and found a spot on the street that was far enough from the corner streetlight that I didn't feel like I was calling attention to myself. The park wasn't large and well-manicured, but there were still lots of trees and rows of neatly trimmed bushes. At night, walking down a path lined with trees, even well-spaced trees, can feel spooky. I had been at this park with the kids once in the daylight and vaguely remembered the winding path to the kiddy pool. It would be easy for Ashley to waylay me in the dark. Still, I agreed with Grant and Yuri that she probably wouldn't attack until when and if she knew what I had on her and felt confident that she could stop me from using it. One way or another.

When the door opened on the passenger side of the car I was startled. I hadn't seen anyone coming. I turned, expecting to see Yuri or Grant. Instead, there was Ashley with a gun pointed at me. She obviously wasn't going to adhere to our plan.

"Let's go," she said. The former Seafair Princess wasn't smiling. In that moment, she didn't look like reigning royalty. More like Uma Thurman in Kill Bill.

"Where?" I said. Come on Yuri, Grant, you can save me any time now.

"I said 'let's go.' Start the engine."

"Why can't we talk here?"

"Because my guess is that you don't have the original picture with you. That's what blackmailer's do. They leave the original in some safe place so they can keep asking for more. Well, that's not going to happen to me. We're going to wherever you have the original and any copies. We're going to end this little charade right now."

"I don't think you want to do that," I said, stalling for time.

"Just start the car." She nudged me with her gun. There was a clunking sound as her gun met my gun. "Oh, what's this?" She reached over and put her hand in my pocket. "Expecting trouble?" she asked with a smile that definitely did not give me a warm feeling.

"There doesn't have to be any trouble," I said, trying to sound reasonable.

"Start the damn engine!" she yelled. The sound of her angry voice echoed in the small space.

I switched on the key and floored the gas without putting it in gear, trying to flood the engine. It didn't work. Any other time it would have, but this time my car simply roared with energy. "Sorry," I said. "You're making me nervous. But you really don't want me to go to my place. It's my mother's bridge night. And the kids have friends there. It will be public."

She paused. Then she said, "If you behave, nothing will happen. We will go in and get the picture, and that will be that."

"But you will be seen. How do I explain you being with me?"

"I'm sure you will think of something. You're a clever woman." Somehow it didn't feel like a compliment.

"You do know that I got it online." Stall for time, I kept telling myself. Stall for time.

She hesitated then said, "One picture doesn't prove anything."

"You're right," I said, perhaps too quickly. "I just hoped I could draw you out with it." She seemed to hesitate again; perhaps my screwy logic was making some sense to her. Then the expression on her face changed, from mean to downright nasty.

"You're just like them," she said angrily. "You think you can outsmart me, take advantage of me."

"Them?" I asked.

"They think we're all west coast bumpkins."

Bumpkins? Somehow that didn't sound like a word in Ashley's vocabulary, maybe Randy's though. "You mean the Mann family?" Come on, keeping talking.

"Yes, the precious Mann family. It's all about helping their Bobbykins get elected. They don't give a shit about me." She seemed eager to talk, to voice her frustration. But the fact that she was willing to tell all to me about her family problems was not encouraging. Still, as long as she was talking, she wasn't shooting.

"But you're his wife, you're in all of the campaign pictures. They need you."

"Really? You think so?" She suddenly sounded hopeful, like I was confirming her dream. Then the corners of her mouth turned down, back to the wicked witch look.

"His 'we're so good because we're from the east coast' mother even went so far as to inform me that we shouldn't start a family yet. Can you imagine? She wants to control everything about our lives." Mom was right, the family considered Ashley expendable. If it hadn't been for the gun pointed at me, I might have felt sorry for her.

"That makes sense to me. Campaigns can be stressful. There's plenty of time later to have children."

"And if he loses, that would make it easier…." Her frown grew deeper, lines appearing on her otherwise smooth forehead. "Not that I wanted to ruin my figure with a baby anyway."

"What does Bobby say?"

All at once her voice went up a few octaves, loud and emotional: "He goes along with his family, no matter what. That's why…." She stopped talking and the gun wavered. I thought briefly about making a play for it, but before I could make a move, she steadied the gun and pointed it at my midsection.

"That's why I gave Brian the lowdown on some of the family's less savory activities."

"You?" I admit it, she completely surprised me with that bit of information.

"He promised not to use anything I told him until after the election. Then he crossed me by talking to that reporter friend of yours. I had no choice but to tell Randy."

"Ouch. I bet he didn't like that."

"He's an officious asshole."

"That's something we agree on."

She looked at me with an almost wistful look. "I'm sorry about this, but I have to protect my husband."

"I'll give you the picture," I said again. "Then it's over."

"That's what Jim said. But I knew he couldn't be trusted." She paused. "And I don't think you can be either." She took a deep breath and said firmly, "Let's go. Now!"

I couldn't think of any other way to postpone the inevitable and was about to put my car in gear when everything was suddenly lit up. As if someone on a set had yelled for lights. Against the glare I could barely make out a car with its brights on facing us; there was another one behind with its brights on. We were blocked in and spotlighted.

"This was a set-up," Ashley said, her voice and her gun shaking.

"Yes, and if you shoot me, I think they will probably shoot you. So why don't you put the gun down and get out of the car." Please put the gun down. Please put it down. Please don't shoot me.

Someone tapped on the back window on the passenger side and I hit the button to lower it before she could tell me not to. Yuri leaned in and put his gun against the back of her head. "Drop it," he said, somewhat melodramatically.

For just a moment I thought she was going to shoot me out of spite. Instead, she put the gun on the dash and said, "You can't prove anything. She pulled a gun on me and I defended myself." She was quick with the excuses, very quick and almost convincing.

"Step out of the car," Yuri ordered.

Ashley straightened her slim shoulders and got out of the car. As I watched I noticed another car down the block. A dark sedan. It hadn't been there when I first arrived. Was it Ashley's? Why hadn't I seen it drive up?

Grant had a pair of handcuffs and turned Ashley around to cuff her. "You can't do that," she said.

"I just did."

"I'm calling Connolly," I said.

Out of the corner of my eye I saw the dark sedan drive off. Not Ashley's car after all.

Connolly answered on the first ring. When I gave him a brief overview of the situation, he immediately said he was on his way, and that he'd have officers on the scene within minutes.

"You aren't police," Ashley said. "You can't detain me like this." She was still agitated, but she was starting to sound less crazy. She tried to shake off Grant's grip on her arm, but he held on. Meanwhile, Yuri turned off the brights, but left both cars where they were.

"The police are on their way," Grant said. "You'll get a chance to tell your side of the story."

"You can't do this to me," she said again. Then she started crying and whipping her body from side to side. "Let me go!" she screamed. "You let me go!"

"It's over, Ashley. You killed two men. You're not going anywhere." This was my chance to get her to say something incriminating. Unfortunately, she might be scared and frantic, but somewhere in the back of her mind, she was still thinking rationally about what was in her own best interest.

"I don't know what you're talking about. You were trying to blackmail me. You're the one who should be in handcuffs."

She was good, I had to admit it, but in her panic, she'd never asked about where I'd gotten the photo. "Ashley, how could I possible blackmail you with a photo that's in the public domain. I don't have the original. I came across it searching back issues of the newspaper."

Her expression changed for just a moment as she processed the information. But then her mask dropped back into place as the squad cars pulled up. Yuri handed the officers her gun and gave a high-level summary of what had taken place. Ashley demanded that they take off the cuffs, and Grant agreed to do so if the officers promised to keep an eye on her until Connolly arrived.

The officers looked confused, but fortunately they had been instructed to keep all of us there and wait for Connolly. When he arrived just a few minutes later, he also looked confused. I tried to explain why we were all there and what had occurred even as Ashley kept talking over me, accusing me of accosting her with a gun and trying to blackmail her. She was obviously distressed and at times more emotional than coherent. Grant tried unsuccessfully to intervene a couple of times to get her to calm down. Yuri just stood back and watched.

In the end, Connolly couldn't put all of the pieces together while standing on the sidewalk surrounded by bewildered police officers and chaos. He instructed one of the officers to take Ashley to police headquarters and asked Yuri and me to get in Grant's car and follow him downtown. On the way I called Mom to tell her I was going to be later than I'd anticipated and wasn't sure exactly when I'd be back. "I'll expect an explanation tomorrow," she warned when I declined to say more.

It turned out to be a long night, a very long night. We all had to give individual statements. And Connolly insisted on personally talking to each of us one at a time. Grant was thc first to be released. There was some question about his right to handcuff Ashley, but under the circumstances, he wasn't going to be charged with assault. He left a message for us saying that he would try to contact P.W. and let her know what was happening. Apparently, what we had done qualified as an "emergency," or else Grant felt like his long relationship with P.W. gave him the right to make a judgement call in spite of Blaine's directive.

Since what we had done had not been a sanctioned part of any existing assignment, I couldn't help wondering if this was it, if this time we had finally crossed a line that would result in ending our employment with Penny-wise. I felt bad that I had involved Yuri and Grant. But at the same time, I was also very thankful that I had.

Yuri was told he could go next, but he hung around and waited for me. Connolly read me the riot act before asking about the pictures. When I admitted I'd been bluffing and I had indeed found the photo by combing through old newspaper reports on the campaigns, he almost smiled. Almost. "It was a hairbrained idea, and you put the lives of you and your colleagues at risk. You do understand that, don't you?"

"But she's guilty of murder," I protested.

"You don't have any proof," he countered.

"If things had gone as planned, I would have recorded our conversation. But just given how she responded to my mention of a picture of her and Jim together, don't you think she's guilty?"

"What I think doesn't count. It's what I can prove that does."

"Doesn't what happened tonight give you enough to at least search her home or something?"

"She's got a lawyer on the way here now. My guess is she won't say anything more than she already has, he'll make noise about how anything she said tonight was under duress and can't be used against her, and she'll be released.

Just like the three of you. No judge will issue a search warrant based on these conflicting stories."

"But you know I'm telling the truth."

Connolly looked sad. "Yes, I believe you. But the best I can promise is to look into it."

"Thank you."

"And in return, I want you to promise me that you won't even think about talking to anyone related to the campaign until I get back to you. Got that?"

"Got it."

"And no reporters. If they come after you, the phrase you'll be using is 'no comment.'"

"Got it."

He added one last thing as I left, "And, Cameron, watch your back."

An officer told us there was someone waiting downstairs. When we came out of the building there was Grant, our reliable team member. He hadn't left when he'd been released but had hung around to make sure we were okay and to drive us back to our cars. On the way he reported on his conversation with P.W. The bottom line was that although she'd been annoyed, she hadn't been surprised. We were all to be in her office first thing tomorrow.

That was becoming a habit.

CHAPTER 21
END GAME

THE GOOD THING ABOUT KIDS is that they usually don't ask many questions about the lives of grownups. My kids are no exception. Unless I'm doing something that directly affects them, they don't show a lot of interest in my life. And that morning I was thankful that the conversation was about what they were looking forward to in their day rather than them asking about where I'd been the night before.

Fortunately, Mom slept in, so I wouldn't have to face her questions until later. By then I would hopefully know what my employment situation was and could spin things accordingly. I gulped down my coffee and went to Pennywise to hear the verdict.

P.W. was her usual fashionable self. Her burnt orange jacket, dark brown slacks and flamboyant scarf featuring the outlines of orange and brown leaves proclaimed "winter is on its way." Yuri looked tired. And concerned. Grant looked rested, like he'd somehow managed to squeeze eight hours of sleep out of five. I didn't know how I looked. I'd put on something comfortable and run a comb through my hair. That was about it.

"You act like you're facing the coach after soundly losing the game," P.W. said, looking first at Yuri then me. "And, Grant, I know you were just trying to protect Cameron, but did you consider trying to talk her out of it?"

"Yes, I did consider it. But it seemed worth a shot to me."

"And yet it was almost a disaster."

"Ashley surprised us," Grant admitted. "We shouldn't have let that happen."

P.W. was being remarkably restrained. She hadn't once reached for her cigarette. "What you do on your own time is up to you," she began. "But if you had asked, I would have advised against doing what you did. That said, let's hope Ashley doesn't sue you. Although I think that would be unwise on her part."

"My guess is that if it doesn't get in the news, she will let it drop," Yuri said.

"What I'm hoping is that the police find something to implicate her in the murders," I said. "Detective Connolly promised he'd look into it."

"Without our assistance, I assume?" P.W. raised one eyebrow and waited for confirmation from each of us. "Then, unless either Ashley or the police decide otherwise, let's get back to normal. Understood?" Each of us gave a nod of understanding. And I gave a silent sigh of relief.

Back in the pit, Yuri gave me a surreptitious thumbs up that I acknowledged with a subdued smile. Another slide for us.

I never seriously thought Grant's job was in danger, but I was sorry I'd put him in an uncomfortable spot with P.W. When I tried to apologize, he waved me off. "You were doing what you thought was the right thing. That's why I agreed to help. Please don't ever hesitate to ask for any kind of assistance—at work or outside of the office." I was thankful to have such a supportive and smart colleague. I owed him big time.

There was very little kidding around in the office the rest of the day. Everyone worked quietly, eyes on their computers, taking the occasional coffee break, talking about the election, avoiding talk of Ashley. I regretted not being able to torment Yuri with a reference to a cauldron of bats and a prickle of hedgehogs, but that would have to wait for a less somber moment.

Detective Connolly called early afternoon to let me know that Ashley had been released not long after us. She had apparently threatened to sue everyone who had been involved, from the three of us to the police officers who detained her at the scene to the police station admin who had brought her what she labeled as swill, not coffee. Her lawyer had somehow managed to calm her down, but it wasn't clear whether they would eventually press changes or not. If she didn't and we didn't, it would be a wash. All of the weapons were legal, and although it could be argued that Grant had thought he was doing the right thing by detaining her, her lawyer could probably twist the facts to make it seem like Grant had overreacted. Despite the fact that I "claimed" she had pulled a gun on me. It was probably in everyone's best interest if the incident didn't make the news.

Connolly also said that the press had been sniffing around, but he was pretty sure they were sufficiently distracted by the election turnout and several tight races. I didn't ask what direction his investigation might take after what happened because I didn't think it was any of my business, and I knew what his answer would be anyway—that it was none of my business.

That evening Yuri came over for pizza while we watched the election returns come in. Mom joined us. Mara grabbed some pizza and retired to her room to avoid what she considered to be a drawn out, unexciting event. Even Jason seemed bored with all of the lead up to the final count. He hung around for a while, then decided he would rather watch the returns on his computer so he could switch back and forth when he wanted to instead of having to fight us for the remote.

We hadn't shared enough about Brian's research with my mother to make her as concerned about the outcome of the congressional race as we were. Nor had I told her about what had happened with Ashley. There would be time for that later.

Since she knew nothing of the quagmire of political intrigue behind the scenes, it wasn't surprising that Mom zeroed in on the trappings of the evening, who was attending which party, what people were wearing, what they were being served.

The Mann party had a lot of celebrities, the movers and shakers from our neck of the woods. And it looked like the Mann campaign had spared no expense on their event. The food was being served on silver platters placed artistically on tablecloth covered tables. There were waiters in black attire circling the room offering plates of hors d oeuvres to well-dressed guests. They were putting on a good show, as if a win was a sure thing.

"I wish they would zero in more on the food," Mom said. "I'm curious about what's written on that huge cake at the end of the table."

"Pretty presumptuous to have a victory cake," I said.

I could tell that Yuri was struggling to come up with something clever to say about the cake in advance of knowing the outcome of the election. Mom saved him by pointing at a couple just coming into view on the screen and saying, "Is that who I think it is? The Mann camp has certainly attracted the creme d la crème of our local elite."

Whenever the station switched to the Knight campaign, Mom lost interest. Admittedly, the contrast was startling. An upscale adult party versus a student get-together. But in both instances the energy level was high. Both camps still expected—or hoped—their candidate would win.

The Knight-Mann returns continued to jockey back and forth for the lead as the district votes were tallied. At one point, Mom said, "Poor Ashley. She is probably off biting her nails somewhere, anxiously waiting to find out if her dream of becoming the wife of a congressman is going to come true."

Yuri raised his eyebrows in question, and I gave him a quick "no" nod. "Later," I mouthed. Mom deserved to know. After all, it was what she had said about Ashley that had inspired me to try to entrap her. But now wasn't the time. Not until the election was over.

"She's been looking exhausted," Mom continued. "Not her usual bubbly self. She's probably in a room at the hotel, resting until the announcement is made. It will be interesting to see what she wears. I wonder if she chooses her wardrobe based on whether her husband wins or loses?"

Whenever they went live to the Mann campaign party, I scanned the screen for members of the Mann family, and specifically for Ashley. But there was no sign of her caught on camera. Occasionally one of the Manns was approached by a member of the press, but all they said was that they remained optimistic about the outcome and they looked forward to Bobby winning the seat. Everyone at campaign headquarters looked upbeat and seemed to be celebrating in anticipation of a win.

The Knight campaign party was lively but a bit more subdued than the Mann event. It had been a tough few days for them, fighting against the tsunami of negative ads. Even though they had as much reason to expect a win as the Mann campaign, there wasn't as much bluster when reporters pressed campaign officials on how they thought things were going for their candidate.

I went into the kitchen to open another bottle of wine, and Yuri followed me in. "I know we can't do anything more, but I can't get the thought that she's a killer who is going to get away with it out of my head."

"Me neither. And there's one thing I haven't mentioned. I forgot about it given everything that happened last night. But there was another car there, just up the block. I didn't remember it being there when I parked. At first, I thought it might have been Ashley's, but it drove off when Grant cuffed her. I can't quit thinking about that."

"Are you suggesting that she may have had an accomplice?"

"No, I think she was on her own. But what occurred to me was that maybe I'm not the only one to be suspicious of her."

"You mean the family?"

"The beloved family. I think they were keeping an eye on her."

"If that's the case, they are probably tidying up loose ends as we speak. Damn. No breaks in this case. Not a single break."

CHAPTER 22
ELECTION RESULTS

We continued to watch TV returns as first Mann and then Knight took narrow leads. Mom finally got bored and went upstairs. The kids stayed in their rooms, briefly coming out to say goodnight when they decided to turn in. Yuri and I continued our vigil.

When 66 per cent of the districts had been counted, Knight started pulling ahead. Slowly, very slowly, he began to take the lead. The Mann supporters began to appear less jubilant and the crowd at their party thinned out a bit. Bobby had showed up late, at a time when it looked like he had a chance to win. He continued smiling and glad-handing, maintaining appearances on the outside, but most likely mentally preparing his concession speech. The rest of the Mann family seemed to have vanished.

"Wonder where Ashley has been all evening?" I said.

"Isn't she supposed to show a brave front, stand by her man?" Yuri's sarcastic question made me even more skeptical about her absence.

"The question is, will he stand by her?"

Meanwhile, there were more and more people gathering at the Knight headquarters, including reporters.

I recognized several who had apparently abandoned ship at the Mann party. Now they were maneuvering through the growing crowd, pausing occasionally to thrust a microphone in someone's face. "How do you feel about what looks like a positive outcome for your candidate?" we heard one ask. Stupid questions like that always irritated me. How did she think the volunteer felt? Then again, the reporters had just spent the better part of an evening filling in the hours with inane chatter while waiting for results. Maybe it was too much to expect that they would have any creativity left.

"I've had enough," Yuri announced. "You going to stay up until it's called?"

"No, it looks like Knight is a sure thing at this point. Although not by much." It crossed my mind that Brian would have been pleased. At the same time, Knight's win would take the sting out of what Gretchen hoped to accomplish with her article. There were always tangential winners and losers in any political race.

After Yuri left, I turned off the TV and went to bed, hoping I'd wake to good news about the Knight campaign. I like to review election results in print, so I figured I'd pick up the local paper and a cup of coffee on my way to work and savor the good news once I got to the office. The next morning, however, the headline wasn't about election results. Instead, it read:

Bobby Mann's wife commits suicide.

"Damn." I briefly wondered what Mom would say when she saw the news. Personally, I very much doubted that

Ashley had committed suicide. It seemed to me that it was more likely the Mann family had tidied up loose ends before they packed up and headed back east, but I doubted we'd ever be able to prove it. I looked at the headline again. They hadn't even honored her by using her name in the headline.

Underneath the headline the election numbers showed that Knight had won by a tiny lead, one that might normally have ended in a demand for a recount. Instead, Bobby Mann had conceded. According to the article, he was devasted by his wife's suicide. Bobby had refused to comment, so they had interviewed his brother, Randy, about her death.

"The stress of the campaign was just too much for her," Randy was quoted as saying. He added, "But my brother is a survivor. He will get through this." The implicit message as I understood it was that he would deal with his grief and try again for office at a later time.

Yuri was standing by the coffee maker when I arrived. "An overdose. Pills. Can you believe it?"

"I wonder where she got them."

"You're not thinking what I'm thinking—?"

"Probably. She wasn't 'family.' And mourning your dead wife isn't as damaging to a political career as visiting your convicted murderer wife in prison. I wouldn't put it past them to have provided pills and a 'strong suggestion' that she avoid a murder trial by taking them."

"Can you force a person to take pills?"

"I don't know. Maybe they tricked her, told her they were something else. I just don't believe suicide was her idea. I think she would have gone for bluff and bluster.

People that live a privileged life always think they can get away with anything. Even murder."

Yuri was quiet for minute. "I think you're right," he said as he poured himself a cup of coffee. "And if you're right, I hate the thought that the Mann family might skate. That guarantees Bobby Mann will simply move on and run again. Nothing will have changed."

"Except that three people are dead."

The telephone rang. It was Gretchen. "Mum's the word, but I wanted you to know that I found two images," she said. "You were right—there was a connection between Ashley and Jim Gossett. He could have been blackmailing her."

"Or, maybe she was his Mrs. Robinson," I countered.

"Well, I'm opting for the former. I also found two Mann campaign volunteers who remembered her asking questions about Brian. At this point, I think I have enough bits and pieces to string together a fairly convincing argument."

"You don't feel a little bit sorry for her?"

"Because she took her own life rather than face two murder charges?"

"Well, there's that. But I think she paid a heavy price for marrying onto that family."

"Hey, my focus is still on bringing down the Manns, making them pay the consequences for their greed and underhanded dealings. But now the story is not only a tale of political intrigue, but one of murder and suicide. Even though Bobby lost, I think I might be looking at a Pulitzer. Or maybe it's the basis for a book. True crime. Who knows?"

Later that morning, Yuri and I returned to the now familiar topic of Ashley as murderer. "What I can't picture is how she managed to get away with murder, twice, without getting caught." Yuri still didn't see her as anything but a trophy wife.

"I've thought all along that killing Brian was a spur-of-the-moment decision. And it's doubtful that either Brian or Jim had reason to fear her. That would have given her an advantage."

"But what about the weapons? Both were killed with blunt instruments. Did she bring them with her? And what happened to them?"

"Good point. You'd think her victims would have noticed if she was carrying a baseball bat," I said. "Or a Neanderthal type club." I was kidding, but that gave Yuri an excuse to jump to a new topic.

"Neanderthals have been unfairly stereotyped, you know."

I groaned. "Sorry I mentioned that." Before he could head off on a trivia tangent, I continued my argument. "Seriously, there could have been something handy at the campaign headquarters. And she could have concealed a weapon in a large purse when she went to see Jim."

"I'll give you that. It's possible. But there's still the issue of how she disposed of the weapons."

"She wasn't a suspect, so she had plenty of time to dump them somewhere. In a lake, a dumpster, down a ravine. They may never show up. Sometimes even inept criminals are just damned lucky." Although in Ashley's instance, her luck had run out.

"Think Randy helped her?"

"I doubt it. But I bet he hired Devine to look for Brian's research."

"And someone to burgle Gretchen's house."

"Then there's the mysterious dark sedan at the park. The more I've thought about it, the more convinced I am that whoever was driving the sedan had been hired by the family to keep an eye on Ashley. They may or may not have suspected her of the murders, but they undoubtedly considered her a loose cannon."

"Do you think the person in the sedan would have stopped her from shooting you if Grant and I hadn't showed up?"

"I guess it depends on what their orders were."

"Another thing I can't decide is whether Ashley's the one who shot at us in the parking lot. I still think it could have been Randy. Or someone Randy hired."

"And I still think that Randy somehow got his hands on Brian's research."

"Or it could have been someone else who was on the list."

"Either way, we'll probably never know."

EPILOGUE

ASHLEY'S PARENTS CLAIMED that the lack of a note and the fact that no one bothered to check on her that evening made her death seem suspicious. But after Gretchen's article was published, the suicide seemed especially plausible. Without coming right out and saying that Ashley was a murderer, the article nevertheless laid the groundwork for suggesting she had both motive and opportunity. The suicide could have been an understandable act of remorse.

The icing on the conspiracy cake was getting Lisa, Brian's girlfriend, to admit Brian had mentioned a conversation he'd had with Ashley. He'd referred to her as a desperate woman who was going to be disappointed in life. Lisa also admitted that she knew a little about Brian's research and had passed along her concerns to her mother, Ashley's schoolmate. If you drew all of the connections on a whiteboard, Ashley was clearly at the center of the chart. She'd committed two murders to help her husband win his race. But it couldn't be proven, so there was no real closure. Unless you counted her death as closure.

The police put the murders of Brian Norcross and Jim Gossett in the "solved" pile. Brian's research hadn't surfaced, but Gretchen's follow-up article raised enough questions about the Mann family's business practices that their legal problems could hound them for years. Still, as Randy Mann had pointed out to me earlier, with their resources and connections, they would probably go on living the good life and doing as they pleased.

Meanwhile, life at Penny-wise returned to normal. I received an assignment to investigate a young boy being bullied at school. It wasn't exactly a ho-hum case, but it didn't feel like a nail-biter either.

Everything returned to life as usual on the home front, too. More or less, that is. Mom had another three-person date lined up. This time she had requested a recent picture before agreeing to meet for dinner. I had a vision of someone having to hold up a newspaper with the date on it as proof the picture was current, but I didn't ask how she went about it. As far as my love life was concerned, Mom managed to casually mention the very polite and attractive detective several times, before she finally gave up. I did agree he was very polite and very attractive, but I didn't tell her that. Meanwhile, Jason continued watching too much news on TV. Mara spent too much time on the phone. I ripped the latest article on single mothers off my refrigerator and tossed it in the garbage. And we still hadn't named the dog.

Two weeks later, Yuri and I went out for a drink on a Friday evening before heading home. He was wearing new glasses that looked just like his old ones, but at least they didn't tilt. We had just placed our order when I got a call from Will. "Hey," he said. "I'm at my favorite bar and guess who else is here?"

"Who?"

"P.W."

"Why are you calling?" I asked. I put the cell on speaker, and Yuri and I leaned over it in anticipation.

"Because she isn't alone."

"Come on, Will," Yuri said impatiently. "There must be more to this—you wouldn't call just to tell us that."

"No, I wouldn't, would I?"

"Sooo?" I prompted. "Come on, spill it."

"Okay, okay. Drum roll…." He made some thumping sounds on his phone. "Because … she's with an attractive Russian man, that's why."

"How do you know he's Russian?"

"I'm not an investigator for nothing," he said. "How do you think?"

"The old drop something and listen for a minute trick?" Yuri asked.

"They shouldn't sit near a low wall if they really want privacy."

"Did you get a picture?" I asked.

"What do you think?!" I could almost hear Will's smile through the phone.

"You did good," Yuri said, giving Will rare praise. "We can put Adele on it on Monday."

After I hung up, we held up our glasses for a toast. "To discovering the story behind the woman," Yuri said,

"Hear, hear. To P.W. and the pursuit of truth."

ACKNOWLEDGMENTS

THE VOLUNTEERS WHO WORK on political campaigns perform an exceptional service to our country. They spend long hours on fundraising, menial tasks, and promoting their candidate. All with no guarantee they will end up on the winning team. Unfortunately, I know what it feels like at the end of a hard-fought campaign to find yourself cleaning up the headquarters after losing the race. Still, it was an exhilarating experience overall. And I cherish memories of the dedicated volunteers who gave their best for our candidate. (Although I still think the "best man" didn't win.)

I also want to thank my agent, Donna Eastman, and the supportive women of Amphorae: Kristina Makansi, Laura Robinson, and Lisa Miller. Finally, I want to thank you for reading my book—I hope you will continue reading the Discount Detective series.

Visit my website at www.charlottestuart.com.

ABOUT THE AUTHOR

IN A WORLD FILLED with uncertainty and too little chocolate, Charlotte Stuart has always anchored herself in writing. As an academic with a Ph.D. in communications, she wrote serious articles on obscure topics with titles that included phrases such as "summational anecdote" and "a rhetorical perspective." As a commercial fisher in Alaska, she turned to writing humorous articles on boating and fishing. Long days on the ocean fighting seasickness required a little humor. Then, as a management consultant, she got serious again. Although even when giving presentations on serious issues she tried for a playful spin: Stress—Clutter and Cortisol or Leadership—Super Glue, Duct Tape and Velcro.

Her current passions include pro bono consulting for small nonprofits and writing lighthearted mysteries. A curious mix of problem solving: pragmatic and fantasy. Charlotte lives and writes on Vashon Island in Washington State's Puget Sound and spends time each day entertained by herons, seals, and eagles and hoping the deer and raccoons don't raid her vegetable garden.

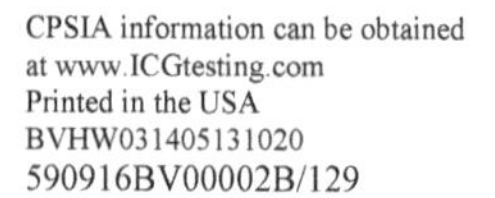

CPSIA information can be obtained
at www.ICGtesting.com
Printed in the USA
BVHW031405131020
590916BV00002B/129